BRANDON KOWALLIS

CURSING *at*
MOUNTAINS

This is a work of fiction. All characters, organizations, and events portrayed in this story are either a product of the author's imagination or are used fictitiously.

Visit the author's website at: www.brandonkowallis.com

CURSING AT MOUNTAINS. Copyright © 2025 by Brandon Kowallis.

The Library of Congress has cataloged this edition as follows:

Name: Kowallis, Brandon, author
Title: Cursing at Mountains / Brandon Kowallis
Identifiers: Library of Congress Control Number: 2025921795 (print) | ISBN 978-0-9964597-1-6 (paperback) | ISBN 978-0-9964597-2-3 (hardcover) | ISBN 978-0-9964597-3-0 (ebook) | ISBN 978-0-9964597-4-7 (hardcover w/dust jacket)

FIRST EDITION PUBLISHED IN 2025

Book Design by Brandon Kowallis

Published by StonefirePress

STONEFIRE
PRESS

Acknowledgements

This book would not have been possible without the love, support, and encouragement of so many wonderful people in my life. First and foremost, my wife Michelle and my two amazing children for encouraging me and believing in me through endless years of my attempts to balance family, a full-time job, and writing.

For those who took a first read in the early stages of this book and gave me the brutal feedback I needed to go back to the drawing board and make it better: Gretchen Baker, Jill Mower, David Harris, Jacob McCoy, Dann Hurlbert, Jernae Kowallis, Kory Kowallis, and Kim Mobley.

For my editor Ted Olson at Story Road for helping me cut out my ramblings and focus *Cursing at Mountains* on its most important messages.

For everyone else who showed interest when I jabbered on about my work-in-progress and encouraged me to keep writing until it was done.

And finally, for you dear reader. For your willingness to pick this book off the shelf and take a leap of faith to discover what it might have to offer you. May your journey through these pages be filled with beautiful insights.

This book is dedicated to everyone with a desire to improve their life during this short mortal journey as we travel along strange and exciting and sometimes painful roads.

Shadows

Chris hunched over to catch his breath as he broke into a small clearing within the jungle. Drenched in rancid sweat, he fumbled against the open air for a few steps, growled a few incoherent words, and felt his shin sink deep into something soft and warm. Another off-balanced step, and red-brown slime swallowed his knees. He tugged at his right foot, and his left sunk deeper. His heart reached his throat and crescendoed to a dull throbbing inside his head. The taste of metal filled his mouth, and the salty film that covered his entire body crept into his eyes distorting his visual reality.

He wiped the sweat from his eyes and stared up at the dark green canopy bowing ominously toward him. He couldn't remember how long he had been running through the choking heat of the rainforest underbelly; how long he had torn his way through the green, before the mud. He didn't even know why he was running, only that he had to run. Had to escape from something horrible.

He inhaled a stabilizing breath and his heart slowed and he stopped sinking into the red mud. A dark cloud of mosquitos formed around his face and arms. He could feel their tiny proboscises sinking into his exposed skin as he contemplated his next move. Behind the wall of leaves, primates screamed on high alert and colorful birds cackled threatening songs, until Chris could no longer handle the relentless pandemonium. He closed his eyes hard and immediately the world fell silent.

He held his breath for a suffocating moment, hopeful that the hot air filling his lungs might lift him from his predicament. In the quiet, his heart knocked furiously against his chest betraying the silence, and he knew the *it* that had been chasing him would hear; knew it would come.

He opened his eyes and scanned the impregnable wall of vegetation encircling the mud trap. Leafy demons drenched in their own perspiration swayed back and forth in his imagination waiting for him to disappear beneath the muck. The more he fixated on them the darker the forest became until the shadow of their twisted limbs rested over the entire landscape and reached into the heavens, snuffing out pinpoints of blue in the canopy above and eclipsing the world below in premature night.

He drew in a ragged breath and noticed the outline of a raw-boned tree resting diagonally across the surface of the mud pit. The tree's thin, gnarled trunk angled upward and then disappeared into a cluster of ferns lining the mud pool. Chris strained to examine the escape route and caught a shift in the jungle wall at the edge of his vision.

A sudden, deep thud from beyond the movement set off a shockwave that pulsed through the ground and into his body. Tremors gripped his legs and hands while another subterranean boom thinned the mud beneath him. He began sinking faster. Chris tightened his fists and swallowed hard. The sound was closer now. To his side, the wall of ferns and trees rippled unnaturally.

He panicked and lunged for the fallen tree against the pull of his hopelessly cemented legs.

The sudden movement caused Chris's chest to pivot into the mud with a loud smack. Pudding-like sludge splashed onto the tree's branches and the mud encased his collapsed body. He tried to claw his way toward the nearest branch, but the mud held him back. High-pitched, futile cries involuntarily issued from Chris's mouth, and the more he fought against the mud the more the branch retreated against the tar-like waves.

Behind the jungle wall, sticks and branches snapped with a new intensity. Thunder from beyond the tree-enshrouded horizon grumbled across the sky and funneled unnaturally into the air around Chris before passing into the now churning, pulsating vegetation at his side.

Chris's arms burned near exhaustion as he attempted to swim to the fallen tree against the mud dragging him into its depths. His hips, now hopelessly entombed beneath the brown slime surface, pulled like a deadweight against his torso. In a final desperate act of survival, Chris's entire body erupted into spasms. He opened his mouth to scream and a pathetic whimper trickled out, and the one forearm that had resisted entombment collapsed.

The jungle wall pulsed harder now—spinning into some fluid, green-black hole, from which emerged the horrid sound. Chris froze and his throat closed in. Mud slid up his neck and around his jaw as living darkness crawled from the hole, twitching and vibrating toward his sinking body.

The creature moved as though it hovered between a fragile state of death and life. Hunting. Determined. Wisps of darkness scaled off the organism in smoke-like trails as it thrashed through the air and then poised over Chris. A deep and unearthly drone issued from its core and into Chris, and smokey black particles scattered across his face. The flecks of darkness stung like venomous mosquitos.

Almost beyond his awareness the mud rose to Chris's ears. He could feel the penetrating clay working its way into his inner ear, silencing the jungle with a tormenting tickle. The bitter clay continued to rise until it swallowed his mouth and nose. He breathed a non-breath and gagged a convulsive gag as the sludge-worm worked its way into his sinus, throat, and lungs. A single eye remained above the surface now; wide and watching. Taking in the horror as the unholy creature reeled frantically, lunged toward him, and the world went dark.

CHAPTER 1

Falling

C hris jolted awake, with the terrible, guttural scream of the creature echoing in his ears. His head throbbed. He opened his eyes and lifted his head from the desk. A light knock at his door drew his attention, and he glanced over as it slowly creaked open. A stout, gray-haired woman in a casual business dress timidly poked her head through the door.

"Are…you…okay…Chris?"

Chris wiped the drool from the corner of his mouth and sat up.

She opened the door a little wider and stepped in, scanning the office for signs of trouble. Behind her, a small crowd gathered, gawking awkwardly over her shoulder.

"Uh, yeah." His head spun. "Why? What's up?"

"Uh. We heard you making… noises. We were concerned."

Chris blushed and tried to compose himself. He looked at the people gathered in the hall.

"What kind of noises?"

She drew in a deep, awkward breath and held it for a beat. "Screaming?" She replied timidly.

The blush turned hot.

"Seriously? Wow. Uh. Yeah, no, I'm fine. I must have dozed off." He paused for a moment, scratching the back of his head. "Did I really scream?"

The woman—an administrative assistant—nodded.

Chris was sweating profusely, and he straightened his shirt. The people who had gathered in the hall began to disperse.

"Well, I'm just glad you're OK. We weren't sure whether we should come check on you or run for our lives."

Chris chuckled embarrassingly and shook his head. "Geez."

Neither of them spoke for a moment while Chris rubbed and slapped his face.

She looked at her watch. "Well, since no one appears to be dying, I'm going to head home. Is there anything you need me to do before I head out?"

Chris leaned on his desk staring at her blankly, his face resting against his hand. When the question finally registered, he blinked and nodded. "I...I think I'm good for now. Thanks Sandra." He stared at the ground and then turned to Sandra. "Did I really scream?"

Sandra smiled and closed the door. When it clicked shut Chris reclined in his chair and waited for the haze to pass.

Once his mind had returned to reality, he stood up and made his way over to his third-story window. It was 4:30 now and well-dressed men and women began trickling out of the multi-story brick buildings scattered across the campus. Most pushed through the doors, more interested in their phones than in the well-manicured urban gardens where students sat reading, flirting, and philosophizing. As he looked down at the scene below, he noticed his transparent reflection in the window.

Geez, I look like crap. He lifted his chin to get a better look.

His desk nap had flattened his dark hair on the left side of his head. Half of his shirttail hung from his waist like a broken wing. The armpits of his blue shirt sported dark sweat circles. And his face looked older. Dark bags hung beneath his eyes next to wrinkles he hadn't noticed before. He stepped back and sucked in his gut in an attempt to boost his own confidence.

It hadn't even been a year since he had accepted the promotion as Director of Human Resources at Queens Mount University, and he was already beginning to see physical evidence of the mental toll it had taken on him.

He let his gut fall back into its natural position and sighed.

Nine months of dealing with difficult people, hitting endless resistance to his team's improvement ideas, pinging Slack channels, nonstop email chains, and pointless meetings, were all a far cry from what he had initially envisioned when he accepted the position.

Down below Sandra left the building and walked toward the bus stop. One by one across the campus, lights flickered off in office windows.

"What is wrong with me?" he asked his reflection.

His cell phone rang, and he walked over to his desk to pick it up. It was his wife.

"What's up?"

"Are you home yet?"

The blood rushed to Chris's head and his palms went clammy. *It's her depression talking, not Emily,* he told himself, closing his eyes, and drawing in a full breath.

"You're going to be late again, aren't you?!" his wife snapped, her voice teetering on the edge of an emotional breakdown.

The electrical storm that had been firing off in his brain all day immediately shut down. Chris opened his eyes and looked out the window in numb silence.

"I'm sorry, Emily." He walked over to his desk, and began mindlessly organizing the papers scattered across it. "I've been in back-to-back meetings all day, there's a ton of email I need to get through, and..."

"*Need* to get through or *want* to get through?"

Chris took a deep breath and held it. He felt helpless. "Don't say that, Emily. You're killing me here. It's just that I showed up an hour and a half late today after helping out at home this morning and now I've got some catching up I need to do. I'll be out of here by six o'clock once I put in my eight hours."

"So it's my fault then?"

"What? No. That's not what I said."

"Yes you did! You always point the finger back at me. Everything's my fault!"

In the background he heard a bang, followed by a pause, and then a child's scream. The scream grew louder as his daughter, Kira, approached her mother.

"Peter knocked over my tower!" She bawled.

Chris was about to ask what happened, when he heard the familiar electronic tone indicating Emily had hung up. The tension in his jaw and face were turning into a migraine. He wanted to smash his fist against his window and scream at the impossible task that haunted him. Every day now for the past three months, he had watched his wife sink deeper into her depression. He was having to constantly choose between job and family. And he was failing at both.

He decided to take a walk.

✳

It was well after dark by the time he arrived home and greeted his six-year-old daughter and three-year-old son. The two children sat in the middle of the living room in self-made nests of dirty laundry, glued to the flickering TV screen. Toys and half-eaten microwave dinners spotted the once blog-worthy decor. They barely noticed their father as he walked past them and made his way to the kitchen.

The open garbage canister filled his lungs with the stench of three-day-old rotting food as he passed by it. Dirty dishes filled the sink and empty Lunchable boxes teetered on the edge of the counter. He lowered the garbage lid as he passed by, quietly closed the half-opened fridge, and then opened the freezer to find something to eat.

From the stack of microwaveables, he grabbed a frozen pizza and popped it into the microwave. As the pizza spun slowly inside the oven, a strange sensation passed over Chris as though someone were standing immediately behind him. He knew it was insanity to look. There was no way that someone had crept into the house and, without his knowing, had snuck up behind him. But he had to look.

He turned slightly, glancing over his shoulder, and the feeling immediately disappeared.

"I'm going nuts," he whispered, rolling his eyes.

He turned back to the microwave and immediately the sensation returned. Chris shook his head and rubbed his eyes.

When the microwave finally beeped, Chris placed the pizza on the counter to cool and walked into the living room to start getting the kids ready for bed.

He clapped once. "Okay, guys, it's time to turn off the TV and get to bed."

The kids moaned at the request.

"Come on, squirts."

"Aw, Dad. It's almost over. Can't we finish watching it?" Kira protested.

Chris grabbed the remote off the couch and turned it off. "Come on. I need you guys to pick up your toys and get your teeth brushed."

Peter hopped out of his nest as though the protest had never happened and began placing the toys in the square wicker boxes on the white Ikea shelf while Kira threw a fit in protest.

"You know, Kira," Chris made eye contact with his daughter and then glanced over at a box on the top of the bookshelf, "don't worry about it. I'll go ahead and take care of it."

Slowly, he began making his way toward her favorite doll. Kira's eyes bounced back and forth between the toy and her dad, widening the closer he got. When he was a few feet away from the toy, she stopped crying, hopped out of the nest, and began hoarding all of her toys as quickly as she could, keeping a wary eye locked on her dad.

Five minutes later, the crankiness faded as Peter and Kira sent stuffed animals, action figures, and Legos on living room adventures that ended in Boxland. In the background, Chris supervised, stepping in occasionally to help the toys arrive at their destination sooner than later.

Thirty minutes later, the house was livable, the kids were in bed, and Chris finally settled down to enjoy his cold pizza. Between bites, he worked on tidying up the kitchen, telling Peter to get his butt back in bed, and catching up on email.

When he sent his last email and closed his laptop, he slumped forward and stared blankly at the center of the table.

Tension radiated across his neck and shoulders and his mind felt numb. He thought about the days before children, before marriage, when he could do whatever he wanted, whenever he wanted. Now those days felt like a distant dream in which an ambitious Chris would work late into the night and then wake up early to focus on things he was excited about. A dream where friends would call him and invite him to hang out with them, and where he felt giddy about spending time with his girlfriend who would later become his wife.

Those days were gone now. His ambitions had faded long ago. His friends were caught up in their own busy lives.

✳

After staring at the table for a while, Chris made his way down the hall toward the bedroom to try and work through his earlier conversation with Emily and subsequently relieve his own emotional suffering. With each step down the hallway, however, his anxiety increased.

Emily's depression had changed her perception of reality and altered her ability to talk rationally about anything. Chris had tried for months now to get her to see a therapist; He read up on depression and anxiety and tried to help her see the world from a more positive lens. He invited her to join him and the kids outside in the sun, walking around the block. He kept the house clean and comfortable when he could so she could feel a little more comfortable. But the more he tried, the more she retreated into the darkness. And the more time she spent in bed, the more she demanded from him.

By the time he made it to the bedroom door, his hands were shaking. An orange glow lined the edges of the door. He wasn't sure whether Emily and the baby had fallen asleep with the light on or if they were still awake. Their bedroom door often creaked, so Chris opened it carefully. As the door opened, he could see Simon sleeping in his crib, his little infant chest rising and falling peacefully.

He pressed harder and the door creaked. Chris held his breath and watched Simon squirm for a moment before settling back into that peaceful, rhythmic breathing. A shuddered breath exhaled quietly from Chris's lungs and he stepped cautiously through the door.

He expected to find an accusatory glare, but thought that maybe tonight things would be different. He turned to slow the momentum of the door before it creaked again and saw from the edge of his vision the woman he loved reclined in bed. She was void of expression, disconnected and staring at the crib. Her matted hair covered half of her face, and her pajamas sported days-old spit-up mark stains. The only sign that she felt anything at all were her red, swollen eyes. The anxiety Chris felt gave way to despair. Any hope that they might be able to talk things through tonight toppled with Emily into the recesses of that dark abyss into which she had retreated.

Chris closed the door behind him and crept quietly across the room, slipping into his pajamas, and then carefully sliding under the covers next to Emily. The second he settled into bed she sank into her covers and rolled onto her side, away from Chris.

For several minutes, Chris lay there staring at the wall, his mind and body consumed with emotional pain. He placed his hand gently on Emily's side, desperate to connect and heal what was broken. The moment his hand touched her, she shrugged it away.

For what seemed like an hour, the two of them lay there without speaking. Chris assumed Emily had fallen asleep. By 1:30 the baby began to fuss. Chris climbed out of bed, picked up Simon, and wandered back down to the kitchen to go through the usual routine: warming the bottle, changing his diaper, trying to keep his son from wailing, watching the clock, looking for a snack. His life had become so routine that most days he felt half asleep, half in a dream. Lost in a living nightmare.

Thirty minutes later Simon's voracious sucking had slowed to an occasional half-conscious sup, and his eyes rolled shut. Chris swapped out the bottle with a pacifier and made his way back to the bedroom. It was 2:36 a.m. when Chris finally closed his eyes and fell asleep.

✳

At 6:03 a.m. a faint glow from the bedroom window woke Chris. He rolled out of bed and hobbled over to the crib to see if Simon was still alive. Emily had always been certain that each of their children were at high risk of sudden infant death syndrome. Chris hadn't worried about it at first, but the more she talked about it, the more she indoctrinated him with obscure news articles, the more he worried. When he finally saw Simon's chest rise and fall, he sighed and began quietly preparing for another day.

Before children he had loved mornings — the silence, the time to sit and reflect, to be alone, to let his mind wander down creative paths and work through difficult problems before the distractions of the day steamrolled him. But kids changed everything. It was as though each child had come equipped with a built-in disruptor switch that was somehow triggered by Chris's consciousness. No matter how early he woke, the kids seemed to rise from their sleep shortly thereafter.

Today was no different. No sooner had he pulled cereal from the kitchen shelves than he heard the sound of little feet making their way down the hall. Moments later, a bleary-eyed little boy came around the corner rubbing his eyes, a half-dazed smile on his face.

The second he noticed the brightly colored Froot Loops cereal box on the counter Peter erupted into bird sounds as he circled the kitchen flapping his arms.

"Peter! Keep it down," he whisper-snapped.

Down the hall he could hear Simon beginning to fuss. Immediately his heart rate increased, and his face and shoulders tightened.

Peter fluttered over to his seat while Chris rolled his eyes and began filling Peter's bowl.

The second the cereal tumbled from the inner plastic bag, the room began to spin, and a deep whooshing sound popped his ears and drew his attention toward the cereal and the bowl.

Each colored O that splashed into the milk sounded as though someone were pounding large metal sheets with rubber mallets. Chris felt suspended in time, hyper-aware and yet completely oblivious. The thundering grew louder as the cereal continued to pour.

He felt trapped in a bowl watching sounds and colors morph into a swirling mass. As the cereal continued to fall from the box, the rainbow of fruit colors shifted to a muddy gray and then deep black. The sharpness of the sound dulled and deepened into that a horrifying, familiar drone. A wave of panic rushed over him and he felt an unexpected tap on his back.

Chris jolted around and made a pathetic groaning yelp. Behind him, Kira rubbed her eyes, one arm around her stuffed giraffe, the other now tapping the air.

"Simon woke me up, Daddy," she whined, oblivious to the panic on her father's face.

"Kira." Chris panted. "You about gave me a heart attack."

Kira stopped rubbing her eyes and looked up at the counter behind Chris. "Daddy, why are there Froot Loops all over the counter?" she asked groggily.

Chris turned and looked at the mess. Peter's bowl was now mostly hidden in an enormous pile of Froot Loops.

"Geez!" Chris cursed. "I swear I'm losing my mind." He leaned against the counter for a moment trying to catch his breath.

Down the hall, Chris heard Emily stagger out of bed and Simon's crying subside. His mind was already beginning to concoct worse-case scenarios about the day. How she would beg him to stay home the moment he opened the door to leave. How she would likely blame him for the kids watching TV all day and eating junk. How she might beat herself up until she became non-functional and dumped everything on him.

Chris closed his eyes, inhaled deeply, and turned his attention to getting Kira breakfast and packing her lunch for school.

Once the kids had been fed and the dishes cleaned up, Chris made his way back to the bedroom to check in on Emily and Simon. Shockwaves of anxiety pulsed through his body with each step. At the bedroom door, he paused, took a deep breath, and then pushed the door open slowly.

Emily had finished feeding Simon and had returned him to the crib where he lay wiggly and content. Cute baby noises issued from his little body as tiny hands, legs, fingers, and toes haphazardly explored the space around him. Emily stood in stark contrast beside the crib, staring beyond Simon, completely detached.

Chris's heart sank as he watched his wife. He approached her slowly, knelt down beside the crib, and watched Simon squirm and babble through the bars. Instinctively, Chris began making weird, adult, baby sounds back at Simon, contorting his face to match the sounds. Simon stared at Chris curiously for a moment and then released a joyful giggle, followed by a rumble from within his diaper.

Simon's giggling face immediately knotted itself into a concentrated grunt, followed by more rumbles. Chris looked up at Emily, chuckling softly, hoping the moment had sparked a flicker of light to her emotionless face. There was nothing. The anxiety, bitterness, and anger festered throughout Chris's body and he turned back to Simon, drawing from near-empty reservoirs of emotional strength to playfully coach his son through his morning bowel movement.

When Simon had finally finished doing his business, Chris could feel the full weight of Emily's emotional state pressing down on him. He swallowed hard, bit his lip, and stood up to change Simon's diaper.

"The strangest thing happened this morning," Chris said, as he walked Simon over to the changing table. Chris turned his head slightly toward Emily as he worked on Simon's diaper. She hadn't moved.

"I need you to stay home today, Chris," Emily whispered despondently. "I can't do this anymore."

Chris continued to change Simon's diaper without saying a word. His heart began racing, and he breathed deeply. Deep breaths seemed to have a way of keeping him from saying things he would later regret.

"Please," Emily begged, turning slowly toward Chris.

Chris tried to hold it together. "I want to Emily. I want to be able to stay home more and help out like I did those first three months after Simon was born.... it's just... I've used up all my leave. I've got nothing left. You're not working now and I can't just not work. You've got to know that I'm doing everything I can to help you out."

"So it's my fault?"

Chris could feel himself losing control. He placed Simon back in the crib and began pacing the bedroom. His breathing was quick and shallow now, and his mind a lightning storm of dark thoughts. He paused at the nightstand beside the bed and fixated on a crayon mark spanning the length of their brand-new nightstand.

"That's not what I said."

"Yes, you did. You said because I'm not working you can't help."

Suddenly, something inside of Chris snapped, as though a switch, over which he had no control had tripped. With everything he had, he kicked the side of the night stand over and over, releasing the pressure built up inside him. Emily grabbed Simon from the crib and took a step back, eyes wide.

"I can't do this either!" Chris screamed. "What am I supposed to do, Emily? You lay in bed all day and refuse to get help while I get the kids breakfast, take them to school, help with the baby, and show up at work two hours late. My coworkers and boss are starting to make up stories about what's going on. I wouldn't be surprised if they let me go soon. Then I come home after working late, clean the house, get the kids dinner, get them to bed, and you are right here where I left you. And all you seem to do is ask me to do more."

Chris's hands were shaking. He clasped them together and brought them to his mouth. Emily stared at him and held Simon close. She shook her head, tears streaming down her face. Simon began to cry.

She walked over to the rocker in the corner and sat down. Simon wailed louder as she attempted to place a pacifier in his mouth. The volume increased with each passing second and Emily began to bawl.

"Just leave!" she shouted, trying to get the pacifier to stay in Simon's mouth.

Anxiety, frustration, fear, anger, and guilt churned inside of Chris like an unstoppable vortex. He wanted to run and stay, collapse at her feet and punch the wall again, and again, and again. He wanted to comfort his wife and son whom he had hurt, apologize until they knew how sorry he was. But he couldn't.

Chris closed his eyes, took a deep breath, and bolted.

From the living room, his daughter had stopped playing and stared down the hall as Chris came storming out of the bedroom. Peter sat next to her, oblivious to anything other than the Duplo Legos in front of him.

"Daddy, why were you talking in your loud voice?" Kira asked.

Chris rushed past her without a word. Kira followed.

In the kitchen, Chris gathered his things for work: keys, lunch, laptop bag, and a report he had been working on. He felt a repetitive tug on his shirt that annoyed him beyond his capacity to deal with it.

"Daddy? Why were you talking in your loud voice? Huh?"

He wanted to turn and slap her, but the thought of striking his daughter cut him to the core. He clenched his fist, drew in a deep breath and turned to his daughter.

"Sometimes, Kira," Chris responded, his voice firm and controlled, "mommies and daddies fight, just like you and Peter. Right now, mommy and daddy need a time out, just like you and Peter."

Chris could see her little mind trying to make sense of what had just happened and what daddy was saying. He stood there for a moment trying to figure out what else he could say and then sighed, squatted down next to Kira, and placed her on his lap.

"Don't worry, girl. Everything will be fine. Mommy and daddy are just having a rough day."

More than anything he wanted to believe what he told his daughter, wanted someone to hold him, to reassure him that everything would be fine. But when he looked out on the horizon of their relationship, the landscape seemed infinitely dark. In his torment, Chris felt little arms wrap around his neck.

"It's okay daddy."

Kira let go of his neck and handed him a folded piece of paper.

"Me and Mr. Custard made this for you to help you feel better." Chris took the paper and she hugged the floppy, white monkey stuffy she had been holding in her other hand.

A depressed lump formed in the back of his throat, and he wrapped his arms around his daughter.

"Thanks Kira." He glanced up at the clock and realized school started in fifteen minutes.

"Shoot!"

Chris set her on the ground, placed the piece of paper in his pocket, and took her face in his hands.

"Kira, I need you to get your school clothes on as fast as you can. Can you do that?"

Kira nodded and sprinted to her room. As she disappeared around the corner, Chris grabbed her lunch, stuffed it into her backpack, and then finished packing his own things. In the background he could hear his wife and son crying uncontrollably. He knew that Peter wouldn't stay entertained with his Legos for long and headed to the living room to turn on the Disney Channel. He watched, heartbroken, as his little three-year-old's natural creativity and curiosity gave way to the zombie-like trance of the flickering screen. He leaned down to give Peter a hug goodbye just as Kira came bounding around the corner in a completely mis-matched outfit, shoes on the wrong feet. Too late to change her outfit, Chris helped her switch her shoes and together they headed out the door.

✳

When he arrived at work, an hour and a half late, his administrative assistant looked concerned.

"Chris, where have you been? Did you not get my text?"

He grappled for his phone that was buried in his pocket, and looked at the screen. It was dead.

"Shoot!" Chris cursed, his voice weak. "I must have forgot to plug it in last night."

"The VP called to see if you could attend the senior leadership meeting this morning. They want to discuss the HR segment of the enrollment task force recommendations. It started twenty minutes ago."

"Where?" Chris asked, feeling as though he were about to collapse.

"President's board room."

Chris rushed to his office, plugged in his phone, and made his way to the board room.

✸

When he entered the board room, Kyle, a young, near-replica of Chris, who had recently become his assistant director, nervously presented to the group. As Chris took his seat, his boss, a tall, bald man in his mid-fifties, glanced over at him disapprovingly through narrow, black-rimmed glasses. Everything in the room felt serious and void of energy — from the suits worn by both men and women to the deadpan expressions etched on the faces of those in the room to the oak-trimmed office decor.

As Kyle spoke, Chris couldn't shake the nagging frustration he felt over the content presented. The ideas he and his team had originally proposed to improve accountability, break down silos, and boost employee morale had been relentlessly shot down and modified over the past few months to the point that only a faint remnant of the original proposal remained.

The defeat he felt, mixed with severe sleep deprivation, and what he could only describe as recent insanity, made it impossible for him to stay focused on the meeting. Lost in the memories of the conflict with his wife this morning, he had retreated to the place where those numb to the world go. While he was there he failed to notice that Kyle had taken his seat and the eyes of everyone in the room had turned to him.

"Chris?"

Chris snapped back to reality and felt the beating glare of those in the room staring down on him — some with concern, others clearly put off by his lack of focus.

"Anything you would like to add?" Jack, his boss, asked, exasperated.

Chris quickly composed himself and cleared his throat. "First of all, let me apologize to everyone for being late. Our three-month-old son was up all night, and we had a little meltdown with the kids this morning I had to deal with," he lied, "So I apologize." The group smiled politely, void of sincerity.

"You know, there really isn't a lot I would add. I think Kyle did such a fantastic job summing up our recommendations." Chris glanced over at Kyle who returned a polite but insincere smile. "Perhaps the only thing I would add would be that I know that what we presented is a change for this institution. I know that change can be difficult and painful. But we feel confident that if the university is willing to take a risk and implement these recommended adjustments to our existing HR programs, we will see a marked improvement in employee satisfaction rates, greater collaboration across departments, and hopefully, as a result, increased enrollments."

For a moment, as Chris looked around at those in the room, he felt strangely confident in what he had said, pleased with his ability to articulate his position and the work they had done. For a brief moment, the incongruence that had haunted him earlier had vanished. He felt certain that this time the proposal would pass.

Wrapped up in that moment, however, he failed to notice the silence that persisted for an unusually long time. Most people in the room were now thumbing through the printed recommendations Kyle had distributed prior to Chris's arrival, without reading them.

"Chris, I admire your optimism," his boss finally interjected, "but the changes you and your team are recommending, while laudable, would be difficult to implement here from both a cost perspective and a cultural perspective."

Chris felt a sharp pain in his chest as though his boss had thrust a javelin through the last particle of hope.

Others within the group nodded. A thin, older woman with a pixie haircut, streaked with gray, leaned forward to speak. Years of administrative monotony had etched a permanent frown across her tired face.

"Jack is absolutely right. Your ideas are good. I just think that given the fragile nature of employee morale right now, we need to explore more subtle ways to invite change at this institution. Thinking both short term and long term. I would hate to implement change that only makes matters worse."

Chris leaned forward and again cleared his throat. "With all due respect, Dr. Price, I'm afraid that the longer we wait to institute changes like these, the worse things will become. As much as I value each employee at this institution and want to see them be successful, the longer we allow poor performers to go unchecked and fail to recognize and reward those who are contributing to the advancement of this institution, the more likely our top talent will start looking elsewhere. I know this sounds harsh, but there are toxic individuals at this institution who, in my opinion, need to either step up or get out."

Chris could feel his heated emotions beginning to flare, and he could see that Dr. Price was not taking kindly to his push back.

"Don't think that we don't recognize that, Chris." Dr. Price rambled on condescendingly about people of influence within the university and how she didn't want to offend them. "I would much rather work with these individuals over time to help them step up than to simply start taking punitive actions as a result of an evaluation tool that HR has developed over the past few months."

Chris looked down and began shaking his head, smiling uncomfortably, as others nodded. The agitation he felt carried over into his voice.

"Our HR and professional development programs have been working with these individuals for years now. The problem is that the people who most need those programs never participate. We can't just sit back and allow deadweights to bring this institution to its demise just because we're afraid to take action against them. Look, I know there will be consequences. I know this will be hard and painful, but the alternative of not acting or taking less disruptive measures will only exacerbate the problem."

Dr. Price's face flushed red and her frown deepened. Others in the room smiled awkwardly and fidgeted with their phones and notebooks. Chris could feel his jaw clenching. He and his team had spent months gathering data, talking to supervisors and their direct reports, and looking into what other organizations were doing to handle the issues they were up against. HR had done more in the last few months than the institution had done in the past few decades. They understood the problem. Senior leadership did not.

"Chris, can I say something?" the president of the institution interjected.

President Reed, a dignified woman in her mid-fifties, smiled gently and leaned forward tucking her shoulder-length auburn hair behind her ear. Her arrival at the institution had been a godsend after the previous dictatorial and mildly unethical leadership of the former president.

"I truly appreciate the time, thoughtfulness, and commitment to the goals of the university that you and your team have put into this project. While your team's efforts and suggestions are commendable and worth exploring, I think it would be wise if we conduct a little more research and consider policy changes before implementing any potentially disruptive solutions." She turned to Jack. "Jack, I'm wondering if you wouldn't mind working with the cabinet members at our next executive meeting to narrow down those areas of focus? Once the cabinet narrows that down, you can guide Chris and his team on additional research they may need to pursue in order to identify better solution recommendations for the cabinet to implement over the next few years."

"Absolutely, President," Jack responded.

"Thanks Jack and Chris, and thank you for all the time and energy your team has put into this. The next item on the agenda is..."

Chris felt like a piece of trash that had been tossed out the third-story window and landed in a pile of pillows. It took him a moment to realize that the conversation was now over. President Reed trailed off and both Chris and Kyle picked up their bags and headed out into the hall, dazed by what had just happened.

As they headed down the hallway neither of them spoke. Once they were outside the building, Kyle turned to Chris and unleashed.

"What a freaking waste of our time. This whole project has been a waste of our time! What do they mean spend more time researching!? And policy changes!? How is that going to make any difference whatsoever? They basically want us to fix the problem without changing anything." Kyle looked down and shook his head.

"Yeah," Chris acknowledged and mentally trailed off.

He felt defeated. The illusion that he or his team could have any sort of lasting impact at Queen's Mount University faded with each meeting he attended, but today felt like the final blow. It was clear to him now, his job was not to innovate, but to maintain. Not to lead, but to follow. Chris could feel his sense of control, his ambition, his motivation, sliding away with each step he and Kyle took across campus.

"I guess it's time to start re-thinking things," Chris responded despondently.

Kyle stopped walking and looked over at Chris. "The only thing I am going to be re-thinking is my job."

Chris paused, sighed deeply, and began rubbing his forehead. "Come on, Kyle. We'll get through this. It's just another bump in the road. Let's give the cabinet some time and see what they come up with. Maybe it won't be as bad as we think."

Kyle glared at Chris, squinting and shaking his head, as though he could see right through the show Chris had been putting on.

"Okay." Chris said, "I'll talk with Jack tomorrow and see if there might be something we could do to revisit the conversation. I mean," he looked down and shook his head, "maybe if we can get them more data before they meet or survey a few more employees. I don't know, maybe that will help."

Kyle took a deep breath and looked up to the sky. "You know," he paused, "at this point I really don't care." Kyle looked back at Chris and then down at the sidewalk. "I think I just need to step away from this for a while. I'll see you when I see you, Chris."

Kyle headed off toward the student center. Chris felt the sun beating down on his shoulders and noticed that it was relatively quiet around campus, unusual for this time of day. But then, he really didn't know what time it was. He felt tired. Not just physically tired, but life-tired.

From behind him he felt a brief, passing touch on his shoulder that took him by surprise.

"You look lost, Chris. You headed to the equity and access meeting?"

He turned toward Angie from Payroll's voice. She slowed her pace to wait for Chris.

"Is it already that time?" Chris asked, reaching for his phone in his empty pocket.

Angie looked at him suspiciously. "Are you okay, Chris? You seem a bit off."

Chris stared at her, half zoned out. "Sorry, no. I. It's been one of those days," he responded. "Here, I'll walk with you."

Angie brushed off her suspicion, and together they made their way across campus to the next meeting.

✳

Two hours later, Chris returned to his office through the back door. He wasn't one to avoid others, but today he needed time to process as desperately as his administrative assistant needed time to talk.

To his relief, most of his staff had stepped out for lunch, allowing him to slip through the hallway unnoticed. Chris sighed, quietly closed his office door, and then sank into his ergonomic chair. Immediately, his left leg began to bounce neurotically. He made a conscious effort to control it, but his mind trailed off and his leg resumed its compulsive shuddering.

His drained phone popped into his head, and he reached over to unplug it from the charger. He thought about the remark someone had made in the last meeting about one of the college advisors getting arrested for inappropriate behavior. He wiggled his mouse to wake his computer and look up the story on the local news site. His phone dinged as he searched, and he picked it up to see who had pinged him. Nothing important. He returned to his search. When the news site loaded, he skipped to the sports section and decided to take a quick detour.

What am I doing? He knew he was wasting his time, knew he had more important things to do, but he couldn't seem to stop himself.

Outside his door he could hear Kyle and Tara making their

way down the office hallway. Tara's petite Asian figure, long black hair, and confident personality had captured the attention of most single guys in the office, even though most of them were too intimidated to talk to her; except Kyle. Ever since Tara had joined the team as the new Equal Employment Opportunity Officer a few months earlier, the awkward attraction between the two of them had driven everyone in the office bonkers.

Chris rolled his eyes as they flirted outside his door. As much as he loved his window view, the thin walls had always bothered him.

After what seemed like an eternity to Chris, Tara's giggling began fading off as their conversation shifted to less flirty topics.

"So how did it go in your meeting this morning?" she asked.

"Honestly?" Kyle responded.

"Well, yeah."

There was a pause and then Kyle continued in a more subdued voice. "It sucked."

"Chris again?" She was talking so quietly now that Chris had to focus hard to understand what she was saying.

"His light's out. Probably out to lunch. Here, we should probably step into my office." Kyle's tone was serious now.

Chris could hear the door next to his open and then close. The second the door closed, Kyle let loose.

"I have about had it up to here with Chris," he shot out. "I have climbed out on a limb for him, how many times now, and for what? For him to come along and screw it all up. Senior leadership was so close to buying in to what we've been working on, and then Chris shows up a half an hour late, starts doing a rah rah monologue about how change is difficult but necessary, gets all heated with Dr. Price about ousting slackers, and now we are back at level zero. Then he acts like it's no big deal — we'll just see what the cabinet wants us to do and get through this — which is another way of saying what they want *me* to do. I'm telling you,

Tara, I am done with this place."

There was another pause and some shuffling before Tara continued quietly as though she were afraid someone might be listening. "I was talking to Leslie the other day and she was like, we barely see him in his office. No one has any idea what he's doing. It's like he is avoiding us or something. Jan says she thinks he's getting a divorce, probably cheating on his wife."

"It wouldn't surprise me," Kyle said, completely apathetic. "But you know what, at this point, I really don't care."

"So what are you going to do?"

"I don't know. I've put out a couple of applications in the corporate world. The tech industry is hot right now. Not as fulfilling as higher ed, but then the last few months working with Chris have not exactly been what I would call fulfilling."

Another long pause.

"I haven't really mentioned this to anyone," Chris heard more shuffling and then Tara continued, "so don't say anything, but a friend of mine just launched a tech startup and they've been growing like crazy. It's like a data warehouse or something. Supposedly they acquired a huge amount of investment capital, and she keeps begging me to join her."

"You should totally take it," Kyle jumped in excitedly. "I mean, you're single, you have no commitments, you're really good at what you do. This could be a chance of a lifetime."

"I don't know. My friend seems like she is working 24/7 and I kinda like my weekends." Another short pause. "But you're right, the climate around here has been a little rough lately."

"Think about it. You could craft whatever culture you wanted, and after a few years when things got settled, I'm sure you would get your weekends back, and, with your salary, you could probably spend them in Paris. And tell her you know a guy with several years of HR experience that would be your assistant."

Tara giggled and Chris heard an "Ow!" which he could only assume was a flirtatious punch to the arm. There was another brief pause as the laughter died down.

"Shoot! I've got a meeting," Chris heard more shuffling and then the door next to his opened.

"Hey," Kyle said as the door closed. "You doing anything tonight?"

As they finalized the details for their date, Chris slumped back in his chair hurt and furious. He wanted to sit in the corner of his office and cry, and then fire Kyle and Tara to help them escape their nightmare they were both apparently living. Kyle and Chris had been friends before Chris's promotion. In fact, it was Kyle who had encouraged him to apply for the job in the first place.

Out of the lower corner of his eye, he noticed a tiny movement and looked down at his lap as a small brown spider scurried across his leg. His entire body reacted the second it registered, and the panicked movement hurled his weight backward, tilting his office chair to a point of near-perfect balance. Chris hovered there for half a second swatting frightfully at the spider while he swung his arms in the air to counterbalance his chair's precarious angle. The second he managed to brush it off, he passed the point of no return and his chair shot out from underneath him, toppling him heals over head to the ground.

For several minutes he lay there breathing his way through his damaged pride. Whatever made him snap earlier that morning with Emily welled up inside of him again. He had no one to turn to. His wife was checked out. His friends had distanced themselves from him years ago. He thought he had a good relationship with his coworkers but obviously not.

He had to get out. Had to breathe before he exploded again. In the darkness of his thoughts, he barely noticed himself picking his body up off the floor, stuffing his phone into his pocket, stepping out into the hallway, and making a beeline for the back door.

The second he stepped outside, an alert popped up on his phone. It was a text from Emily.

Please come home! Peter is throwing a fit. I CAN'T DO THIS!

He squeezed the phone so hard he was certain it would shatter in his hand. He wanted to throw it across the street; watch it smash into a thousand pieces. For a fleeting second, he thought he might do it, but he didn't want to make a scene. He stuffed the phone in his pocket and walked as fast as he could toward the surrounding row-house neighborhoods. When he had cleared the main flow of people, the walking turned to jogging and the jogging to a full out run.

The sprint only lasted a few blocks before he entered the city park and collapsed onto a bench completely winded. He could feel his pulse in his ears as he gasped at the air to catch his breath. His mind raced maddeningly from one negative thought to another: his fight with Emily, the condescending tone of Dr. Price, Kyle's betrayal, the chaos at home, his TV anesthetized kids.

He placed his head between his knees and started to shake. He couldn't breathe. His chest felt tight.

I'm having a heart attack.

His ears began to ring — a loud and piercing blare that rushed and morphed into a monstrous, unearthly drone.

"Oh God!" He groaned and looked up to the sky.

All around him people he hadn't seen before stopped and stared at him, hatred singed on their faces.

Chris glanced fearfully at the crowd. *I'm losing my mind. I'm losing my mind. I'm losing my mind.* He curled into himself, covering his face with his hands.

The sound grew louder with each passing second, grinding into his eardrums. It was unbearable now, emanating from and permeating into everything around him. The eyes of the crowd bore down on him, as though they were only inches away. He smelled their acrid breath.

A loud mechanical whir jolted him from the terror. He opened his eyes and watched. The wing of a large passenger jet clipped the buildings in front of him and pivoted the body of the plane directly toward his bench. A second later the world went black.

CHAPTER 2

Airplanes

W hen he finally came to, burning debris covered the ravaged cityscape. Fallen electric lines hummed and snapped around him. The masses of angry people had disappeared. To his surprise, it was night now, and the bench he sat on, like himself, had been completely untouched.

He glanced around at the devastation through dream-clouded eyes. The building in front of him had partially collapsed from the plane's impact. Surrounding buildings were charred, their windows blown out. Smoke billowed up into the night sky, illuminated by small, crackling fires scattered throughout the area.

He expected to see bodies or body parts lying around him, but he was alone. *Maybe they were obliterated. But how am I still alive?* He took in the scene, trying to make sense of what had happened. Everything felt surreal and strangely peaceful. He stood up and listened to the flames and the electricity.

"Is anyone there!" he yelled, looking around for any signs of movement. "Hello!"

A sickening thought slipped into his mind.

"Hello! Is anyone there?" he demanded. His voice felt different. The sound. It didn't carry like it should. Something wasn't right.

"Oh God," he moaned, looking toward the sky. "I can't be dead. Oh God, please don't let me be dead."

"Oh, you're not dead," a matter-of-fact voice commented from behind him.

Chris spun around as a prophetic looking man dressed in a stylish casual business suit stepped out from behind a large piece of wreckage. The man coughed and choked on the smoke that billowed up around him. He maneuvered his way through the debris piles, careful to avoid smudging his suit.

Chris stared curiously at the man who appeared to be a few inches shorter than he was. He carried a brown leather shoulder bag that he guarded carefully as he negotiated the debris. When he arrived at the bench Chris had been sitting on, he sat down with a sigh.

"Not a lot of time," he said as he brushed off dust and ash that had settled on his suit, and began fumbling through his bag.

Chris stared at the man, confused.

"Chris Alexander, right?"

"Excuse me?" Chris replied, his tone guarded.

The stranger thumbed through a folder he had pulled from his bag. "That's your name, right? Chris Alexander? Two first names, hah."

"Do I know you?" Chris asked suspiciously.

"No, you don't know me. You've never met me before. But I know you. Know everything about you." He flipped through the folder. "You have three children, your wife has major postpartum depression, which is just a flare up of her life-long struggle with chronic anxiety and depression."

He turned a couple more pages, scanning them with his

finger. "Looks like you were excited about your job when you started, what, nine months ago, but now you dread going to work and feel completely deflated by it." He turned a few more pages. "Huh. Says here that just today you heard your coworkers venting about how lame they think you are as a leader. Wow, and strange dreams, meltdowns with your wife. Sounds like you could use a therapist or something," he said nonchalantly.

"Where did you get that?" Chris demanded, on the verge of yanking the folder from his hand. He wasn't sure whether this was a sick practical joke or if someone was trying to defame him.

"No, Chris, this is not a practical joke. No one is spying on you or your family and no one is trying to drag you through the mud," the stranger replied. He looked up from the papers at a now wide-eyed Chris.

"Geez." Chris rubbed his head and studied the devastation surrounding them. "I'm going nuts." He paused for a moment and then turned back at the stranger. "So who exactly are you?"

"The answer to that question is a bit complicated, Chris. I supposed the easiest answer is to say I'm David. But that's not usually what folks like you are looking for when they ask that question. So what I like to tell them is that I'm sort of like a well-timed teacher. I help people see things they can't see, that they need to see, when they need to see them. Sometimes it's subtle, you know, but other times it requires a bit more—" he paused and stroked his beard, "—*intervention*, shall we say."

"So, what are you, like a guardian angel or something? Or is this some sort of weird, other dimensional, wormhole thing I stepped into?"

David chuckled. "I think you've spent a little too much time watching late-night television. The reality, Chris, is that people from different cultures and religions would likely call me, call *this*," he continued, gesturing to the scene before them, "something different based on their life experience, perceptions, and choices.

But regardless of what they call me or think of me as, it ultimately doesn't change the reality of who I am, what I am, and why I'm here with you today.

"Knowing who or what I am isn't relevant to what you and I need to accomplish right now. So, forget about trying to make sense of or understand what *this* is and accept it for what it appears to be. When you do that, you'll find that you're closer to the answers you need than you thought. Can you agree to do that?"

Chris stared at David for a moment and then shook his head and muttered under his breath. "I'm losing it. It's just a dream. Just a weird, bad dream."

David continued to smile at Chris, waiting patiently.

Chris studied the wreckage around him and then turned back to David. "You sure I'm not dead?"

David shook his head quietly, his smile receding a little.

Chris sighed, "Well, it sure doesn't seem like a dream. Too real." He paused and looked around at the scene again.

"It's as real as you and me," David added.

Chris shook his head again and started pacing. "Then, why am I alive? I shouldn't be alive. This doesn't make any sense."

"Doesn't need to make sense," David sighed. "A lot of things that happen in life don't need to make sense. You, Chris, have done way too much rational thinking in the wrong direction up to this point in your life. It's time for you to stop trying to make sense of things, open your mind, and accept what this life is trying to offer you."

Chris shook his head and bit his lower lip "No." He chuckled nervously. "No." He reached into his pocket and pulled out his cell phone. No signal.

"They will be fine," David reassured him softly. He paused and half-glanced over his shoulder as though he were talking to someone else. "Always worrying about things they have so little control over. Making things out to be far worse than they are."

He turned back to Chris who was mumbling to himself and fixated on his phone. David's hint of a smile faded and he glanced down at his watch and sighed loudly. "You're avoiding my question. Can you agree to stop trying to fit things inside your little box so we can get on with what needs to be done here?"

Chris put his hand up to his mouth and looked around. Beads of sweat trickled down his forehead and into his eyes. The salt-soot combination burned and he wiped it away with a trembling hand. He looked over at David, eyed the side street he had come from, and took off at a sprint, dodging and scrambling over debris. David sighed and shook his head.

All around Chris, the acrid smoke billowed up from crippled buildings and flaming debris. He hacked as he maneuvered through the rubble, pausing occasionally to get his bearing. The wreckage seemed endless, as though he were living in the infinite space between facing parallel mirrors. Everything felt both unfamiliar and familiar. The street he was on should have opened onto campus several blocks back. At the same time, he was certain that the campus was just ahead on the right.

Twenty minutes into his graceless escape, his half-tucked, button-down shirt dripped with sweat and he hunched over to catch his breath, wheezing and coughing. The skies above glowed starless and muddy orange—a ceiling of smoke illuminated by the fires below. He stood in silence looking around at the scene, certain he had entered another stress-induced dream.

"Hello!" he shouted. "Anyone!"

In the distance, a low rumble rose from an unseen horizon and passed through him. Its vibrations rattled his body and brought back distant memories. He held his breath and didn't move. The sound intensified with each passing second, twisting itself into that familiar drone that had haunted his darkened mind since his nap in the office. Only this time, as strange as this dream was, it didn't feel like a dream, it felt real. Before long the sound had grown into a column of black smoke swallowing the city. Chris covered his ears to block it out and immediately it stopped, as though blown away by some unseen force.

"Strange, isn't it?"

Chris jolted toward the now familiar voice. A half block away, David walked calmly toward him.

"In this place, you can run forever and never find what you are looking for. Most people spend their lives running in the wrong direction; searching in the wrong places, blinded by shallow questions that reinforce their perceptions of reality. Stuck in a loop like the one you are in now." He reached down and picked up a piece of brick. It disintegrated into black ash and poured between his fingers. "But it's all an illusion, one we have unknowingly crafted for ourselves. In this place, to get what you want, you often have to do the opposite of what you feel compelled to do. The more you follow the compulsion and react, the deeper you go into the loop, and the darker it gets. But if, instead of yielding to habit — to compulsions that drag you down — you pause and listen to the voice inside that invites you to turn and walk in the opposite direction, you will find that what you thought you wanted was nothing but a distraction to keep you from what you really need."

"But it's your choice, Chris." David brushed the ash off his hands. "You can continue to run or you can stop running for once, open your mind, and choose a different path."

Chris looked at the ground, still trying to catch his breath. Sweat dripped from his forehead. He picked up a piece of debris and hurled it at one of the nearby buildings. David's words made no sense. This place made no sense. But as much as he wanted to scream and continue to run, he knew David was right. He was tired of running.

"Chris," David said softly, stepping up to Chris and placing his hand on his shoulder. "Your job, your family, your wife, they will be fine. In fact, they will likely be significantly better..." He leaned in until his eyes met Chris's. He took a deep breath and turned serious. "... if you can pick your fat, out-of-shape self off the ground and trust someone beside yourself for once in your life."

Chris frowned at the fat comment and clenched his fists. Immediately, he heard his hands squish and looked down. Sweat dripped off his arms and hands, and his shirt's light blue fabric clung tight to his drenched gut. A belly button crater marked the pinnacle of his bulge, and his stomach hung out over his belt beneath his untucked shirt. David was right.

He let out a deep sigh and relaxed his fists. "Fine." Chris looked up at the sickly, gray-orange cloud cover. "So where do we go from here?"

"Now *that* is a good question," David replied, a smile returning to his face. "If you'll walk through this door over here to the left, you'll be back in your office, and everything will be back to normal."

"Really?"

David laugh-snorted. "Of course not, this is just the beginning. I was only playing with you."

"Geez man." Chris sneered at David's odd sense of humor.

David slapped Chris on the shoulder and began making his way back down the street. "Come on Chris. Life is way too short to take everything seriously. It's like you're a college administrator or something."

Chris stared blankly at David and then hurried to catch up. The two of them turned down a side street and within a block had returned to the crash site where they had started. Chris couldn't believe it.

Toward the far end of the park, between toppled trees,

crumpled metal, and scattered slabs of concrete, were the partial, smoking remains of the plane's fuselage. David and Chris wormed their way carefully through the debris toward the gaping hole in the rear end of the fuselage where the tail had detached.

David stopped a few feet from the rear of the fuselage and gestured to Chris. "After you."

Chris stared at David and glanced back and forth between the bearded man and the smoking, dark hole in the rear of the plane.

"You want me to climb up there?"

The nose of the fuselage had buried itself into the earth lifting the rear of the plane perhaps six feet off the ground.

"Here, I'll give you a hand." David bent over and linked his fingers together so that Chris could use his hands as a step to boost himself into the hull filled with dislodged passenger seats, scattered luggage, and exposed wires.

Chris shook his head but knew it was pointless to argue with David. He placed his foot in David's hands, grabbed hold of the torn metal edge of the fuselage, and gracelessly flopped himself into the plane. The second his body cleared the edge, everything changed, as though he had passed through some invisible portal.

The fuselage was clean, quiet, and like new. Fluorescent lights illuminated the center walkway, and rows of rigid, blue upholstered chairs—three in a row to each side—lined the walkway. Above, luggage compartments had been left ajar as though the plane had just been vacated. Chris pulled himself to his feet, and immediately, the cockpit doors opened. The captain stepped out and rounded the corner to exit the plane. A second later he returned and made a quick, inspective glance into the fuselage before re-entering the cockpit. He didn't seem to notice Chris standing at the back of the plane. Chris could hear the sound of passengers entering the Jetway and moments later they began filing into the plane looking for their seats.

Everyone seemed oblivious to Chris as they filled in the front row.

"There's someone I want you to meet," David said from behind.

"Geez!" Chris gasped. "Don't sneak up on me like that." He watched as people continued filing in and then turned back to where the hole had been. "This is so surreal."

"Let's head up front there." David continued, nudging Chris forward.

Chris scanned the plane in a daze as the two men wove their way through the aisle, pushing past people who were beginning to notice the two men. When they arrived at the first-class section, David motioned toward one of the empty seats next to a fashionably dressed, young man in his mid-thirties.

"Go ahead," David said, gesturing toward the seat.

Chris eyed David suspiciously but didn't argue.

The man, who was settling into his own seat, glanced at Chris as he sat, and then let out a disgusted sigh. "Typical." He rolled his eyes as he fidgeted with his carry-on under his seat.

"Excuse me?" Chris was on the verge of a blow-up now with so many people pushing him around today.

"Oh, sorry," the stranger replied, his voice littered with inconvenience. "Didn't mean you. It's just that this whole day has been such a bore."

"Definitely not a bore for me," Chris mumbled. He looked over at the man and then gestured to the cabin. "So are you in on all this too?"

"In on what?" The man stared at Chris suspiciously.

"I guess not," Chris said quietly and turned to the seat in front of him. He felt like an idiot.

For a moment, the two of them sat there without speaking. Something about the whole thing felt strangely familiar to Chris. He glanced over at the stranger who had reclined his seat and closed his eyes. The man's entire body emanated discomfort, disgust, something unpleasant. Chris stared at him for a moment, and then it clicked.

"Matt... Taylor?" Chris asked hesitantly.

"Who's asking?" he said, his eyes still closed.

"You're the head of People and Culture at Moth IO right?"

Matt opened one eye and looked over at Chris suspiciously.

"Look man, I'm sorry. I read your book about the crazy things you guys have been doing in the human resources space; radical transparency, unlimited leave, salaries based on value-add to the company, in-house employee services, public performance dashboards." Chris paused. "I've been trying to get our institution to buy into the ideas you mention in your book, but talking to our leadership is like talking to a brick wall. How do you do it?"

"Right," Matt responded with complete disinterest and closed his eye.

Chris couldn't believe his lack of interest in the topic. He stared at Matt for a moment and then sank back into his own chair and glanced around the cabin. *Where is David?* Maybe he was going crazy. Everything seemed so real.

"So, what are you," Matt asked, eyes still closed, "like, HR director in some government institution?"

Chris turned back to Matt, shaking away the insanity thoughts. "Yeah, that's right. Queens Mount University. How did you know that?"

"No offense dude, but you're all the same." He opened his eyes and looked over at Chris. "You all seem to think that people operations in tech is like the pinnacle of what HR should be like. You think if you can just convince your leadership to roll out similar programs in your organization, it will change everything." Matt paused for a moment and bit his lips. He seemed to be struggling internally with something that was about to burst.

He leaned closer to Chris, squinted, and lowered his voice, "I'll tell you what though, the only thing that taking radical HR measures will change is how entitled everyone at your organization becomes, and how much work it creates for you to maintain their expectations, just so they don't take a better package somewhere else. And when they do move on, guess whose fault it is?" His lips tightened, and he jabbed at his chest with his index finger and then turned and reclined back into his seat.

"Our job," he continued, rolling his head toward Chris and gesturing with his finger between the two of them, "you and me, is to keep entitled people from leaving and help people work out stupid, petty problems they should be able to work out on their own. That's the bottom line. Only difference between you and me, between your industry and mine, is I work longer hours with more pressure and make a lot more money. But I can tell you, the money, it's not worth it."

Chris could feel the foundation upon which he had constructed his entire world view of HR crumbling. *What a freaking fraud! How could someone who published bestselling human resources books and become a model for everyone else be so caustic about the work he's been claiming is so great?* From behind him Chris felt a tap on his shoulder followed by the sound of a man clearing his throat.

"Um. Excuse me. I believe that's *my* seat you're sitting in."

Chris turned and saw a middle-aged man, about fifty pounds overweight, standing above him. Sweat dripped off his balding head and stained the armpits of his white, button-down shirt.

Before Chris had a chance to respond, the man began yelling to the flight attendant. "What is going on here? Why is this man in my seat?"

Chris stood up and tried to step out of the man's way. "Hey man, I'm sorry. I didn't know..."

"Didn't know? Didn't know? Where is your ticket? Stewardess!" his voice cracked. "I was supposed to have my own aisle. This is ridiculous. Look I paid for two seats."

"There must have been some sort of mistake," Chris interjected apologetically, "I'm really sorry about this."

The man ignored Chris's apology and continued shouting toward the flight attendant. "I can't sit there. This seat needs to be sterilized. Stewardess!"

The flight attendant, a petite African American woman pushed her way through the crowded aisle from the back of the plane. Chris felt embarrassingly irritated by the man's childish temper display. All around him, gridlocked passengers began expressing their frustration.

"I'm sorry, sir." The flight attendant squeezed past the last few passengers. "What seems to be going on?"

While the man ranted about the injustice he had suffered, the flight attendant listened patiently. Once he had finished unloading on her, the flight attendant asked the two men for their tickets.

Chris fumbled through his pockets and scanned the floor. "Huh. I must have dropped it somewhere," he lied. The passengers seated nearby glanced around to help him find it. The disheveled, sweat-stained, businessman handed his ticket to the flight attendant and glared condescendingly at Chris. He wanted to deck the man.

The flight attendant watched Chris fumble through his pockets and sighed, "Sir, if you could come with me, we'll get this sorted out."

The flight attendant escorted Chris up the Jetway and out of the gate where crowds of passengers had gathered for zone two.

"I am so sorry about that sir." She stepped behind the counter at the gate and tapped at the keyboard. "Do you have your ID with you?"

Chris dug through his pockets nervously and pulled out his driver's license. She typed something on the keyboard and then squinted her eyes.

"Huh. There doesn't seem to be any record of you in our system."

Chris leaned in on the counter and tried to act surprised. He felt stupid.

"Here, let me give my manager a call and see if she can help get this sorted out. You are welcome to take a seat if you'd like. This might take a few minutes." The flight attendant picked up the phone to call her manager and was interrupted by one of the three passengers who had been standing behind Chris.

While the flight attendant helped the next person in line, Chris made his way to a vacant seat next to a stout, African American woman. The moment he sank into the blue, pleather-wrapped metal bench, tension gave way to exhaustion. Thoughts he couldn't let go of raced frantically from one explanation to another, trying to make sense of what was going on. He released his breath and stared at the passengers filing into the Jetway. From off to his side, he could feel someone watching him. He turned toward the sensation and saw the woman he had collapsed next to eyeing him up and down.

"Rough day, hun?" she sympathized, her I-might-womp-you-across-the-back-of-your-head-with-my-purse expression fading away as she finished sizing him up.

She shuffled a little in her seat and adjusted the off-white, wool cardigan covering her burgundy dress. Her curly black hair was pulled back tight in a bun, and her sudden, genuine interest in his well-being immediately disarmed Chris.

"It's been a weird one for sure." He sighed and turned his attention back to the boarding passengers.

The woman stared at him for a moment and then continued. "Well, I'll tell you what, ain't nothin' a little of mama's homemade taffy can't fix." She leaned over with difficulty and grabbed her large purse. She shuffled through it for a second and pulled out a wax paper wrapped piece of candy and handed it to Chris. "Now that right there is some of the finest saltwater taffy east of the Mississippi."

Chris looked over hesitantly and took the candy. The woman shuffled as she attempted to push her bag back under her chair.

"If you want any more you just ask," she said, and then settled back into her seat. "What's your name, hun?"

"Chris," he replied unwrapping the taffy.

"Well ain't that a fine name? My brother's name's Chris. He passed away a few years ago from the cancer, but he was the sweetest soul to ever gift God's green earth." She reminisced for a second and then extended her hand toward Chris. "I'm Freda."

Chris popped the candy into his mouth and took her hand. "I'm sorry to hear that. Wow, you're right, that is good taffy."

"Mmm hhh!".

She smiled and then turned to the current of people moving up and down the terminal. "Well, I never."

She struggled to get to her feet and made her way toward the central walkway.

"Can you believe the nerve of some people?"

Between the opposing flows of travelers, an older Hispanic man in dark navy coveralls hunched over next to an airport sign and struggled to clean up a large puddle of water that was rapidly spreading across the floor. Beside him a man in a business suit pointed at the cuff of his slacks and shouted profanities that faded into the noise of the airport crowds. The custodian stared at the floor timidly until the exasperated businessman shook his head and stomped off.

The old janitor struggled to right the tipped bucket just as Freda arrived. Chris watched as she placed her hand on the old man, grabbed a clean rag from his sanitation cart, and began sopping up the water from the floor and wringing it into the bucket. The old man said something to Freda who protested and continued helping until the floor was spotless. When they finished, the man shook her hand with both of his. Freda smiled, said something to the man who smiled back, and then returned to her seat.

"That was nice of you to help that man out," Chris said as Freda settled back into her seat. He felt ashamed at his own inaction.

"We sanitation experts got to look out for our own."

"Really? You're a janitor?"

Freda's confidence and determination, along with her well-dressed appearance, was the last thing he expected from someone working as a janitor.

"Sho nuff," she responded with pride, sitting up a little taller in her seat. "I been helpin' people keep their spaces workable and fine fo the last twenty years."

"That's amazing," Chris replied. Her authenticity and conviction toward what Chris always thought of as menial work threw him off. "I mean, most janitors I've met sure aren't as enthusiastic about their jobs as you are."

"Oh, I get that. When I first wandered down this career path, I was anything but enthusiastic. I mean me! Bein' a janitor! Forever! No, that wasn't who Freda was. I was better than that. I was gonna do *big* things one day. Then, after several months of feeling sorry for myself, I said to myself…I said, 'Freda. This sour, I-hate-my-life attitude is gonna carry you straight to the grave. Maybe one day you'll go to college. Maybe one day you'll find a better job. But right now that ain't happenin', so you better change your attitude or you gonna make yourself and everyone around you miserable.'"

"Really?" Chris replied, certain now that the woman was an actress in whatever strange play he had been cast in.

"That's right. I decided to start looking at my job as more of a *calling*. You know what I'm saying?"

Chris leaned back in his chair and stared at Freda in disbelief. She glared back at him as though she had lowered her reading glasses.

"Soon as I started figurin' out how my work was making a *difference* in the lives of people in my building, things started gettin' better."

Chris nodded distantly, his gaze drifting toward the ground.

"I know that sound kinda strange and all, but it's the truth. Me taking out that awful smelling trash made it easier for the vice president to concentrate. Me keeping the bathroom clean helped Ryan, who was a hypochondriac, feel a little more comfortable so he could get more sales. So you see, my job became critical to the success of the company and the well-bein' of everyone there. And you know what happened?"

"What's that?" The show was getting old now.

"I found my dream job." Freda smiled. "Sure it have it's days, but I tell you what Chris, when you love what you do and who you do it for, those days, they don't matter one bit."

Chris snickered briefly and stared at Freda who raised an eyebrow at him. His inner skeptic took a back seat to matter-of-fact warmth.

"Passengers in Zone three for flight 3657 to Jacksonville are now invited to board," a voice interrupted over the intercom.

"Well, that's me," Freda reached down to gather her things.

Chris barely noticed, his gaze now fixed in a distant, brow-furrowing stare as he attempted to process what Freda had said and the fakery of the whole situation.

"Freda?" he said.

As Freda slung her purse over her shoulder, she looked over at Chris who snapped out of his stare.

"Any chance I could have another piece of that taffy?"

"Oh," she laughed, "you tried the Koolaid, and now you can't stop." Her entire body shook as she chuckled gleefully. She reached in her bag, pulled out a handful of candies, grabbed Chris's hand and placed them in it, holding his hand for an unnaturally long time.

"It was a pleasure meetin' you, Chris."

Chris looked up at her and smiled as she released his hand and took her place at the back of the crowd now funneling into the Jetway.

Chris turned to the janitor working behind the crowd. He was hunched over his mop and seemed to struggle as he made his way along the endless airport corridor. All around him busy, well-dressed passengers flowed by, oblivious to his presence or the work he was doing. Lost in the river of people, the old man paused for a moment and leaned on his mop. He looked exhausted, ready to keel over at any second. He wiped the sweat from his forehead and made a shy awkward glance toward Freda.

In the airport dream world, Chris saw a flash of a smile rise from the side of the old man's mouth and then vanish as quickly as it appeared. The man seemed to cower between his shoulders in the absence of caring. Chris could feel his pain and the brief warmth Freda had brought into his life as the crowds flowed past him and swallowed him in their busy lives.

"So, did they figure out your ticket issue?"

Wrapped up in his thoughts, Chris hadn't noticed that someone had taken Freda's seat.

Chris turned to the familiar voice sitting next to him. "Right." He rolled his eyes and shook his head. "My ticket issue."

Hidden behind his beard, David's smile faded. "I'm sorry you feel that way."

"Come on, man." Chris reclined back into his seat and then immediately fidgeted forward, elbows on his knees, staring at the floor. He glanced at David and then shook his head dismissively and began playing with his wedding band.

For a moment the two of them sat in silence.

"So, what did you think of the two people you just met?" David asked. "Very different, they were," he commented, almost to himself, stroking his beard thoughtfully.

Chris thought he sounded like Yoda and furrowed his brow trying to decipher what David was getting at. "Actually, I take that back," David said. "They're quite similar, but what you experienced was very different."

Chris sat up a little and looked over at David. "Similar? I have no idea how you could call Matt and Freda similar."

"How did you feel about the conversations you had with each of them?" David stroked his beard again.

Chris looked at David, suspicious and annoyed. "What are you, my therapist?"

David stared at Chris, completely unfazed by Chris's accusatory tone. "I'm curious. Plus, what else have you got to do? You have no ticket. You have nowhere to go and nothing to do."

"Thanks to you." Chris sneered at David.

"Right." David cleared his throat and continued. "Well, here you are, and here you'll stay until you open your mind to what they have to teach you. So let me ask you this, why do you think Matt was a cynic and Freda was an angel?"

Chris sighed and shook his head. "You sound like my wife, you know."

David smiled.

"Fine." Chris stretched back into his chair and looked up to the ceiling. "I don't know." He rubbed his head trying to come up with something to get David off his back and get on with whatever they were getting on with. "My guess is that Matt Taylor has a God complex or something like that because he gets so much media attention. I think he was putting on a show back there because he is tired of talking to everyone about it.

"Freda, on the other hand, is one of those anomalies that is happy all the time. We have a few of those at work. Always finding the good in things no matter how bad they are. Sometimes it gets a little nauseating. She probably had like a messed-up childhood or something like that, but determined she was going to be different. Like Oprah." Chris raised his eyebrows and smiled at David insincerely. "How's that?"

David shook his head and frowned. He squinted at Chris like he was about to slap him across the face. "Chris, you and Matt are like two peas in a pod. Are you really so thick headed you can't see that?" David whacked him across the back of the head.

"Ow." Chris rubbed his head. "What did you do that for?"

David sat up like a thunderhead about to erupt.

"You think you're so smart. You think you know all the answers to running a solid human resources program. You see yourself as one of the few people in your organization who are open to new ideas. But if I were to take you back and place you in Jack or Kyle's seat this morning when you went head-to-head with Angela, you would see yourself as clearly as you perceive Matt Taylor now — a burnout who's egotistical, self-centered, and afraid of the world around him."

Chris sulked under the pain still radiating from the back of his head and glanced reluctantly toward David. "I don't think you're seein' the whole picture," Chris mumbled.

"And that is the crux of it all," David interjected. "You believe that you *are* seeing the whole picture. But were you thinking, *well, maybe Angela is right*, when she disagreed with your way of seeing the world? *I should consider her perspective*. Did you think maybe Kyle and Tara both had good points when they criticized your leadership style behind your back?

"Of course, you didn't. From your limited perspective, you knew you were right and that they were the ones who were blinded by ignorance. You were oblivious to other perspectives in the same way you were blinded to the fact that everyone in the board meeting this morning saw you just like you saw Matt Taylor a few minutes ago."

Chris stared straight ahead and bit his lip. His breathing became shallow, and his restless knee was getting out of control. "This is stupid," he muttered.

He felt David's hand come to rest on his shoulder.

"Chris." David's voice was quiet now. "Five years ago, Matt accepted his position at Moth with the same enthusiasm you had when you accepted your position at Queens Mount University. Matt's wife was expecting, and they were both excited about the opportunity. For the first few years, Moth was everything you would imagine it to be: fast-paced, creative, entrepreneurial, visionary. And Matt was a huge part of that. But just like with any new job or company or marriage, the honeymoon eventually wears off after a year or so, and then it's just work. Matt was no exception.

"The more the company grew, the more the insanity of the ambitious adventure and life-sucking work hours began to take their toll on Matt. It was all he could do to survive the endless barrage of problems. Before long he found himself buried in the quagmire of email, drawn-out meetings, and paperwork. People he'd hired threatened to go elsewhere if Moth didn't up their HR game. From the outside things looked great. But behind closed doors, a lot of those creative initiatives had spawned monstrosities they hadn't anticipated. At home it was no different."

Chris's defensive mechanisms began to falter as David pried open his mind and poured in new perspectives.

"Children have a tendency to test the limits of any relationship, especially when they first arrive."

Chris nodded almost imperceptibly; his gaze now distant.

"When his baby finally arrived, Matt began to bury himself

in what was slowly becoming a very unfulfilling job in order to escape an increasingly unfulfilling marriage. He was tired of the screaming matches, the accusations, the endless diapers and sleep deprivation."

Chris stared at the floor in front of himself vacantly.

"Last week," David continued, "Matt filed for divorce, and turned to the bottle."

Chris didn't move.

"You see Chris. Often the way we perceive the world and the people around us is a far cry from the snapshots we experience in any given moment, or in the pictures people paint of themselves."

David squeezed Chris's shoulder and continued. "When Freda first took that janitorial job she told you about, her husband of twelve years had just walked out on her. He left her for a twenty-year-old he met at the bar, leaving Freda to take care of four young children by herself. She hadn't worked for over nine years and her highest level of education was a high school diploma.

"Custodial work was the only work she could find. She cried every night that first week and all through the weekend. Not because she wasn't grateful to have a job. She was, but she hated the work and the way people treated her there. Her supervisor was a sexist and a racist. He demeaned her, not just with the work he assigned to her, but he also added so much to her list of responsibilities that it was impossible for her to get everything done. And to make it all worse, he would follow her around, criticizing her work, and peppering her with sexist remarks and other forms of verbal abuse.

"A few weeks later, he came on to her and threatened to fire her if she didn't sleep with him. Freda was terrified. She wasn't the strong, confident, caring woman you met today. It took everything she could muster to stand up to the man. And as a result of that decision, if things weren't already bad, he found ways to make them worse. She endured that hell for the sake of her children for the next six months. Then she and some of the other female custodians, who were mostly African American and Hispanic, faced their fears and spoke up to the general manager. The supervisor was fired shortly thereafter."

David leaned forward, mirroring Chris, and inhaled deeply.

"How do you think it is Chris that one person could land their dream job and then come to loathe it and another could be forced into a nightmare of a job and come to refer to it as a calling?"

Chris didn't move for a few moments and then shook his head almost imperceptibly and half-turned to David. "I have no idea."

"Let me ask you this," David added, "Why did *you* take the position at Queens Mount?"

Chris turned his attention back to the floor, scanning the recesses of his memory. "I don't know." He began fidgeting aggressively with his ring. "I suppose, at the time, it just seemed like there was a lot of potential to really make a difference. To take us out of the nineteenth century and build a culture where people collaborated with one another instead of being so siloed. Where lazy people were held accountable and those who delivered results were rewarded. I fooled myself into thinking that human resources was the key to improving the student experience and that if we did HR well it would increase our overall enrollments."

"Sounds like you were pretty excited about your job."

"Yeah." Chris felt his eye twitch.

"And how did you feel about your job after your meeting with the cabinet today?"

Chris exhaled loudly and closed his eyes. "I realized how delusional I'd been."

"Pretty deflated, huh? Would it be safe to say that after this morning's meeting you felt as though the part of your job that had brought meaning and purpose into your life up to that point was essentially tossed into the furnace and incinerated into oblivion?"

Chris chuckled through his nose. "That's definitely a colorful way to put it."

"It is, isn't it?" David stretched out his arms around the back of the seats to his sides. He looked around the terminal at the people sitting in back-to-back rows of blue pleather benches, absorbed in their electronic devices.

"You know, Chris, whenever I'm around people who are traveling, it reminds me of a story."

Chris half-glanced over at David and then turned back to the people gathering in front of him.

"Years ago there was this woman who dreamed of traveling the world, so she saved up her money and began booking flights. She traveled to Asia, Europe, South America, Iceland, and even the Arctic, experiencing the most beautiful and exotic places on this planet. She took lots of pictures, checked off her bucket list, and then impressed her friends and family with her stories of the places she had visited. Exciting right?"

Chris had the feeling David was trying to make another point.

"The interesting thing is that she would return from each trip with an unshakable feeling of emptiness gnawing at the back of her soul. An emptiness that only seemed to grow deeper with each trip. She assumed that more adventures, more novel locations, would fill that void, but they didn't.

"After decades of traveling the world, she arrived at the end of her life with one question haunting the back of her mind. Do you know what that question was?"

Chris looked slowly over at David.

"So what?" David answered. "Her question was, so what?"

Chris stared at David while his mind chased the question, trying to make sense of it. A moment later his gaze faltered and drifted toward the thought.

"In those final moments of her life, she saw the places she had traveled, the experiences she had enjoyed, the coworkers, family members, and friends who had endured her endless stories. And then she saw herself, there in that hospital room, alone.

"Being alone wasn't anything new. Flying solo was what set her apart. But now that she looked back on all she had done, she saw for the first time how little she had accomplished for anyone but herself. Her purpose was clear, but her approach and reason for pursuing that purpose was skewed. She had lived a completely self-centered life, void of contribution. Consumed by thrills that diminished with time."

David paused, watching the crowd dwindle into the Jetway.

"Sometimes Chris, people may be driven by purpose, but they fail to tap into the aspects of that purpose that lead to lasting fulfillment. The adventure of pursuits that align with our purpose might excite us, but it's the positive contributions to the lives of others that keep us charged and fulfilled.

"You can travel and see the world, or you can travel and change the world. Changing not only the world, but yourself as well. In a way, purpose without contribution and change is like a phone without a battery.

"Imagine if this young traveler had used those opportunities to contribute and had spent less time bragging and more time collaborating with other travelers and non-profit organizations. Maybe she could have helped dig a well, or aided research, or taught English, or used her photo skills to make family portraits for those who couldn't afford them. What if she had written articles for a magazine to call on others to stand up and help address world problems they were unaware existed? It likely would have required more effort to do that, but her exit from this life to the next would have been free from regrets."

The terminal had quieted down now as the last passengers trickled down the Jetway.

Chris sunk into his seat and slowly shook his head. "I don't know. I get what you are saying, but I don't think having some altruistic purpose is going to magically make someone happy who isn't."

David smiled reflectively and looked off toward the Jetway. "You're right, there is no end-all, quick-fix solution for happiness and fulfillment." He turned to Chris. "But every small, positive change you make is one step closer to a fulfilled life. And grounding yourself in purpose is one of those small changes that yields massive returns."

Chris's eyes drifted again, chasing wandering thoughts. "So where do you think they are on figuring out my ticket thing? I'm assuming we need to get back on the plane to wrap this little session up."

"Oh, you don't want to get on that plane." David shook his head nervously.

"Why's that?" Chris suddenly felt uneasy.

"The thing with making changes to your life is that the sooner you make them the better."

Chris looked at the gate and then back at David.

"David, why don't I want to get on that plane?"

David cleared his throat and looked up at the flight schedule on the large flat-screen TV. "Three days ago in a small town in northern Virginia, there was a crash that was all over the news. Do you remember that?"

Chris thought back, trying to recall a crash. He had been responding to emails after putting the kids to bed when he heard it on the news and was only half paying attention. "I have a vague memory. It was bad, right?"

"That's right. Everyone died. It was headed to Jacksonville Sunday afternoon, and as far as they can tell, it hit turbulent weather, which caused a system malfunction, which lead to the crash."

Suddenly over the intercom, Chris heard the final boarding announcement.

"Last call for flight 3571 to Jacksonville".

Chris looked up at the display and saw the date, September 8th. Three days ago. The time was 3:53 PM.

Chris glared at David. "This is all just a show, right? Actors and actresses teaching Chris a lesson. None of this is real."

David shook his head. "We already went over this, Chris. Plus, you saw Matt for yourself. Not an actor. Nor was Freda."

"Well, we've got to do something. Is that why I'm here? Is that the point of this—" Chris fumbled for words and waved his hands at his surroundings. "—whatever this is? Am I supposed to change the past or something?"

David sat back and looked straight ahead. "There's nothing either of us can do, Chris."

"There are women and children on that flight. Innocent people."

"You're right." David's voice was distant now.

"Well, we have to at least say something."

David stared straight ahead, expressionless. Chris shook his head in disgust and rushed over to the information desk.

"Excuse me ma'am, there are problems with that plane. You need to cancel that flight."

The attendant, who was on the phone, rolled her eyes.

"Excuse me one second." She positioned the receiver away from her mouth. "Look, sir, the pilots go through a lengthy pre-flight check to ensure the safety of the passengers, and our planes are inspected regularly for mechanical issues. I can assure you that the plane is perfectly—"

"Look, I know this sounds crazy," Chris interrupted, "but someone really needs to inspect that plane before it takes off." He could feel himself shaking with frustration now.

The attendant rolled her eyes again. Over the radio he could hear the pilots making their final preparations.

"Sir. Like I said, there's nothing to worry about. Now if you could just—"

She wasn't taking him seriously, and that infuriated Chris. His thinking became muddied. *None of this is real. Why am I even doing this?* But what it if was? What if there was something he could do? What if David was right and it was real?

He glanced quickly back and forth between a young man in a neatly pressed airline uniform securing the strap on the Jetway entrance barrier and the attendant in front of him. Before he realized what he was doing, Chris bolted for the Jetway, ducked under the barrier strap, and rushed gracelessly down the ramp.

"Sir! You can't go down there." The young man turned to the woman at the desk. "Call security!"

As Chris stormed down, the lights in the Jetway faded. Something felt off. Not only did the Jetway feel unnaturally long, but it was becoming progressively more difficult to make out the walls.

What am I doing? He gripped the rail firmly with his right hand and continued pressing forward into darkness. The door to the plane had to be just ahead, but after several minutes, nothing materialized. An uneasy feeling settled over Chris until he finally decided to turn around.

Behind him, the light he had expected to see spilling in from the terminal was gone. He white-knuckled the rail and rested his forehead against the plastic wall. *This is madness.*

Chris filled his lungs with an uneasy breath and began working his way back toward the gate. He could feel the ramp sloping upward, feel the stale carpet against his shoes. For a brief moment he released his grip on the rail to feel for the opposite wall. He took a step. Then another. Either the hallway had widened or the wall was no longer there. He reached back for the rail, but it too had become a distant memory.

From the darkness, a deafening bang destabilized the endless carpet floor. He crouched for cover and brought his hands to his head. The sound of screaming passengers and the whirring of failing turbine engines filled the space around him. Despite the chaos he could distinctly make out individual voices. A male voice with an Australian accent screamed profanity over and over. A shrill, girlish scream from the obnoxious businessman pierced through Matt's profanity.

Chris placed his hands over his ears to block out the flood of screaming and panic and immediately the screams faded to the soft and gentle hum of another familiar voice rising from the maelstrom.

"It's gonna be OK baby."

Though all he could see was darkness, Chris could feel Freda comforting a panicky little girl next to her as she sobbed for her mama. It was as though he were the one within Freda's close embrace. She hummed a gentle song that ushered a quiet calm into the chaos. He could feel her joy and satisfaction for a life well lived passing through the little girl and into his own soul. He listened to that beautiful song, to the sound of the little girl's cries fading to sniffles.

And then it was over. An ear-splitting crash knocked Chris off his feet and sent him rolling across the never-ending Jetway floor. The sound of bodies being torn apart and plastic and metal crumbling into a cratered pile of unrecognizable debris ricocheted like shards of glass through his once comforted soul and then faded into oblivion. They were no more. Matt and the egomaniacal businessman. Freda and the little girl. All gone. Chris sank into the surface he'd come to rest on and bellowed out in agony, sobbing for people he barely knew.

"Fleeting, isn't it? This life. Very unpredictable." David's voice echoed through the darkness. Distant, and yet so close it seemed to originate from within Chris. "Most people get wrapped up in the minutia of their lives and forget their time will come, and so they live as though it won't."

Chris stopped sobbing and curled into a ball on the floor.

"They think that *one day* they'll be in a better position to do, and to be, and to accomplish the things they really want or need to accomplish. They think that *one day* they will carve out time to work on changing the things they know deep down that they need to change right now." David paused. "But it's easy to let that time slip by until we find ourselves sitting on our own flight 3571."

David's comment echoed through the darkness for a moment and then faded to silence.

Chris lifted himself off the floor. "That's cold." He sniffed.

"Maybe. Then again, maybe it's just a matter of perspective."

Chris shook his head and sat up, hugging his knees.

"This morning you were miserable and hopeless. But now you've been given a chance to re-examine your life through the experiences of others and think about what regrets you might have carried with you had you been sitting on that flight three days ago. No one's death is in vain if we allow their life to influence the direction of our own.

"So, I ask you Chris, what have you been putting off over the last year because it's too hard, too time consuming, too energy intensive, or too painful?"

The question stirred Chris's tormented mind. He swallowed hard and shook his head. He thought of his family falling apart. Meaningless work that filled him with frustration and kept him awake most nights. Friends who had faded from his life. He thought about how distant and disconnected he had felt lately with everyone around him. For a fleeting moment, he wished that he had been on that flight. Wished the pain had all been wiped out three days ago along with Matt and the screaming banshee businessman.

His voice was a labored whisper. "I don't know."

"I think you do, Chris, but I think in the ocean of pain you've lost your bearings. Purpose and meaning get fuzzy when life gets stressful, and lately your life hasn't exactly been... easy?"

Chris lifted his head, stared off into the darkness, and began to rock.

"You know, there is a reason for that, Chris. There is a reason for discomfort or *dis-ease* in your life. Physical symptoms of discomfort help doctors identify diseases of the body. *Dis-ease* is life's attempt to wake you up to the grim reality that either your life is on the wrong trajectory and needs a course correction, or that it's time to develop a new way to deal with your current challenges. You, Chris, need both."

Chris took a deep breath, closed his eyes, and listened.

"The farther you allow yourself to travel down the wrong path, Chris, the longer and more difficult your journey back, but that option to turn back and find a better route is always there waiting for you. Are you ready to turn back?"

Chris stopped rocking.

CHAPTER 3

Letting Go

Immediately, the darkness around Chris lightened to a mottled gray, as though the world around him was coming into focus. The air turned warm and dry and dusty. Beneath him the flat, matted carpet of the Jetway transformed into dirt and gravel. He stood up and brushed up against what felt like dry grass, something prickly. His khaki pants caught on something and he heard a tear as he pulled his leg away.

The scene was sharper now. He squinted and strained his eyes and thought he saw sagebrush and distant mountains. The hot sun illuminating the landscape increased in brightness until Chris could no longer keep his eyes open.

He closed his eyes tight and cringed as the light and the heat bore down. From somewhere the beyond the mirage, the sound of a thousand pilings being driven into the soft and distant ground unnerved him.

When his eyes finally adjusted to the light, he blinked rapidly and gaped at the world before him in disbelief. The Jetway was gone now. Not a single sign of humanity remained. Before him, a vast desert landscape expanded out in all directions. Far away he could see sepia mountains covered with pale-green junipers and pinion pines. The sky washed muted blue and cloudless, and the valley in which he stood rolled gently, scattered with small stocks of dried grass, sagebrush, and tiny desert shrubs.

Behind him, over a barely discernible knoll, the pounding intensified and the earth began to rumble. Dust rose from behind the knoll and a swarming herd of cattle crested into view, thundering toward Chris no more than a hundred yards away.

Chris turned in a panic and ran. The cattle closed in to fifty yards. In his khakis and dress shoes, he struggled and slipped across the uneven terrain. All around him the desert vegetation tore at his clothing and knocked him into a continual, graceless stumble.

Chris screamed as the herd finally overtook him. Dust rose from the ground and filled his eyes, mouth, nostrils, and lungs. He coughed uncontrollably and stopped running. A sea of mooing and snorting cattle bumbled around him, drowning out the sound of the slumped over, hacking and choking, well-dressed man.

Suddenly, Chris felt a hand reach down, grab him by his collar and toss him over the back of a dust-covered horse.

"What in Sam Hill are you doing out here, son?" A gruff voice shouted over the thunder. "You nearly got yerself pulverized there."

Chris clawed desperately for something to grab onto while the cattle flowed past them. He could taste the horse's sweat as his face pressed into the animal. The man on the horse tried to steady the now agitated creature, but the thundering cattle made the job nearly impossible.

"Well, git yourself upright and hang on!" The stranger commanded.

Chris grabbed hold of the man's dusty leather vest and pulled himself up. He wrapped his arms around the stranger and felt the horse lunge forward.

"On with ya!" he yelled, and he slammed his heels into the side of the animal. The horse let out a loud snort and bolted forward.

When they had finally woven their way through the cattle and slowed to a trot, Chris could make out, through chalky eyes, a transparent stream up ahead in the middle of the sagebrush wasteland. Around the water's edges stood cottonwoods and willows, creating an oasis for the cattle to stop and drink and for their drivers to shade themselves for a few minutes before heading on.

The old cattle rancher stopped his horse and dismounted. "So what on God's green earth are you doin' way out here in the middle of the Nevada desert?" He took off his hat, wiped the dirt and sweat from his deeply grooved forehead, and then cleaned his hand on his tan field jacket.

"Nevada?" Chris slid gracelessly off the back end of the horse and stumbled backward a few feet. "I have no idea." His entire body slumped on the verge of collapse.

The cattle rancher stared at Chris suspiciously and then shook his head. "Well. If you don't know, it won't do much good for either of us to try and figure it out. Name's Bert." He took a step toward Chris extending his hand.

Chris stared at Bert's hand and then extended his own. "Chris." His breathing was labored.

Bert squeezed hard and watched as Chris glanced despondently around at the scene, cringing against the harsh, desert sun. The creek and a gentle breeze from the west felt strangely calming. Almost instinctively, he reached into his pocket and pulled out his phone, holding it up to catch a signal. No service.

"You ain't gonna have much luck with that there device out here son." Bert turned back to his horse and began tightening the saddle straps.

Chris sighed and placed the phone back in his pocket.

"It's about three days journey back to the ranch with the herd and all, but you're more than welcome to tag along and use our landline when we get there. Shame we didn't cross paths a few hours ago. One of our cowboys came down with something nasty, so we sent him home on the water truck a few miles back."

Chris looked around and began rubbing the back of his head; an ineffective stress-coping habit he'd carried with him since childhood.

"Course, you're welcome to stay here." Bert paused, looked around at the landscape, and then chuckled softly to himself. "But then, unless you've got some sorta transportation that I don't know about, you've got yourself a mighty long walk to the nearest road, about forty miles that way." Bert gestured with his chin to the northwest.

Chris sighed, hunched a little more, and placed both hands on the back of his hips. He looked around and weighed his options. Bert squinted and glanced slowly back and forth between Chris and the invisible road.

"Tell you what, Chris." he finally said, stroking his handlebar mustache. "If you don't mind giving us a hand, we may be able to move this herd a little faster. Might get us back to the ranch a day early." He looked Chris up and down and chuckled softly through his nose. "Course, that there outfit that you're wearin', probably ain't gonna look too pretty when you're done."

Chris sighed again, reached into his pocket, and pulled out his phone a final time to see if a signal had magically appeared.

"I suppose I don't have too many options do I?"

He stared at the photo of his wife and kids on his home screen and then tucked it back into his pocket. A rush of stress flashed through his body as sweat dripped down his face, mixing with the desert dust. He imagined how worried, or angry, or depressed, his wife must be by now. Probably to the point of a complete emotional breakdown. He worried about his children under those circumstances and realized that someone should have picked up his daughter from school an hour ago, if the time was right on his phone. He didn't really know what was real and what wasn't anymore.

"That's a mighty fine-lookin' family you got there. Most of mine are all grown up now, moved back to south Arizona to connect with their roots I suppose. Don't see 'em as much as I'd like these days."

"Thanks." He tightened his grip on the phone in his pocket.

"Welp. We'll getcha in contact with 'em soon enough."

The two of them turned their heads as a young man in his early twenties came riding up to Bert and Chris. His horse snorted as he brought her to a halt and dismounted with ease. When his boots hit the ground, a cloud of dust erupted from his field jacket and jeans.

"Hey Uncle B. I think that's the last of 'em," he said. He opened a small satchel on the side of his saddle and pulled out a canteen. "You think we'll make it to the Worthington's before nightfall?" He hadn't seemed to notice Chris until he finished his question. He stared cautiously at the new stranger.

"I think that should be doable. Especially now that we have an extra hand." Bert gestured to Chris.

The ranch hand continued staring, took another swig of his water, wiped his mouth, and extended his hand toward Chris. "Howdy. Name's Seth."

Chris shook his hand and introduced himself.

"So you camping out here? Didn't see your truck." Seth eyed Chris up and down suspiciously.

"It's, uh..." Chris stared at the ground, not entirely sure how to explain his situation without sounding like a lunatic. "It's complicated."

Seth turned to his side and spit. "Fair enough." He took another swig and made his way over to the creek.

"Chris here's gonna be joining us for a couple of days," Bert interjected. "Said he's always been wanting to learn about cattle ranching." Bert looked over at Chris and winked.

"Sounds great." Seth said as he knelt by the water and began splashing the dirt off his face. "How long you want to let the cows water here, boss?"

"Oh," Bert said, staring at Chris, "let's give 'em thirty minutes or so."

Seth doused his head in the creek and stood up. "Oh man, that feels real nice."

He took another swig from his canteen and then wandered over to a rock under the shade of a cottonwood tree and reclined against it, tilting his cowboy hat over his eyes.

Bert turned toward the tree and gestured to Chris to join them. He walked slowly and crouched down against the trunk of the cottonwood with some effort, reclining with a deep sigh.

Chris didn't move. He still couldn't believe where he was standing and how he had gotten here. He could feel the dust in his teeth. Taste it against his tongue. He walked over to the stream and splashed water on his face. It did feel nice. He scooped up a handful and poured it over his dust-covered hair.

"So, Chris." Bert shifted a little and tilted his hat down over his face. "You ever ride a horse before?"

Chris walked over to where the two men were resting and sat down on an uncomfortable rock, a stiff contrast between the two nearly sleeping men. "When I was a kid, my mom let me ride the ponies on the pony carousel at the state fair. Does that count?"

Chris's comment hovered in the air for a minute or so. He wondered if they had fallen asleep already.

"I suppose that's better than nothin'," Bert replied. "Seth, why don't you grab Pablo's horse? He's going to need something to ride." Seth didn't move. "And the condensed five-minute version of Horseback Ridin' for Dummies." Bert smiled under his hat.

"Sure thing, boss." Seth didn't budge until one of the cow dogs wandered over and licked him in the face. "goldarn it, you stupid mutt." He brushed away the matted, dust-covered collie and picked himself off the ground.

"Good boy, Wallace," Bert said to the dog from under his hat. Seth hobbled over to his horse, hopped on, and headed off at a gallop.

Under the tree, Bert didn't move. He reminded Chris of his grandfather, only ten times stronger. The cattle surrounding them grazed the desert vegetation, drank from the stream, and startled Chris with random unanticipated bellows. Wrapped up in stress-provoking thoughts, he hadn't realized he'd been rocking back and forth. He made a conscious attempt to stop but nearly fell off his rock when Bert unexpectedly broke the silence.

"Now, when you get on Pablo's horse, Picante—"

"Geez." Chris cursed to himself. Chris could feel his heart pounding in his chest and leaned forward to catch his breath.

"—the one thing you need to remember is that you're the one in control. Don't ever let that horse think otherwise. If she thinks you're soft," he chuckled, "you'll be in for quite the ride."

Bert lifted his hat and sat up. Chris could hear the distant thud of hooves approaching and felt the knot tightening in his stomach. The idea of telling a creature five times his size that he was in charge seemed completely backward. But the idea of falling off and getting trampled was equally terrifying.

As Bert rose to his feet, Seth came into view, ponying another horse behind him. The two horses snorted as they came to a halt in front of Chris and Bert. Seth dismounted and led Picante over to Chris. The closer she got to him the bigger she seemed. Her dark brown, dust-covered body towered over him, muscles twitching to ward off the flies. Chris swallowed hard. She stared at him with profoundly deep brown eyes that seemed to go on forever. If anyone could see his fear, it would be those endlessly dark eyes.

"Well, Chris, she's all yours." Seth extended the reins toward Chris.

Chris glanced over at Bert. He wasn't sure why. Reassurance maybe. A chance that Bert would change his mind. His breath was shallow and rapid now. Bert nodded, gesturing toward Picante. Chris turned back to Seth and took the reins.

"So you're gonna want to step into the stirrup there with your left foot, grab the horn at the top of the saddle and just pull yourself on over. Like takin' a big ol' step into a jacked-up pickup truck." Chris looked up at Picante and hesitated. "Go on now."

Slowly Chris lifted his left foot to the stirrup, reached for the horn, and then stumbled backward, catching himself before he crashed into the ground. He could feel his nerves beginning to fray, took a deep breath and looked back up at Picante who snorted and took a step back.

"Whoa there, girl." Seth grabbed the reins Chris had dropped and patted her neck. He turned to the side and spit out the shell of a sunflower seed he'd been working on, and then turned to Chris. "Second time's the charm."

Chris picked up the remains of his damaged ego and walked back over to Picante with a renewed, but cautious, determination. Seth passed him a re-affirming nod as Chris took the horn, lifted his foot into the stirrup and pulled with everything he had, and flopped himself onto the saddle like a walrus working its way up a rocky shore. Picante shifted as he shuffled into the saddle and immediately Chris felt the blood flush to his feet.

"Whoa girl. It's okay. You settle down now." Seth's voice was calm and reassuring. "Not too bad there, rookie."

Chris closed his eyes and breathed deeply as the blood returned to his head. Seth glanced over at Bert hesitantly who nodded at him to continue.

"Alrighty then." Seth turned back to Chris and breezed through the basic rules and techniques for horseback riding while Chris tried to take it all in.

When he was done Seth turned back to Bert. "Anything else, boss?"

Bert rose slowly from the ground and made his way over to his own horse. "I think that about sums it up."

Seth handed Chris the reins and turned toward his own horse. "She's all yours."

"Best be gettin' on our way." Bert mounted his own horse. He settled in and turned to Chris. "You ready, son?"

"No, not really." Chris sat board stiff in the saddle.

Bert smiled and then nudged his horse forward. "Relax those shoulders, boy. You'll give yourself a neck ache."

Chris attempted to let go of the tension in vain.

Bert and Seth took off at a trot alongside the creek. Chris looked down at Picante who seemed virtually oblivious to him. He kicked her hard, and she started walking. Up ahead Bert and Seth picked up the pace. Chris watched as the distance between the cowboys and him widened.

"Let's go, girl," he said timidly. "Come on!" She continued to walk slowly. "Giddyup?" He gave her another hard kick.

Bert glanced back from up ahead to see how Chris was coming along. "Tell her like you mean it!"

Chris looked down at Picante and frustration began simmering. Feelings stirred thoughts, and in the back of his mind he replayed the executive cabinet fighting back against his recommendations. He watched his wife as she quietly refused to help out at home. He saw the kids whine about picking up their toys.

The animal beneath him became the embodiment of his thoughts and he drove his heals into her side with everything he had.

"Gaaaaaah!" He screamed like a maniac, and Picante lunged forward.

Bert and Seth stopped the moment Chris screamed. Picante barreled toward them at a full gallop. Chris could see the men up ahead preparing for the worst as he rapidly approached them. He pulled back slowly on the reigns and immediately, his horse slowed to a trot, then to a walk. Seth and Bert relaxed as he led Picante over to the two men, gave the reins a final tug, and came to a stop a few feet in front of them.

Bert released his breath and chuckled quietly. "Good heaven's Chris. A little less enthusiasm next time, all right? And Chris—"

Chris looked up at Bert.

"—don't forget to breathe."

Chris felt lightheaded and realized Bert was right. He exhaled a long sigh through pursed lips and felt a little better. Where they had stopped, a sage-covered valley rolled on for dozens of miles toward arid, rocky mountain ranges. The only sign of humanity was what appeared to be a fence line maybe ten miles away. The moment—the place—felt surreal. A half-dream made more bizarre by the strange silence that settled over the desert. A silence interrupted, only occasionally, by the rush of a soft, dry wind, or the song of a meadow lark, or the buzz of a fly.

"Terrain here can be deceptive," Bert commented to Chris as he gazed across the landscape. "Hills can turn into cliffs, salt pan into mud traps, and some areas can be a lot steeper than they look from a distance. What I'm saying is that what might look like the easiest way forward, well, sometimes it ain't. So for the most part, we're gonna be following this range north. Stick to the herd and you'll be fine. If one of the cows wanders off though, best not to follow her. Just let Seth or me know, and we'll track 'er down."

Chris nodded silently.

"I think what we'll do is have Seth take the right, Chris you ride left, and I'll follow behind and keep 'em movin'."

Bert stared off into the distance for a moment, frozen in time.

"All right boys, let's get moving." Bert turned his horse back toward the cattle herd and took off at a trot.

Chris watched as Bert and Seth began riding off toward the perimeter of the herd, driving the stragglers back to the center of the black mass. Chris followed suit the best he could with the assumption that the side neither men was working was the left side he'd been assigned. Once the herd had gathered in, Bert, Seth, Chris and three dogs nudged the cattle to the north under Seth's lead.

Over the next several hours they followed the west bench of the mountains to their right. Bert seemed intuitively aware of the needs of the cattle, alternating between walking and grazing the herd, and wrangling in the stragglers. Occasionally they would stop for a brief rest, but for the most part, they pressed forward until the sun dipped low along the western horizon.

✳

By day's end, Chris could barely get off his horse. His legs, back, and shoulders ached beyond anything he had ever experienced. And the chafing; he'd heard marathon runner horror stories, but this was something else. He hesitated a moment, then he dismounted Picante, moaning.

"Takes a few days." Bert removed the saddle from his own horse.

Chris dusted himself off, hobbled over to a large rock, and sat down. In the background, Bert dropped his saddle over a makeshift stand made of three old logs that had been lashed together like a pointless section of fence in the middle of nowhere.

"Ain't nothin' to be ashamed of," he said as he made his way back over to his horse and checked her hooves. "Happens to all of us when we get back on after not riding for a while, or in your case, ever."

At the edge of the horizon, the sun kissed the top of the mountain and ignited the landscape with orange light. Humiliated by his condition, Chris barely noticed. Feelings of inadequacy flooded him with self-deprecating thoughts: his wife begging him to stay home followed by his shameless reaction—walking out the door; the way the executive cabinet looked down at him like a silly, little, foolish HR director with his head in the clouds; his out-of-shape body that couldn't even handle a few hours on the back of a horse.

"Chris?"

Hearing his name knocked him out of his mental mud trap, and he jolted toward the voice. Immediately, a surge of pain shot up his leg and into his back. He moaned and saw Seth peering down at him from his horse.

"Y'okay there buddy?" He looked concerned.

Chris cringed as the pain began to ease up. "Sorry. Guess I zoned out there." He shifted carefully to a more comfortable position.

"Beautiful. Isn't it?"

Chris turned toward the horizon and watched as the sun dipped behind the mountain, setting the clouds ablaze.

"Wow." For a moment the pain disappeared.

"Sure beats sittin' in some cubicle, don't it?" For a few minutes no one spoke, lost in their own thoughts.

"Anywho," Seth continued, breaking the silence, "just finished countin' the herd and it looks like two of our heifers wandered off somewhere. Seein' as how the boss's already put his saddle away, you think you got it in ya to come take a gander and see if we can spot 'em? Four eyes is always better than two. I reckon they're not more than a mile back."

Chris sulked internally at the thought of getting back up on Picante, but the idea of looking softer than he already was gnawed at his pride.

"Sure thing," Chris responded, attempting to hide his pain as he rose from the rock and made his way slowly over to Picante.

Lost in a physically exhausted daze, Chris came in from behind the grazing horse, grabbed the horn of her saddle, put his left foot in the stirrup, and attempted to pull himself up onto her back. Immediately, he realized he had done something wrong. Picante lifted her head in a panic, neighed wildly, and bucked hard. Chris could feel himself hurling through the air, and before he could comprehend what was going on, he came down with a loud thud. Bert turned to see what the commotion was and rushed over to get Picante under control, while Seth jumped off his horse and ran over to Chris.

On the ground Chris choked and gasped as he attempted to reclaim the breath that had been knocked out of him. Seth squatted down next to him and put his hand on his shoulder. He gave Chris a moment and then helped him to his feet.

"Man, that hurt," Chris coughed.

He hobbled over to the rock he had been sitting on, with Seth hovering alongside. In the background, Picante fidgeted, wide-eyed and breathing heavily as Bert held the reins and spoke to her softly.

"Suppose we should have mentioned that it's not a good idea to mount a horse that don't know you're there." Bert commented, his attention half on Chris, half on Picante.

Chris sat down on the rock and hunched forward trembling. "Yeah, that would have been nice to know." He moaned.

Seth sighed and glanced back in the direction they'd come from. "Well. Best be gettin' after those missing heifers 'fore it gets too dark."

He scanned the horizon and then looked down at Chris and gave him a painful slap on the back. Chris cringed as Seth wandered over to his horse, stroked its neck, spoke quietly, and then climbed onto its back and rode off.

Chris watched Seth disappear over the knoll and then looked around at the place they had stopped. The ground under a small grove of junipers had been dug out and flattened, and a few feet away from where he sat appeared to be the remains of a primitive fire pit. Behind him, trickling water caught his attention and he turned to see a rusted out, galvanized pipe protruding from the ground surrounded by green moss.

"There's a lighter in the saddle bag there." Bert led a now calm Picante across camp to the post where he had tied his own horse. "If you want to go ahead and get a fire going, I'll grab us a couple cans of chili to heat up once I get Picante situated." He paused and then turned to Chris. "You do know how to build a campfire?"

"As long you've got a lighter." Chris shifted his weight forward and stood up slowly, cringing as he rose. "You wouldn't happen to have any lighter fluid or gasoline would you?"

Bert turned toward Chris, eyes wide.

"I'm kidding." Chris said as he hobbled over to the juniper grove.

Bert shook his head and turned back to Picante.

There wasn't much wood around the camp: a handful of thorny sticks, some dried grass, and a few dead, gnarled sagebrushes. Chris reassembled the disheveled pit and replaced the small plants growing in its center with stacked grass and desert wood. Flames from the lighter leapt quickly from the dry grass to the sticks, and by the time Bert had finished removing Picante's saddle and getting her settled in, the fire was in full bloom.

Chris, who had dragged his rock over for a seat, was lost in the flames when Bert came over to join him. He pulled over a rock of his own and set it down opposite Chris.

Bert settled in and stared at the fire. "So how many youngins you got there at home?" His tone was deep and his rhythm slow and intentional.

Chris had been too tired to think about his family. Too tired to think. The question revived an anxious knot in his stomach. He thought about the anxiety they must be experiencing with his disappearance, the uncertainty. He stared into the fire for a minute and then began rubbing his dust-covered face. "Three. A seven-year-old daughter, a three-year-old son, and a baby boy."

Bert smiled and stared into the fire letting Chris's response hang in the rapidly cooling, desert air.

"Those are hard ages." Bert paused. "Don't get me wrong, little ones are adorable at that age, but boy are they a lot of work. How's your wife holding up?"

"She's fine." Chris responded coldly.

Bert looked up from the fire and scanned Chris slowly, his eyes penetrating the facade.

"I'm glad." Bert turned back to the fire. "You know, when my first couple of children came along, my wife struggled something fierce." He paused and became distant. "So did I."

"We pert near, landed ourselves in the deevorce court. She was struggling with what today doctors might call 'the depression'. Laying in bed all day, neglecting the kids, and I'd come home to a mess. I was pretty riled up after a hard day's work. Here I'd been working my behind off, and she was just laying around shirking her duties."

Chris glanced over at Bert whose gaze was locked hard on him. He could feel his stress mounting the more Bert talked, but for the first time since his children were born he didn't feel alone in his pain.

"Took me a long time to learn how to deal with it, but I sure am glad I did; otherwise, I'd be a lonely ole coot right now. Cows are nice and all, but they sure don't take the place of a good woman when it comes to companionship."

Bert reached down, grabbed a stick, and stirred the fire. Chris watched sparks spray off the wood and rise into the air, flickering out about five feet above the pit. After stirring, Bert tapped out the fire that had clung to the stick and set it aside.

Chris could feel questions welling up inside of him. Questions he was terrified to ask. But he had to know.

"So what did you do to deal with it?" Chris finally blurted with obvious forced nonchalance.

Bert didn't budge. "Now, that there is a mighty fine question."

The coals of the fire were glowing now, bright orange, their luminance near that of the ambient light. Bert reached over, pulled a few cans of Hormel chili out of his bag, and used his pocket knife can opener on them. Once they were opened, he ground them into the coals to keep them from tipping over.

He placed the knife back in his pocket and settled back onto his rock. "Today, when you fell off Picante, what do you think happened?"

The question caught Chris off guard. He glanced over at Bert who was lost in the fire again.

"Uh. I... don't... know. I guess, like you said, I surprised her?" Chris shook his head in confusion, wondering what had happened with that *mighty fine* question he had asked.

"That's right. You see, horses, any living creature for that matter, when you catch 'em off guard, typically don't respond well. They like to feel they're in control of their situation." He paused and turned to Chris. "Just like people." He stared at Chris for an uncomfortably long time and then drifted back to the fire. "When horses, or people, lose that sense of control, it usually ain't pretty.

"Funny thing is though, this idea of control, it's like a mirage in the desert that draws a thirsty man toward it. He expends his last ounce of energy trying to get there, only to realize he's been duped. Key is realizing that sooner than later. That way you can use your strength to dig a well, instead of chasing illusions that lead to nowhere but suffering."

Chris racked his brain trying to figure out what any of this had to do with his question and Bert's relationship with his wife. Maybe, he thought, he was just an old man rambling.

"Let me put it this way—" Bert turned back to Chris with that penetrating stare. "— The more you try and control the things or people around you, things and people you have no control over, the more miserable you and everyone around you become.

"When Red here, that's my horse, and I first met, Red was not in the mood to be controlled any more than I was in the mood to deal with a stubborn horse. The more I tried to get him under submission, the more he fought back. Wasn't until I realized I needed to stop trying to make him be the horse I thought he should be, and work with him to become the horse he had the potential to become. That's when things started working out a little better for the both of us.

"If all I ever did was beat ole Red into submission, we'd get our job done, sure, but both of us would be miserable in the process. Nowadays, we've got what you might call a mutual agreement. I take care of Red by letting him have what he needs when he needs it, and of course avoid mounting him when he ain't aware of my presence." He smiled and winked at Chris. "And he in return helps me wrangle these here cattle.

"My wife, and most people for that matter, are no different than horses." Bert paused and chuckled in a way shook his entire body. "Course, don't ever tell my wife I said that. I'd be sleeping on the floor for a week with that there comment."

The chili started to bubble, and Bert reached into his jacket pocket and pulled out a pair of dusty leather gloves and a metal clamp. He put on the gloves and reached into the fire to remove the cans with the clamp. He wrapped the first can in one of the gloves, placed a spoon in it, and handed it to Chris.

"Careful now, that there can'll cook your fingers like sausages."

Chris carefully took the can from Bert, placed it in his lap, and began stirring the chili while he watched the orange glow of the coals shift against their blackened wood curtains.

"I don't know. I sort of see what you're saying, but if I were to let *my* wife—" Chris realized he had said too much and cleared his throat. "—I mean my kids, or let's say my staff, do whatever they wanted, nothing would ever get done. They'd sit around doing just enough to not get in trouble, and then I'd end up having to do everything. Or in the case of my kids, they'd likely grow up to be criminals." Chris cursed himself for letting down his guard. "I guess, sort of like a horse that never becomes rideable because you let it do whatever it wants." Chris attempted to hide a smile and felt his self-loathing dissipate a little.

Bert stirred his chili, took a spoonful, and began blowing on it.

"And how's that been working out for your stress levels?" Bert glanced up from his chili and looked down at Chris.

Even though they were on the same level, Chris felt small, insignificant, and completely exposed. He wanted to push back at the man who had pointed out the obvious. But the quiet desert night, the warmth of the fire, the steady crackle of the coals, and the fearlessness in Bert's voice made the comment sink deep. He thought about all of the frustrating moments he'd been through with his wife over the last few months: trying to get her to get out of bed, do the dishes, clean the house, and everything else a stay-at-home mom *should* be doing. He thought about how frustrated he was that she never wanted to go out anymore and spend time with him. He thought about how often he had yelled at his kids lately, trying to get them to stop fighting, eat their dinner, pick up their toys, behave in public. He thought about his frustration with others at work, not fulfilling or supporting his unspoken expectations. He tried to recall the last time he felt anything other than exhausted and stressed at the end of the day.

He bit his lip and glanced sheepishly at Bert and then back to the fire, jabbing his spoon more forcefully into his chili. Finally, he closed his eyes, inhaled deeply, and turned to Bert. "It's exhausting."

Bert turned back to the fire and took a bite of his chili.

"It ain't easy letting go of control." He chewed slowly for a minute and then continued. "We convince ourselves that the way we think things should be is, well, the way they must be. There are a lot of shades of gray between black and white. Letting go of control helps us find those shades."

Bert took a few more bites of his chili and let the thought linger.

"Ya know, life don't get much more challenging than trying to reign in a bunch of little critters who don't know the difference between what's safe and what's not, what's appropriate and what's not. And who have a whirlwind of emotions running through their little bodies twenty-four-seven. My hat's off to you for doing your best to get through those years." Bert swallowed. "There's a difference though between guiding a child, or an adult for that matter, and trying to control 'em. You can usually tell whether you're guiding or controlling based on how you feel in the process and afterward."

The humble pie Chris had swallowed was starting to have a decent aftertaste. "What do you mean?"

"Well, when you try and make your kids get to bed and they don't want to, that can be real frustrating for most parents. Hell, it's frustrating for me when I watch my grandkids. That's cause getting to bed just ain't optional; it's something they need to thrive and so they ain't rascals the next day. Plus, I'm tired after watching the grandkids all day, and grandpa needs a rest."

Chris smiled and nodded almost imperceptibly.

"A person who's tired and frustrated though might, in a fit of anger, decide to tie 'em to the bed until they eventually fall asleep in a pool of tears. Never mind the fact that the child also has a part to play in falling asleep. That approach might hit the target but it leaves both the parent and the child resentful, angry, guilt-ridden, and exhausted. And it probably scars the kid for life. That there's what controlling looks like.

"On the other hand, when you realize you're not the only one in control here, that getting to sleep is a mutual journey where you control the expectations and consequences and they control the sleep, that opens the door to a lot more options for figuring things out. And it's a heck of a lot less stressful and more productive to work together controlling the things you can control than stepping into someone else's territory and trying to control things you can't.

"When my kids were young, my wife and I had to figure this out the hard way. Oh they were bad sleepers." Bert shook his head at the thought. "I got so frustrated at one point when one of our boys kept coming out of his bedroom that I flipped the doorknobs so we could lock him in. He pounded on the door in a screaming tantrum for what must have been an hour, while my wife cried and begged me to open the door and let her comfort him. All the while I sat on the sofa a fumin' mess and feeling like the world's worst father. Finally, my wife and I had a sit down and decided that trying to force him to sleep wasn't working and that it was time for both of us to stop worrying so much about the part we had no control over. At that point, we started paying closer attention to what rewards and consequences motivated our son and the others and then used that to get 'em to lay still, close their eyes, and relax."

Bert set down his can of chili and grabbed a few more sage-logs to toss onto the fire.

"When your motivation is trying to help 'em learn the importance of getting a good night's sleep, and you're respecting their God-given right to make age-appropriate choices and suffer the consequences of their decisions, they learn from those decisions and your frustration levels are gonna be way lower than if you try to force 'em. Probably not all gone, but certainly lower."

Bert picked up his can of chili, took another bite, then pointed his spoon at the fading sunset beyond the jagged horizon.

"Imagine how frustrating it would be to try and force that there mountain to move out of your way instead of just traveling around it. It may be aggravating that the mountain's blocking the shortest, most direct path back home, but no matter how badly you want it moved, it ain't moving. So you might as well accept that and find your way around it or over it. People who try to control things waste a lot of time and energy cursing at mountains. Time and energy that could have been spent getting around 'em and on to their destination."

Bert stopped talking and turned his attention back to his chili. For several minutes the two men said nothing, watching as the flames danced in front of them above a carpet of shape-shifting, black-orange coals. Bert's comments permeated the silent space between crackles, the original question still clawing at the back of Chris's mind until he could no longer take it and half-turned toward Bert, mesmerized by the hypnotic flames.

"So how did letting go of control pan out with your wife and her depression?"

"Getting through something like a loved one who's mind is suffering, is probably one of the hardest exercises in letting go of control that a person can face. When my wife was toiling with the blues, I started realizing, that no matter how much I argued with her, criticized her, attempted to persuade her, or talked to her about her depression, that there was nothing I could do to force her be the woman I wanted her to be. I couldn't force her to get out of bed, clean the house, do the dishes, take care of the laundry, or stop asking me to handle the responsibilities she needed to be takin' care of, any more than I could get that mountain to move or ole Red to budge. You know why?"

Chris shook his head quietly.

"Because who *I* wanted her to be was not who *she* believed she could or should be. I was convinced that my way was the best way, the only way, and I wanted things that way right now. Black and white thinking." Bert paused and looked up at stars peppering the dark side of the horizon opposite the twilight glow. "It's not that she didn't want to get out of bed and take care of her share o' the chores. She did. She really did, but she carried a burden I didn't with her distortions seeing the world around her, which made it impossible for her to get things done in the way I expected. She needed to do it in her own way and in her own time. She needed someone to walk beside her, not someone to push her from behind.

"I used to do all the dishes and clean up the clutter, so I didn't have to listen to her gripe about it and so things were the way *I* wanted 'em. But all that did was make her feel like she had a little less purpose in her life and fewer reasons to get out of bed. After a spell she started *expecting* me to do 'em for her. Once I quit doing *her* chores *my* way, the pain of letting the dishes and clutter sit for a week outdid the pain of doing 'em. That pain drove her to get out of bed, push herself a little, and muster the strength to get 'er done *her* way and in the way *she* wanted 'em. That and my being there by her side when she was ready, instead of pushing her back into bed with my criticisms and accusations. But it was a hard journey for both of us... " Bert paused and reflected. "... for a time. Struggles always pass in time, and new ones always seem to take their place."

He grabbed another dead sage and tossed it onto the fire.

"Yeah, they do." Chris whispered.

Bert looked over at Chris who was lost in something more than the flames. He watched him patiently for several seconds before turning back to the fire.

"Abraham Lincoln once said, 'The worst thing you can do for those you love is the things they could and should do for themselves.' The more you give in to someone's requests or demands or manipulations to do something that they can or should be able to do themselves, the more they start to expect that you're always gonna do it for 'em. Then they stop learning and growing. At some point you have to draw the line and deal with the bellyaching that follows. It's their way of controlling you, even though most never realize that's what they're doing. Same way I didn't recognize it for a long time."

He paused to adjust the logs in the fire. More stars had appeared across the sky now, and the ambient light was no more than a faint glow along the western horizon. Bert lay the stick at his feet and adjusted his position on the rock.

"Once you stop trying to control the people around you, and accept what they might have to offer," he grunted, as he settled into a more comfortable position, "you start to realize that there's a real beauty to the challenges that certain people bring into your life. It's those experiences that make life worth living ... even though it don't seem that way at the time. Hasn't been a single trial I've had to face in my life that didn't spit me out for better in the end."

Chris nodded almost imperceptibly. "That's interesting."

"Ain't it?"

Bert nodded and drifted off into the fire. Darkness had engulfed the desert now, and the light from the fire faded off in all directions. In the distance, the soft thunder of an approaching horse drew their attention away from the firelight and toward the south. The longer they stared, the more their eyes adjusted until they could just make out the shape of a shadowy figure riding toward them. A few seconds later Seth galloped into camp and dismounted his horse.

"Any luck?" Bert asked.

"They were about a mile back. Heifer and her bull calf. They're safe and sound with the herd now. How's the chili?"

Seth worked on taking the saddle off his horse and led him over to the post with the other horses.

"Oh, I thought you brung your own. Chris just finished up the last can."

Seth stopped in his tracks and turned to Chris, eyes wide. "Ain't kind to eat another man's chili."

He threw the rope he had been carrying to the ground and made a beeline to Chris, shaking his head. Chris leaned back as he approached.

"You know what happens in these parts when one man eats another man's Hormel chili?" He lifted his hand toward the gun he was holding on the leather holster attached to his side.

Chris stumbled as he attempted to stand up. "Hey, man."

"Come on Seth, now just cool it down there," Bert admonished.

Seth's hand was over his gun now, eyes locked on Chris. Chris began backing away slowly along the desert ground.

"Well, you'll find out in the morning when them beans really hit'cha." Seth burst out laughing and dropped his hand from his holster. He wandered over to Chris and extended his hand to help him up off the ground. Once he was up, Seth gave him a hard slap across the shoulder and wandered back over to his horse.

"Oooo," Seth hooted. "I had you good there, Chris." He laughed as he finished tying up his horse and then wandered back over to the fire. "All right boss, where you hiding those cans of chili?"

"Right there on the inside of the fire ring waiting for ya."

Seth settled down on the ground next to Chris, grabbed

Bert's clamp, and picked up the can Bert had tucked to the side to keep warm.

"Ya' did a mighty fine job out there today, rookie." Seth grabbed a spoon while carefully balancing the chili with the metal clamp. "Much better than I handled things my first day on the job. Maybe you ought to think about sticking round here and helping us out."

He settled back into his seat and shoved a spoonful of chili into his mouth, releasing an involuntary gasp and nearly dropping his chili.

"Dang!" he cursed, spitting the chili back into the can. "Shoulda been paying more attention. That's gonna sting for days." He put his hand up to his mouth and wiggled his tongue around, before grabbing another spoonful, blowing carefully for several seconds this time, and then taking another bite.

"Seth's right, Chris. You did a fine job out there today. I'm sure you're anxious to get back to that family of yours though." Bert turned to Chris and winked.

It was pointless hiding anything from the old man. Maybe it was pointless to keep hiding things period. The glow of the fire drew the three men into its hypnotic realm for a time.

Time. What did that even mean anymore?

When the fire finally died off, Seth grabbed another dried sage and tossed it into the fire.

"Well, boys, I think it's time this old man turned in for the night." Bert rose with some effort and stretched.

He stood there for a minute, lost in thought, and then wandered off to settle in.

"Chris, there's an extra couple of blankets in the saddle bags over there. Help yourself to what you need. We'll see you boys in the morning."

✳

It took Chris a while to fall asleep under the deep expanse of endless space and the glow of a trillion stars. It was strange to him, the silence. No drone of ever-flowing traffic, no refrigerator kicking on, or crying waking him in the middle of the night. Just the crackle of coals and the meandering of thoughts.

He watched the lessons of an old man dance around in his mind. Wisdom forged by decades of struggle and hard labor. He saw his wife, distraught by his disappearance, unable to function. In the fabricated reality of his mind, he could see his children crying for their daddy, pushing Emily over her mental and emotional limits. He thought about how controlling he had been toward them, toward others at work, and how messed up his life had become as a result.

Bert was right. Cursin' at mountains. Chasin' illusions. Emily. Need to get home. His thoughts drifted onward, meandering along strange paths toward a sleep as deep as the universe itself.

CHAPTER 4

Wilderness

C hris knew it was morning when the light of the sun illuminated his eyelids, stirring his mind from a profound unconsciousness. The light felt painfully bright, and for a time he lay there, waiting for his closed eyes to adjust.

In the distance, he could make out the almost imperceptible sound of a large group jabbering loudly.

How strange.

The ground felt out of place too; softer and more grassy. And his aches and pains from the previous day were gone now. Even the air was off from where it had been the previous day. He didn't usually notice air, but today it felt less dry. High above him, beyond the reach of the junipers that he had fallen asleep under, a gentle breeze rustled leaves that chattered like rain. In fact, the smell of junipers and sagebrush was gone, replaced by a pungent pine scent.

When his eyes finally adjusted to the light, he squinted them open and felt suddenly disoriented and dizzy. The desert was gone. Bert and Seth, gone. The horses, gone. A collapsed log had taken the place of the rock he had fallen asleep against. It stretched out thirty feet across a grassy meadow half buried beneath wildflowers. At the center of the meadow, peaking from behind the grasses, he could barely make out the reflection of a pond.

At the other end of the log, where the tree had uprooted from the ground, a dense forest of Douglas and White fir faded into a seemingly impassible wall of dark vegetation. Patches of aspens and mountain shrubs lined a forest floor strewn with decades of fallen logs and dried fir needles.

Panic washed over Chris. He sat up quickly and glanced around to get his bearings.

The blanket he had fallen asleep under still covered him. The fire pit was there too, filled with compressed ash. It seemed old, though. Older than the one he had stared into the night before. The rocks that he had adjusted last night were now covered in lichens, half-swallowed by the earth beneath them. Had it not been for the charred, barely legible, red and yellow Hormel chili can laying in the ashes, he would have assumed this pit had no relation to the fire last night.

"I'm going nuts." He rubbed his face and reclined against the log.

The distant chatter was clearer now. A group of young men most likely, whining, teasing, and haggling each other. The sound grew louder until crossing paths with the group became an inevitability. Chris sat up a little taller and looked around. He noticed movement through the forest fifty feet away.

"All right princesses. Welcome to your kingdom for the next two weeks."

Groans and sighs of relief erupted from the group.

"This is bull sh—"

"Damien! Watch your mouth, dude. Do I need to remind you what happens if you can't keep it under control?"

Just beyond the trees, a solid man, wearing a five o'clock shadow, black beanie, and a logoed, black, GoreTex jacket appeared and disappeared behind the trees. The tall, linebacker-of-a-Polynesian boy he was addressing, along with an assortment of boys dressed in black shirts and green cargo pants, did the same.

"Sorry," the Polynesian boy grumbled.

"Okay boys, find yourself a cozy plot of dirt where you can catch your beauty sleep tonight and let's set up camp." The boys began scattering, shoulders slumped under the weight of their packs. "And make sure I can see you from right here!"

Chris waited for the inevitable as the adolescent clones in matching backpacks panned out.

"Hey! There's someone over here." A stocky, overweight, Latino boy froze in his tracks and stared at Chris, not knowing what to do. He glanced back and forth between Chris and the man in charge. Boys that were now scattered throughout the forest froze and turned toward Chris.

"What?" The man in charge, who was now chatting with another adult, stopped talking and made a determined beeline toward the Latino boy.

Chris stood up, brushed off his dust-covered khakis, and began folding the gray wool blanket he had been sleeping on. He felt like a homeless man, surviving on his delusions in the wilderness.

"Hey man, what's up?" The man in charge pushed forward unintimidated through the undergrowth toward Chris. He studied Chris carefully, sizing him up like a military man. "You okay?"

Chris stared at his surroundings, trying to wrap his mind around where he was. "Yeah, I think so. You wouldn't happen to know where I can get cell service would you?"

The leader stared at him suspiciously. "Dude, you are a long way from cell service." He scanned Chris up and down. "Where you from?" Behind him, the boys had begun inching toward the conversation. Without looking, he seemed to know what was going on. "Guys. Get your tents set up, come on." He glanced over his shoulder and watched the boys slowly return to setting up camp.

"Savannah." Chris responded, watching the boys get back on task.

"Georgia?"

"Yeah."

The man in charge looked surprised. "What brings you to the Bob Marshalls?"

"Bob Marshalls?"

"Montana."

"Montana?" Chris turned back to the man in charge. "Really? Huh."

The leader eyed Chris again, while the two of them stood there trying to make sense of it all. Neither spoke. Both scanned the forest for answers.

"Well." The man in charge shrugged and hesitantly extended his hand toward Chris. "I'm Todd."

Chris nodded and extended his own hand. "Chris."

Todd shook his head and half-smiled. "It's an *odd* pleasure."

"Odd would be an understatement." Chris released his hand and glanced around. He felt distant, trapped in a dream. "So how far is it to the nearest signal or landline?"

Todd squinted and stared at Chris. "You sure you're okay?"

Chris rubbed the back of his head. The dust and grit from the previous day broke loose in his fingers. "I suppose I'm still trying to figure that out."

Todd sighed through pursed lips and turned to the east. "Well.

If you head east up the Box Creek trail, you're looking at probably twenty-five miles. West, maybe a little shorter, but you've got some significant elevation gain, and the trail branches *a lot*, so unless you know where you're going, it would probably be best to avoid that route." He paused and stared at Chris. "You're sure you're okay?"

Chris raised his eyebrows distantly, nodded slowly, and turned back to the east. "Yeah. It's just been a strange couple of days. I swear I'm not a nut job though."

Todd shook his head slowly and then shot Chris one last interrogational stare. "Alrighty then. Well, I'm not sure what sort of supplies you've got—" he scanned Chris's camp, "—or what your plans were, but you're more than welcome to hang with us for a couple of days and then hike out with me if you're not familiar with the area. I've been up here with the boys for the last two weeks, and we'll be swappin' leadership in the next couple of days. I've got a truck at the trailhead and can take you as far as Great Falls."

"That'd be great." Chris sighed and watched the boys set up camp. "So what exactly is all this?"

Todd glanced at the boys and then back to Chris. "It's a buttload o' work is what it is." He gestured with his chin toward the other adult wearing a Patagonia fleece jacket. "Shawn and I are with a company called Rise-Up Solutions. We basically help boys, who have hit hard times in their life, work through those hard times using team-based, outdoor leadership opportunities." Todd turned toward the boys and lifted his voice. "Most of these boys have never had to think about anyone but themselves, and we fix that. Don't we, Liam?!"

"Whatever." A slightly overweight, African American boy mumbled back, brushing aside his braided dreadlocks as he dug through his pack.

Todd smiled and turned back to Chris. "Anyway, they're good kids."

Chris cringed at the idea of hanging out with a bunch of teenaged boys for a few days in the mountains. The teenagers in his neighborhood liked to hang out at the park next to his house and always drove him nuts with their loud, obnoxious behavior.

"I hate to be a burden," Chris said, rubbing the dirt from the back of his neck and staring off at the distant mountains. "But given that all I have is this blanket, I don't think I have too many other options."

"Oh, don't worry, we'll put you to work." Todd winked and then turned back to the boys who were unloading their packs and setting up tents at various makeshift sites scattered throughout the forest. "It's probably gonna take these boys an hour or two to get camp set up, and they need to do that on their own. So for now there's not much to do. After that though, I'm sure we'll find somethin' to keep you busy."

Chris nodded and his eyes drifted toward a not-too-distant peak rising beyond the forest. "Well, maybe I'll go do a little exploring while you all get set up. You say an hour or so?"

"Yep, we'll be here."

A soft, cool breeze flowed down from the mountain peaks as Chris wandered through the upward sloping forest. It passed through the pines like water, stirring the air in gentle, patchy currents. Like the Nevada desert, sounds seemed to exist only to emphasize the silence: the occasional buzz of a fly, the click of a Dark-Eyed Junco hopping around the base of the trees, and his own footsteps snapping against the forest floor.

He wondered if, when he returned to camp, Todd and the boys would even exist. Wondered if he would be transported away to another part of the world. The line between reality and fantasy felt frail and fleeting, as did the passage of time. He had been hiking now for somewhere between forty-five minutes and a lifetime.

Up ahead, the trees began to thin out as he approached the ridge, and a vast expanse of canyons, valleys and mountain ranges rolled out across endless horizons. He pulled out his phone to check for a signal: 45 percent battery, signal null.

He placed the phone back in his pocket and sat on a rock, contemplating the expanse, the curiosity of it all, and the oddity of his presence here.

After a time, nearly a hundred feet up the meandering ridge upon which he sat, an explosion of snapping branches startled him. He lurched toward the sound. The second he turned, dizzying, lightheaded tremors rippled across his body as a large grizzly came into view. He half-rose on shaking legs, poised to run as the bear hobbled toward him, rummaging and foraging, and completely unaware that Chris was even there.

When it finally noticed the trembling thing before him, the bear paused and tilted its head curiously toward the dust-covered man adorned in weathered down business attire. For a time, the two creatures stared at each other, uncertain of what might happen next.

Beyond the ridge, wind rose from the canyon below and passed over the ridge, filling Chris's ears with the sounds of roaring water and causing him to stumble. Fixated on the bear and hyper-aware, Chris noticed sounds transforming from a burbling white noise to a deep tornado-like bellow, then to that hideous and terrifying drone that had haunted his hallucinations. The sound circled around him and the bear like a giant invisible snake. It weaved its way around them and drew his attention away from the bear. Chris's eyes widened, and the bear tilted its head toward the sound.

With each rotation the drone closed in, drawing Chris into the eyes of the bear and the bear into Chris. Connected to the animal,

Chris stood as the bear rose to its hind legs, bobbing its head and sniffing the air. Fear drained from Chris's body as he watched the phenomenon through the eyes of the bear. He saw himself twenty yards away through curious eyes filled with compassion. The urge to yawn rose up deep within his throat and the bear opened its mouth as though it would swallow the world. Immediately, the terrible circling drone funneled helplessly into the bear's mouth like water flowing through a drain, gurgling in agony as it passed until nothing but silence remained.

From beside his rock, Chris watched the bear close its enormous mouth, and drop to the ground. It sniffed the air, turned back to the rising ridge and continued on its way, disappearing from view.

Chris collapsed onto the rock and stared at the place where the bear had been. Something was different now, as though he had experienced a forgotten memory from some previous existence only to have it slip away once again, leaving behind an indelible, haunting impression. His enemy was weaker now or maybe Chris was stronger. Either way, the world in which he had been blinded by his own perceptions was coming into focus for the first time.

✸

Chris had been gone for almost three hours when he finally returned to camp. The empty forest he had woken to late morning looked more like a tent city now. Dull green and tan A-frame tents stood among the firs with a fire smoldering at the center. Two rows of makeshift log benches, sheltered under a tarp canopy supported by ropes fastened to the surrounding trees, faced the fire pit like a primitive amphitheater.

At the perimeter of the camp, Chris paused nervously, wondering if he had perhaps once again been transported to another place, another time before modern technology. The second the thought crossed his mind, Todd crawled out from one of the tents and looked over at Chris.

"Hey man. Nice timing. We were just about to get the boys together for our afternoon debrief. You're welcome to join us if you'd like." Todd took the whistle that had been dangling from his neck and blew long and hard.

One by one the boys trickled out of their tents, making their way toward the canopy.

The logs underneath the canopy were set in two rows and had been wedged into position with large rocks to prop them up and keep them from rolling away. Chris grabbed a small stump and propped it up in the back for a seat while seven boys settled down, two to a bench in front of him, eyeing him suspiciously as they took their seats.

Todd sat down on a log up front and waited for the boys to stop jabbering with one another. An unshaven Shawn took a seat next to him, leaned over and whispered something to Todd. Todd nodded, eyed one of the boys, and then brought the meeting to order.

"All right ya buncha' wingless flies." The boys rolled their eyes and their conversations died down. "We have a guest that's going to be joining us for the next couple of days until the trade-off."

The boys turned blank stares toward Chris.

"His name is Chris, and he is out here from Savannah, Georgia."

Chris smiled insincerely and nodded. A pale, scrawny boy with poorly groomed dreadlocks and a drug-worn face eyed Chris suspiciously and turned back to Todd.

"What's he doin' out here, and why are you lettin' him join us? Isn't that against the rules or somethin'?"

"Which rule, Isaac?" Todd challenged.

"I don't know. The one where... I don't know."

The Latino boy next to him, who looked like a dirt-covered version of a teen magazine poster child, punched Isaac in the arm.

Isaac glared back at the Latino boy. "The hell?"

"Andres!" Todd sighed in frustration. "Look guys, Chris needs our help for a few days, and so *we* are going to help him, *because* it's the right thing to do. Got it?" He stared the boys down until they had all averted their eyes.

"What if he's like an axe murderer or something?" a black-haired, olive-skinned preppy boy asked, refusing to take his eyes off Chris.

Todd looked at the ground and shook his head. "Why don't you ask him that yourself, Noah?" He looked up at Noah and watched him hesitate and then turn to Chris.

"So are you like a serial axe killer?"

The rest of the boys rolled their eyes or chuckled and whispered comments.

Chris, who had noticed the sarcastically playful, no-nonsense dynamic between Todd and the boys, closed shyly into himself and began rocking.

"No." He twitched neurotically and sing-songed disturbingly. "I like using my haaaands." The boys lurched wide-eyed toward Chris who stopped rocking, looked up slowly, and homed in on Noah with a creepy smile. Noah's eyes went wide and Chris began to laugh. "Sorry man, I'm just playin' with you, I can't even bring myself to kill a spider."

The other boys turned to Noah and began laughing. "Dude, he had you good."

"Shut the hell up!" he shouted back.

"Hey!" Todd commanded. The boys immediately quieted down and gave him their attention. "For the love of all things holy, can we *not* just let it go? Look, if you're seriously worried that he's an axe murder, which he's not, do you really think a lone unarmed dude in the woods could take down a couple of retired Seals?" The boys stared blankly. "You remember what happened when big Dee got out of control, right? Didn't take too long for us to get him under control, did it? And he was a big dude." The boys shrugged and avoided eye contact. "So can we get on with business now?"

The boys said nothing, and Todd shifted gears from disciplinarian to discussion leader. "All right. Liam, what's the point of this gathering of intelligent young minds?"

Liam cleared his throat and looked up at Todd. "Uh, talk about the hike?"

"Nice work Liam," Todd replied sarcastically. "Maybe next time tell me instead of ask me, okay?" Liam shook his head and rolled his eyes. "All right guys, can someone tell me what our goals were for today regarding the hike?"

The boys shuffled in their seats and looked at one another and then stared at the ground. After a moment of awkward silence, a short, stocky red-headed boy piped in. "Weren't we workin' on watching our pace and tryin' to keep together as a group?"

"You tell me, Chez. Was that our goal?"

The rest of the group nodded their heads.

"Good. Let's plus-delta it; who can tell me what worked well, what didn't work well, and what are we going to do about it?"

The boys stared at the ground. Todd and the other leader waited patiently.

"Damien, why don't you go first." Todd gestured toward the large Polynesian boy who had given him grief earlier.

Damien scoffed quietly, shook his head, and leaned forward. Todd waited until a few of the boys began to fidget.

"Dude, come on," Andres whined without breaking his downward gaze.

"Just shut up," Damien shot back.

Todd looked down at the ground, shook his head and then turned back to the boys. "We are gonna sit here as long as it takes to give Damien time to think about it." He turned to Damien. "Come on man, there's got to be something that didn't suck about today."

Damien sighed and mumbled. "It's nice to be out of that sh--," he caught himself, "crap hole we were in at our last camp."

The other boys nodded.

"Great," Todd replied, "and thanks for catching your language there. Now tell us your delta."

"That's easy. Matias was bein' a wussy and was slowin' us all down."

Matias jumped to his feet and puffed his chest out toward Damien. Damien looked over at the short, overweight boy and then turned slowly back to the ground, unimpressed by his show of bravado.

"Hey man, you try carrying..."

"Whoa, whoa, whoa, whoa, WHOA." Todd interrupted. "Damien, dude, you know what our rule is when it comes to blame. All you're doin' right now is lettin' someone else control your attitude and get the best of you. Is that what you want?"

Damien glanced over at Matias annoyingly, who glared at Damien and then flopped back down on the log. "Hell no." He looked back over at Todd.

"All right. Then why don't you give me that delta again."

Damien frowned and turned back to the ground, bouncing his knee rapidly as he worked through his pride. "I didn't say anything when Matias was drivin' me nuts," he mumbled.

"Good." Todd turned his attention to the group. "Damien wasn't alone in getting frustrated with Matias, was he?" The boys' eyes danced around nervously, while Matias scowled at the lot of them. "As far as I could tell, not a single one of you did or said anything about it other than whine and nag Matias."

Liam turned to Todd. "Dat's cause every time we do, y'all is always gettin' in ah faces."

"Fair enough." Todd glanced over at Shawn who looked up from taking notes in a small journal and nodded. "But if you all want Shawn and me to back off, you gotta stop trying to solve your problems with fights like a bunch of five-year-olds."

The boys fidgeted and looked for something to fix their eyes on that wasn't human.

"If we back off, do you think you can commit to letting go of your egos and engaging in productive conversations with one another that don't end in tantrums or pouting matches like bunch of babies?" Todd asked. The boys looked around at each other hesitantly for a second and then began nodding one by one.

"Okay," Todd continued, "I'm holding every single one of you to it, so expect a follow-up the next time we come together. I want to get back to what Damien said, though. He should've said something, and he's going to next time, but what is the problem that never got solved because he and the rest of you never spoke up?"

Andres half-turned toward the group. "The problem is that some of you are fat and slow cause you sit on your—" he paused and thought carefully, "—butts all day playin' video games, while others of us spend so much time runnin' from the cops that hikin' ain't that big of deal." The boys burst out laughing.

Todd smiled and waited for the laughter to die down. "So you're sayin' that the problem is that some of you are stronger and faster than others?"

"Whatever you want to call it," Andres replied with a faint Latino accent and hunched into his seat.

"So what do you suggest then?" Todd asked.

"I don't know, put the fast guys up front and the slower ones behind?"

A couple of boys shook their heads vehemently. "No way man," Noah interjected. "You do that and Todd and Shawn are gonna make those of us who are fast, sit around and wait for all you slow turds to catch up."

"Yeah," Matias added, "and then those of us who take a little longer will never get a break, because as soon as we catch up you'll take off again."

"True," Todd responded. "So what's your suggestion?"

Noah shook his head. "I don't know, man."

"You could make the fast guys slow down a little," Matias suggested.

"Yeah, I ain't slowin' down for you all." Damien retorted.

"Yeah? And I'm not gonna have a heart attack and die in the middle of the mountains and get eaten by a bear." Matias shot back.

Damien tried to hold in his laughter and snorted, "It would take a whole family of bears to finish you off."

The boys erupted in laughter as Matias scowled and shook his head. It was apparent they exhausted their idea inventory.

"Okay guys, enough dinking around." Todd waited for the laughter to settle down. "Since no one has any better ideas, let's go ahead and roll with Matias's idea for a minute and see where it takes us. How do you slow someone down?"

"Break their legs?" Andres responded.

"Shoot them in the knee," Liam shouted.

"Give 'em some of that nasty water that had Chez runnin' around camp all night with the squirts," Damien added.

The boys burst out laughing again.

"You guys are idiots," Chez shouted back.

Todd waited patiently again for the laughter to die down. In the back, Isaac, who looked too permanently stoned to say anything, tossed out the first intelligent idea. "You could always weigh down the fast guys. If we were all carrying the same amount of weight Matias is carrying around his waist, sorry bro."

Matias fake smiled and shrugged it off. Issac continued, "We'd probably all be moving at the same speed."

"That's a good thought," Todd responded. "Matias, what were you carrying in your pack this morning?"

The boys composed themselves and turned their attention to Matias.

"I don't know. I think I had the kitchen supplies, most of the canned food, water filters, maybe some extra water."

Todd brought the palm of his hand to his forehead and then looked around at the boys, shaking his head as he realized what was going on. "Andres, how about you?"

"I think I had a tarp and some freeze-dried food maybe. Oh and my water bottle."

"Damien?"

"Uh. Sleeping bags, a couple of tarps, Mountain House meals, maybe some utensils, water."

"Nice." Todd smiled at the ground and shook his head. "Are y'all seeing a problem here?

They stared blankly back at him.

"Come on guys. How much does a can of food weigh compared to a freeze-dried meal?"

The boys nodded slowly as the lights came on.

"What were you carrying Matias, like 15 cans?"

Matias shrugged. "Yeah, something like that I guess."

"Plus, the cast iron frying pan, utensils, pots, and probably all five filters? So you were carrying like 40 to 45 pounds of extra weight, while Damien and Andres were carrying what, maybe an extra 10?"

"Man, no wonder I was draggin' behind. I ain't fat, you guys just plain lazy. Makin' me carry all that heavy crap." Matias faded off defensively.

Damien and Andres leaned forward and buried themselves between their knees.

"All right guys, how do we deal with this next week when we

do our next ten mile stretch?"

"We spread out the load!" Matias shouted, glaring around at everyone in the group.

"We could just lay everything out before we pack it up and make sure everyone has an equal load," Isaac added with Rastafarian coolness that immediately disarmed the sarcasm.

Todd nodded encouragingly. "That's a good thought man."

"Yeah, but that ain't really fair because some of y'all are a lot bigger and stronger than us smaller guys. If we all carryin' the same weight, that don't seem fair." Liam interjected.

The boys sat in silence for a minute processing the problem.

"What if we start off equal, and then if someone's goin' faster than the rest of the group, they have to take some of the load off the person who is goin' the slowest?" Noah finally added, breaking the silence.

One by one, the boys began nodding.

"I love it," Todd responded. "So tomorrow we're gonna be heading up the ridgeline for a few miles to get our bearings and scope out the area. How about we test your idea on that hike? If it works great, and if not, we can refine it as we go."

The boys nodded and looked around at each other.

"All right, who wants to volunteer to own this for tomorrow?"

All heads fell in an attempt to dodge Todd's radar.

"Well, don't all volunteer at once," Todd mocked sarcastically. "You guys are all gonna have to own something tomorrow, and this may be the dream job compared to whatever else might come up."

The boys shot timid, brief glances around at each other until Isaac finally raised his hand. "I'll do it. Better than washing dishes."

"Sweet. Thanks, Isaac." Todd pulled a small notepad from his shirt pocket, wrote something down, and then turned back to the group. "Okay, Chez, let's keep going with the plus-deltas. Give us another plus from the last twelve hours."

Todd worked his way through each of the boys, identifying what worked well, singling out problems, coming up with solutions, and making assignments between testosterone-induced jabs and heckles. The boys then reported on past assignments and collectively assessed their performance in something that hovered between board room formality and a cage fight.

Chris thought back to the time-wasting meetings he had both attended and led at the university. He couldn't believe that a bunch of street hardened teenagers with incredibly short attention spans and fuses could be ten times more productive than the educated adults he worked with. Not one of them wanted to be there, but no one was checked out, and everyone seemed to have something to add.

This surreal scene from Cloud Cuckoo Land continued another forty-five minutes until it was obvious that the boys had hit their limits.

"That was insane." Chris combed both hands through his hair as the boys fanned out across camp. Todd finished writing something in his notebook and then looked up at Chris. "Whatever you and Shawn did back there was unbelievable," Chris said.

"Really?"

"Yeah. Ninety percent of the meetings I go to are a complete waste of time. We get together, go around the room so everyone can vomit information at each other about what they're working on. Sometimes we spend half the meeting trying to figure out why we're meeting in the first place. Then a few talkers usually monopolize most of the time, or someone ends up rambling off on some unrelated topic, which means we usually run out of time to solve anything, not that anyone knows what we're trying to solve in the first place. Then we schedule a follow-up meeting and everyone is on their way to the next pointless meeting. I'm probably over-exaggerating a little, but either way it's mind numbing."

"Interesting." Todd's eyes drifted away from Chris to the boys who were settling into their down time. A few of the boys had sprawled out on their sleeping bags, others read, and others sat down chatting quietly with their friends.

"You know," Todd said, watching the boys, "I'd wager that most of these boys probably aren't too different from the people you work with."

Chris stopped watching the boys and turned to Todd. "How do you mean?"

"Most of these boys come from families that mean well, you know. They care about their kids. They want to give 'em every opportunity to be successful, but in most cases there just haven't been any expectations, accountability, ownership, or consequences in their homes. The parents sort of let their kids do their thing, and they do theirs. They're more interested in being friends with their kids than in being parents. Either that or they're just too busy with their own lives to invest the time and energy into helping their kids achieve their potential. When kids or adults end up in those type of conditions, problems almost always occur."

"Not sure I'm following."

"If you watch people closely, you'll see that most adult behavior is just a different flavor of kid behavior, only a little less eccentric and awkward. Well, sometimes."

Todd's attention seemed divided and yet laser focused between Chris, the boys, and his own thoughts, as though he were constantly monitoring everything around him. Chris leaned forward to grab his attention and see if he could decipher where Todd was going with this.

"So I'll give you an example. When parents drop their kids off at our facility, in most cases, most kids are usually dragged in against their will. They come in swearing, yelling, and blamin' their parents for ruining their life. They're completely resistant to authority, and we've even had a few that bolt for the door.

"On the flip side, once they drop their kids off, the exasperated parents or guardians attend a series of parental training meetings. Most of them come into those trainings cursing under their breath that they have to attend a stupid meeting they don't need. They blame their kids for ruining their lives, resist the parenting skills we teach them, and try to get out of the meeting and get back to work as soon as they can. They detest in their children what they can't seem to see or face in themselves."

Todd paused and carefully contemplated his next words while monitoring the boys.

"What I'm tryin' to say is that whatever you think works here for these boys may give you some insights into your own situation.

"Let me ask you a question, Chris. What do the people in your line of work do that drive you nuts?"

Chris thought for a moment and then cleared his throat. "I think the biggest thing at the university where I work is this idea of status quo."

"You're a university man, huh?" Todd interjected. "I was at U-dub in Seattle for a year after I retired from the service. Teachin' boot camp in the fitness program. Anyway, you were sayin'."

"That's cool," Chris stalled for a second to regain his train of thought. "Anyway, maybe you saw this during your time at UW. People in the public sector preach about all these great things they want to do, but then no one follows through. They spend a lot of time talking but won't do anything beyond their core job responsibilities. Either that or they'll accomplish something of minimal impact and then inflate it. They'll flaunt that the fifty thousand dollars spent was worth it for that one student whose life is now changed forever. But they're oblivious that they just spent fifty thousand on one student that could have been used to help hundreds of students."

"Totally."

"Then there's the negativity, backbiting, and gossip. I mean, I thought I had a pretty good relationship with my staff, but then, out of the blue, I find out members of my team are whining about me behind my back. First, they want our program to change, then they resist that change, then they get upset because we're not changing."

"Sounds lame."

"Yeah, right? The longer I'm there the worse things seem to get. It's insane."

"The insane thing is that you just described to a T most of these boys before they entered the program," Todd said. "Not to mention a pretty accurate description of me when I was their age."

"What do you mean?"

"When I was fifteen, all I wanted to do was sit around and play video games and hang out with my friends. That, and be stupid. At the same time, I also wanted to be the lead guitarist in the next big metal band. My friends and I even went so far as to start a band that we based out of my parent's garage. We talked a good talk about how amazing we were gonna be, but beyond getting together a few times each week and dinkin' around in completely unstructured practice, we didn't do squat to make anything of ourselves. We wrote riffs, but no songs. We played sloppy versions of covers. We got bored and then wandered off into the woods to goof around. No discipline. No pushin' ourselves outside of our comfort zones. No commitment.

"My parents didn't help either. They never pushed me to get off the couch and do anything. I ended up getting bored with life, and so my friends and I started smokin' weed and shoplifting for a little excitement.

"When my parents found out, I was almost eighteen, and they threatened to kick me out if I didn't change. Of course, I knew they were bluffin', like they always did, so I kept on doin' my thing. I was a jerk.

"We ended up having a lot of pissing matches, and I probably would have still been sittin' on that couch playin' video games to this day, had it not been for the fact that they weren't bluffing that last time they threatened me.

"After graduating from high school—barely—I found my bag packed on the front porch and the doors locked with a note that said, *'If all else fails the homeless shelter is located at thirteen Johnson Avenue.'* Man, was I ticked off. I hated them more than you could imagine."

Todd clenched his fists and tightened his jaw as he relived the experience. The stillness settling over the forest accentuated the intensity in his emotions.

"For the first couple of days," Todd continued, shaking his head, "I stayed at my friend's house, but his parents were on the war path as well. They told me I was being a bad example for their son and that I needed to get out of their house by the end of the week.

"At that point I started to panic. My parents had let me be lazy for so long that I had no skills. I didn't even know how to look for a job. The only thing that came to mind was the military recruiters who harassed us at school or at the mall. So before the weekend arrived, I found myself enlisted in the navy, and as luck would have it, I was on a bus that very next week."

Todd sighed, relaxed his fists, and stared thoughtfully into the distance.

"Turns out as infuriated, depressed, and anxious as I was that my parents, and my friend's parents, had kicked me out, it ended up bein' one of the best things that ever happened to me."

"Really?"

"Yep."

Todd scanned the camp for a moment and then turned back to Chris.

"So you're probably wondering how my getting kicked out of

the house and joinin' the navy has anything to do with what we were talkin' about."

"You mean my lame work environment?"

"Think about it. The people where you work are happy with the status quo, right? It's comfortable. These boys are no different. They got comfortable doin' a whole lot of nothin', and in their boredom with life, they filled their spare time being destructive to themselves and others. Maybe your people aren't doin' drugs, stealing, and vandalizing people's cars, but trash-talkin' others seems like pretty destructive behavior to me. These kids chose the easy route in the same way someone in a nine-to-five job might choose to coast under the radar and fire off stealthy words at others to avoid the pain of dealin' with problems they don't know how to deal with."

Chris nodded slowly.

"And here's the thing, most people really do want to accomplish something significant in their life. For me it was becoming a famous rock star. For others it might be climbin' the ranks to become the top Fortnite player in the world. Someone else might just be tryin' to be the best mother they can be. Some of your leadership and staff— it's, you know, changin' the world of education, right?"

Chris nodded.

"Problem is, it takes discipline, sacrifice, and doin' things different. And a lot of people have no clue where to begin. Either that or they're just terrified to push themselves or others to take the steps they need to take to get there.

"Kids like these." Todd gestured toward the boys hanging out around camp. "And a lot of adults, especially civilians in the public sector, have never had clear expectations laid out for them on a consistent basis. And if they have, there are no consequences for not followin' through on those expectations.

"If you have no expectations and no consequences, it's

almost impossible to hold anyone accountable. And if no one's accountable nothing productive gets done and no one grows or improves. Sound like what you're dealin' with at work?"

"Well, yeah, but I don't know. When someone joins our team, we go over expectations, and if someone's not hitting their goals, we help them refocus. I even personally check in with each of my staff every month to see how things are going."

"And what do you do in those one-on-ones, Chris?"

The way Todd asked the question put Chris on the defensive. "I suppose what anyone would do. Find out how things are going, see if they need anything from me."

"How *what* things are going?"

"The things they're working on."

"How do they determine what they need to work on?"

Chris felt like he was being interrogated. "They know their jobs, and they do their jobs."

"And beyond what was outlined in their job description when you first hired them, as things evolve and new projects come on board, how do you hold them accountable for those things during your one-on-ones?"

Chris's knee began to bounce. He could feel the tension moving into his shoulders. "What are you trying to get at here?"

"Chris, if I were to ask one of your staff members right now what will happen at their next one-on-one and what Chris will expect them to deliver, what would they tell me?"

The question knocked Chris off his self-constructed pedestal. If he was honest with himself, he couldn't recall a time, beyond their onboarding training, when he had intentionally established expectations with any of his staff. Until now he had assumed that everyone knew what they were expected to do and would do it. They had their job descriptions. They had a copy of the meeting notes and any assignments.

"If I asked your team members right now to tell me what is acceptable and what is not acceptable at meetings what would they say? Would they say dominating the meeting or going wildly off topic is acceptable? Would they say a meeting without a clearly defined purpose is acceptable? Would they say inflating their own limited success or gossip or backbiting is acceptable?"

Chris could feel himself tumbling over a mental cliff. His role in making everything worse for himself and others took center stage. *He* had a clear vision of what he wanted to see happen, but he couldn't recall a time when he had clearly articulated that to everyone around him, beyond occasional one-off comments and soap boxes.

Through a mental haze, he could see the walls they'd likely beaten their heads up against, trying to please him without knowing exactly what it was he wanted. The same feelings that had haunted him throughout his youth. He remembered a time when his dad asked him to mow the lawn and then got on his case because he mowed it vertically instead of diagonally. Remembered getting in trouble for coming home after a curfew no one had told him about, for saying words he didn't know were inappropriate, for not doing chores his parents had never told him he needed do.

His leg stopped bouncing, and he hunched forward with his elbow on his knee and gnawed at his nails.

"Hey man, I'm sorry," Todd apologized. He took a quick, deep breath through his nose and relaxed. "Sometimes I can be a little intense." He glanced around at the boys. "After spending a few weeks with these characters, it's hard toning it down for people who haven't been forced into a wilderness therapy program."

"No. You're absolutely right," Chris replied, half-lost in his own thoughts. "But how exactly do you rein things in? How do you go from ambiguous expectations and consequences to a place where everyone is cool with the standards you establish?"

Todd squinted deep in thought and scanned the camp. "Well,

I can tell ya when I started doing the wilderness therapy thing, there is no way I would have been able to answer that question. In the military, they set the expectations, and you did exactly what you were told, or you'd get the living daylights beat out of you. That's the attitude they drilled into me. I probably would've taken that approach with these boys if this wilderness program had let me, but luckily they have a phenomenal training and mentoring program for therapy non-native yay-hoos like myself. Otherwise, I probably would've imploded the whole program.

"So, typically we lay out expectations for the boys on day one, when their parents drop them off. Like you probably do when you onboard new staff. Those are the big common sense expectations the organization establishes: no fighting, no swearing, firm curfews. You know. We revisit those expectations until they sink in. Formally once a week at a group session and informally when one or more of the boys seems to have forgotten. That list of expectations is pretty small and realistic. Otherwise, these boys—as smart they are—couldn't remember 'em all."

Chris nodded and took it in.

"Since these boys come from environments where expectations either don't exist or they don't mean squat, we often get a lot of pushback and meltdowns. Regular accountability sessions and appropriate consequences are nonnegotiable. If you don't hold people accountable and apply consequences consistently, then your expectations mean absolutely zip and end up driving everyone who has to deal with you nuts.

"Accountability and consequences are at the core of everything we do, and for the first few months, we end up doling out alotta consequences." Todd chuckled quietly and rolled his eyes. "For example: at the end of each day, when a kid gives an account of their assignments and responsibilities, and they admit to the group that they didn't do it when everyone else did, man, does that hurt.

"Sometimes the boys'll verbally lash out at the boy who dropped the ball. Other times, the looks of frustration or disappointment from their peers, or from me, is enough to motivate 'em to step it up and do better next time.

"Then there are the consequences where we make 'em correct the problems that result from not fulfilling a responsibility. Maybe it's takin' the entire group on an extra two-mile hike back to our old camp to recover something that was left behind because someone failed to do a good spot check. Maybe one of the groups now has to sleep in the rain because one of their members burned a massive hole in the tarp when they were dinkin' around with the lighter. It's one thing if *you* have to pay the price, it's another if *your friends* have to suffer along with you because you failed to fulfill your assignment.

In the background one of the boys made a loud, obnoxious sound, followed by laughter. Chris and Todd turned to the sound, as the boys, oblivious to anyone but themselves, settled down. Todd shook his head, rolled his eyes, and turned back to Chris.

"Teenagers."

Chris chuckled quietly.

Todd turned back to the boys a moment. "I'll tell ya though, as a leader sometimes it can be real difficult to let the people you care about suffer the consequences of their behavior, or to follow through on the consequences you've laid out. Sometimes you can see problems coming from a mile away and you want to step in and save them from the consequences. But it's that very response that got them into the mess they're in in the first place. People did things *for* them or fixed their mistakes *for* them, and so they never learned how to be responsible and get those things done themselves."

"Sort of like the saying that the worst thing you can do for someone are the things they can and should be doing themselves." Chris's thoughts drifted back to Bert.

"Exactly. Out here we like to give the mistakes kids make by doing things themselves the spotlight, front and center. Not by pointin' fingers at the boys, but by troubleshooting the problem as a group. That's what you saw us do earlier.

"Shawn and I have to make a concerted effort to redirect them to what worked well, and frequently remind them that failure and problems don't reflect who *they* are. A lot of times you'll hear us say 'We're not talking about *you*, we're talking about the problem.' Once it sinks in that problems and mistakes are neither bad nor good, we can knock 'em off pretty quick."

"It seems like you had some kind of system to do that back there, but I couldn't quite put my finger on it," Chris asked.

"You're a smart dude Chris: review, report, reflect, and assign. That's all there is to it. We review the day and the expectations. We allow each kiddo to report on their assignments. We reflect on what worked well and what didn't, and then talk about how to fix the problem so we don't have to deal with it again. And finally, we make assignments based on the proposed solution with deadline-based deliverables. And when you assign a deadline to an assignment, what does it become?"

Chris shook his head.

"An expectation."

"*Right*." Chris's voice drifted to introspection.

"Expectations aren't a one and done sort of thing. The second you set an expectation and require accountability, people grow, and as they grow, your expectations have to grow with 'em."

"Huh. That makes so much sense."

Todd's gaze bored deep into Chris and then shifted to the boys.

"So what do you do if the people around you push back on that?" Chris asked. "What you're saying makes sense and it obviously works, but I'm just thinking about the people I work with and how resistant they are to change." Chris straightened his posture. He could feel his lower back resisting his efforts.

"I'm gonna be honest with ya Chris. You're predicting a negative future and that future will be your reality as long as you make it so. When these boys came into this program, they were *not* in the mindset of embracing this approach, but here we are now two weeks later and it's workin' pretty well, right?"

Chris looked around and nodded.

"Do you know why that is?" Todd asked.

"That's the thing I can't pinpoint."

"Think about it." Todd rose from his log and stretched. "What does this meeting structure, along with setting expectations, and requiring accountability do for these boys?"

Chris racked his brain for an answer. "That's what I'm trying to wrap my head around. I'm stuck on this fear of expectations and accountability getting out of control. That's one of the things I worry about. Some of my peers at work would probably go way overboard on expectations. I can see them creating ridiculous, micromanaging rules and policies in an effort to control things and mold the world into their perfect ideal.

"On the other hand..." Chris paused and worked through his thoughts, "... if the expectations are relevant, simple, and clear so you remove ambiguity—and you work with others to develop them—it doesn't really feel micro-managerial or dictatorial at all. Expectations, done well, actually empower others to achieve their collective best."

"Bingo!" Todd replied.

Chris nodded and watched the boys who were lounging around camp. These boys had been forced against their will into the wilderness. But they were much more content than his own staff who had voluntarily accepted their jobs at Queens Mount.

One by one his thoughts cascaded down an ever-expanding terrace of questions into an ocean of wonder: his staff's frustration with him, his own frustrations with his boss, his annoyance with upper management and their lack of clarity, lack of clear expectations. A world of ambiguity that left him frustrated. Was it poor communication or was it that they didn't know what they wanted?

"Well, I think I'm gonna lie low in the hammock for a bit," Todd said. "We'll probably start prepping for dinner in an hour or so, if you want to join us, or I can grab you a freeze-dried Mountain House meal now and you can do your thing."

"I think maybe I'll wander down the trail and catch up with you all in an hour."

Ten minutes down the trail, the sounds of the group faded into the forest, and Chris slowed to a steady pace. The world around him fell into a nomadic silence, disrupted only by the brushing of his pant legs and the soft thud of his shoes along the dirt trail. He looked down and noticed the dried mud lining the bottom of his slacks and dress shoes. Whatever Todd and the others were thinking of him, it couldn't be good.

As welcoming as they were, he was certain Todd and Shawn both had an eye on him. No one was that trusting. Or maybe they were in on this whole thing. The illusion. The hallucination. The insanity.

He could feel himself closing inward and placed his hands in his pockets. A small slip of paper brushed his fingertips and carried him away from his insecurities. He pulled it out and unfolded a Crayola reproduction of his family that Kira had gifted him a few days earlier.

He paused and stared at the beautifully imperfect drawing, each member of the family lined up in order by height, a rainbow arching over the top of them and a bright yellow sun illuminating the line-up. He followed the line of smiles, hands linked together in unity, until he arrived at stick-Emily; a single blue tear trickled down her cheek toward the downward arch of her mouth. Chris spiraled inward toward the cesspool that had consumed their family over the past several months.

He needed to be home, needed to comfort his children, to assure them that everything would be okay, despite his doubts. Disintegrating lies inside his head that all was well in Chris-land crippled the flood gates that had held the pain at bay. He folded the paper and placed it back in his pocket and stared up at the canopy.

He felt shaky now, on the verge of collapse. "Oh God!" Chris moaned and a sudden rustle down the trail, just beyond his view, transformed his emotions. Grief to fear. Pain to intimidation. His eyes widened toward the disturbance and his legs waffled in indecision.

Another rustle. Louder this time and closer, followed by the thud of soft and heavy footsteps beating irregularly against the ground like a massive drunken beast. When movement appeared through the trees Chris prepared to run. It was something big.

"Hey, Chris. Fancy seeing you here," a familiar voice greeted, as the man who started it all came into view.

"Geez!" Chris wheezed and collapsed onto a fallen tree just off the trail.

"How's your little adventure going?"

"Bad, David. It's going bad. I swear I'm having a heart attack now." Chris could barely speak through the hammering inside his chest. "What do you weigh, like a thousand pounds? You sounded like an inebriated elephant walking down that trail." He placed his head between his legs and heaved.

David paused and stared down at his gut-free waistline.

"I can't do this anymore, David. I want to go home."

David's compassionate eyes stared down at Chris and listened.

"I feel like I'm stuck in a bad dream, or I'm going to wake up any second in the looney bin. But it's all so freaking real. I get all wrapped up in everything that's going on and forget that I even have a family and that my employer has no idea where I've gone off to. I'm losing it."

"That's good."

Chris glanced up at David in dismay. "Good that I'm losing it?'

"Like I said, the more you let go of trying to make sense of what *this* is... " he gestured to world around him, "... and turn yourself over to the experience, the more you'll find the answers you've come here looking for."

"That *I've* come here looking for? I don't recall any of this being voluntary."

David drove his gaze deep into Chris. "It's not always a single, conscious decision that leads us down the path we are on."

Chris's gaze drifted timidly back to the forest floor at his feet. David took a deep breath, closed his eyes, and released a frustrated sigh.

"It's *not* a dream, you're *not* going crazy, you're *not* dead, and you haven't been abducted by aliens. Can you not, for once in your infinitesimal life, let go of your stupid desire to make sense of everything and just accept what lies before you?"

Chris cringed at the reprisal and his face sagged.

"And your family is fine. Stop worrying about *them* and that little drawing folded up in your pocket."

Chris's eyes widened at David. "How do you even know about that?"

"Oh, Chris." David closed his eyes again and shook his head at the ground. "You *really* need to stop wasting your time and energy on questions that don't matter. Obsessing over things you're not meant to understand is only going lead you to a life of frustration, worry, and regret. Not to mention, rob you of life's most beautiful moments, experiences, and lessons. You need to stop trying to force those experiences into your limited understanding of the world and accept what they have to teach you. If you can do that I can promise you that in time you will come to understand their purpose in your life."

He paused and took a deep breath. "So I'm going to say this one last time; stop worrying about your wife and your children. You will see them soon enough, and *they* will be fine."

For several minutes David's reprimand worked its way through the networks of Chris's mind. David stood patiently a few paces from Chris and watched a vole scuffle through the vegetation. A solitary bird chirped quietly somewhere within the crowded forest and a moment later Chris began bobbing his head.

"Okay," he said.

David moved over and sat down on the fallen tree next to Chris. "I know it's not easy."

"You're telling me." Chris sat up a little taller and looked over at David.

"So what do you think of Todd? Quite the fountain of knowledge when it comes to working with people."

Chris turned his tired face back to the forest floor. "Yeah. He definitely knows his stuff." He shifted and looked back over at David. "So is Todd and everyone else in on this whole teach-Chris-how-to-change-his-messed-up-life thing?"

David frowned and Chris realized he was once again violating David's rule. He turned his attention back to the ground beneath his feet.

"Sorry." He said quietly.

David eyed Chris for a moment and then shook it off with a sigh "No. They're not. Todd, Bert, Freda, they are as real as you and me, and as far as they're concerned, you're just another stranger that has shown up in their lives that they will soon forget. In fact, when this is all over, you could even look them up and learn a little more about them if you wanted. But right now none of that matters. The only thing that matters is that you pay attention to everyone you cross paths with so you can learn the things that *they* have to teach you."

Chris looked up at David and nodded.

"Well, Chris," David stood up and brushed off his pants, "it's been a pleasure." He looked at his watch and began scuffling down the trail. "Just remember to pay attention."

When it finally registered that the conversation was now over, Chris rose quickly to his feet and hurried down the trail to catch up to David.

"Wait a second. Is that it? David?"

Chris rounded the bend in the trail as the forest gave way to a large and vacant meadow, cut through by a trail void of humanity, void of David.

✳

When he returned to camp, Damien and Noah were on the verge of a fight. Chris slowed his approach and watched the bulky Polynesian shove the teen magazine cover model in the chest. Before anything else could break out, Todd and Shawn came running over with a wake of boys trailing slowing behind him.

"That's enough!" Todd shouted, wedging his body between the two boys and placing his hands on the boys' chests. The two boys pressed hard against Todd's hands and eyed each other with contempt.

"I want both of you to lock down on opposite sides of camp until you've cooled off, and then we're going to talk about this. Do I make myself clear?"

Damien and Noah shot a final fiery glance at one another and then moped to their corners, while Todd released a long, steady breath and watched the crowd scatter back to their chores. Out of the corner of his vision Chris shifted his weight and caught Todd's attention.

"Hey man. Didn't see you there." His emotional state shifted almost instantly. "How was your hike?"

Chris let go of the air trapped in his lungs and fidgeted as his mind shifted gears. "It was uh," he looked back at the trail, "a little uncomfortable in these shoes."

Todd eyed Chris up and down. "Yeah, I don't think loafers would be my first choice of footwear for the backcountry, but hey, to each his own, right?"

Chris chuckled. "Right."

"So, you hungry?"

"Starving."

"Great. Come on over, and we'll see what we've got."

Chris followed Todd over to Todd's tent where a bear-proof bag had been strung up in a tree with a nylon rope. He watched Todd untie the rope from the trunk of the tree and lower the bag to the ground.

"So what was all that about back there?" Chris asked, trying not to feel too useless. The pack hit the ground and Todd began loosening the buckles and ties. "I'm guessing you deal with skirmishes like that a lot," Chris continued.

Todd pulled the last cord and began digging through freeze-dried Mountain House meals that filled the bag. "Yeah." His attention was split between examining each meal and Chris's question. "You know the interesting thing is that most problems," he paused and looked closely at one of the packets and then set it on the ground, "can usually be resolved by taking a few minutes to talk through them. Here you go." He tossed a Mountain House to Chris. "Hope you like vegetarian lasagna."

"Thanks." Chris caught the meal and examined it, while Todd pulled out a miniature stove and then sealed up the bag.

"So what do you do when they have a little tiff like that out here in the middle of nowhere? I'd imagine things could get ugly if something like that got out of control."

Todd glanced up introspectively at Chris and then ignited the stove and set water on it to boil. "You know how I mentioned that some behaviors follow us from childhood through adulthood?"

Chris nodded.

"Time-outs are one of those treatments that seem to work really well for childish behavior for both toddlers and teenagers; and for adults. Any human being who gets worked up basically needs time to get out of that emotional state before they can start thinking rationally enough to address the problem.

"It's sort of like being stuck on the side of a mountain. Ideally, you've got to get to the most centered high point before you can see clearly enough to understand what's goin' on and make wise decisions about your route.

"So how exactly do you get them to that point once they calm down?" Chris asked.

"Well, we usually go through a process to help 'em get a clearer picture of what happened. We'll have each boy share *observable* facts surrounding the problem, and then we'll work on finding solutions. I say *observable* facts because most people, kids *and* adults, when they get upset about something, fill in the gaps in their reality with assumptions. And usually those gaps are pretty darn big. It's like when a person on one side of the mountain assumes that what they're seeing is similar to the person on the other side of the mountain. But it's not and they can't see that so they argue.

"Most of the time we have to do *a lot* of digging to uncover the *observable* facts. These kids spend a lot of time and energy covering up the facts with their own assumptions in order to protect themselves. Breaking through takes a lot of patience. A lot of persistence. Once you break through, you help 'em rise a little closer to the summit. And the closer they get to the summit, the more clearly they start to see what happened, why it happened, and can move on to productive solutions."

"That's brilliant."

"Yeah, it's cool when you see those lights turn on. The other thing we do is make each boy repeat what his rival said before he's allowed to make his argument or counter argument. Because if they're not listening to one another there is no way they are going to be able to get a sense of what the view is like from the other side.

"A lot of times they pretend to listen, and then when you ask 'em to tell the other boy what he just said, it's way off the mark and filled with their own biases. When that happens the first boy has to repeat the point he was trying to make all over again until his rival can repeat it in a satisfactory way. In most cases, when they stick to facts and listen to each other, they get to the top of the mountain and find out that it was all just a big misunderstanding or misinterpretation and the issue is resolved."

"That makes so much sense."

The water began to boil and both Todd and Chris tore open their Mountain House pouches for Todd to add the water.

"So what do you do if one of the boys is completely unwilling to talk about it?"

"Clear expectations and consequences. One of the expectations these boys commit to, before we head out, is that if they have a disagreement with anyone, they'll sit down and talk through it. If they don't commit to that, or they won't hold to it, then they get taken back to the lock-down facility where they spend the rest of their time. And I can tell ya," he looked around and leaned toward Chris, "none of these boys want to do that."

"Man. I wish it was that easy with my staff."

Todd placed the stove back in the bear bag and sealed up his Mountain House so it could reconstitute.

"You know, Chris. You and I." He pointed to Chris and then fisted himself on the chest. "We're the ones who establish the culture within our area of influence. We both have people above us who we report to and people in other areas of our organization who we work with that we have no control over, but these boys, and your staff," The meal pouch on Chris lap felt suddenly hot as Todd's intensity, his passion, increased, "we shape the culture on those islands."

"If things aren't working, lay it on the table at your next staff meeting. Tell 'em what observable facts you've seen and heard and then show 'em you want to nip it in the bud for everyone's sake. Show 'em you're easy to talk through difficult topics with. Show 'em you've entered a new chapter of your life, that you really care and are genuinely interested in making the changes you need to make to help everyone work through their differences."

Chris's face tightened in contemplation as a mix of emotions and ideas flooded him.

"Just don't forget to listen and be willing to change. If you expect them to do all the changing and align with *your* way of seein' things on your side of the mountain or you ignore their suggestions, they'll probably think you're just puttin' on a show. They'll know you care more about yourself than about them. You don't have to take all of their suggestions, but at least consider what they have to say and bounce alternatives off 'em until collectively, you find a good solution."

"Right." Chris nodded. "Right."

Todd stared at Chris for a moment and then opened his meal to let it cool.

"You know Chris, one of the things you learn when you spend a lot of time out here in the wilderness is that dealing with most of life's problems is a lot simpler than most of us think."

"Hey T! We need you when you got a second." Isaac shouted from across camp.

"I'll be right there!" He turned to Chris. "This might take a while, make yourself at home. There's a garbage bag in the bear sack. You can put your trash in there when you're done.

Todd grabbed two spoons, tossed one to Chris and then took his own meal and made his way over to Isaac.

For a long time, Chris sat on the stump watching the forest until the light of day's end had faded beyond the horizon. He reflected on how blind he had been to his role in the problems now encompassing his life. For a time that could only be measured by the shifts in twilight, he wandered the vast cognitive fields of his mind, passing by David's reassurance that his family would be all right. Reassurances that everything would be fine. He followed the wisdom of Freda, of Bert, of David, now intertwined within his own subconscious. The deeper he traveled the more he realized David was right. Everything *would* be fine. And then his body collapsed in pain.

✴

From the center of his chest, a sudden and intense pain, unlike anything he had experienced before, sparked and then erupted with explosive force.

Chris opened his mouth to call for help, but the pain had overwhelmed his ability to speak. Panic flushed through his system, trailed by a rush of pain that spread throughout his entire body.

In the distance, the image of Todd and the boys huddling around a fire pit, attempting to ignite a stack of kindling, metamorphosed into a kaleidoscope of repeating colorful images. How could they be so oblivious to him doubled over on the ground, convulsing in the fetal position?

The first embers of a flame took hold of the kindling and he watched through blurred eyes as they gnawed at the wood, consuming it one stick at a time while the pain consumed him. His throat closed in and the flames leapt from one glowing red twig to the next. Burning. Swallowing. The forest folded in toward Chris collapsing into itself like a black hole.

Oh God. Someone see me. The line between reality and fantasy was intertwined now. He craved it to stop, to choose one side or the other, for the pain, the nausea, the sound of the universe screeching in his ears to evaporate and be no more. But it would not.

All he could do was lay on his side, curled in death, watching the boys around the fire, laughing, heckling, staring into its flames, until his field of vision narrowed to a soft-edged keyhole, and then he watched no more.

CHAPTER 5

Coming to

When he finally came to, the pain was dull, achy, and hovering. No longer the overwhelming firestorm that had sent him off into unconsciousness. And the brittle, stoney surface of the forest floor felt soft now, unnaturally so, but strangely familiar. He attempted to open his eyes, but his lids were swollen. He lay there, feeling his chest rise and fall, unsettled about the world beyond his eyelids.

He tried to open his eyes again and strange shapes materialized through the soft-edged sliver of vision. Rectangles. Glowing pills. No trees. Just odd robotic limbs and tubes. Wires.

He strained harder, and rectangles formed into tiles, pills into fluorescent lights, and the robots into sterilized medical equipment. He shifted his body to prop himself up and immediately a fiery bolt of pain shot down his hip and into his leg. The world spun into near unconsciousness and Chris collapsed back into his hospital bed. All around him monitors and machines powered by glowing displays blinked, hissed, and hummed.

His eyes followed a tube, connected to the nearest machine, toward an IV protruding from his right arm. The world spun again and a metal taste filled his mouth. The idea of having a needle embedded in his arm, waiting to pierce its way deeper the second he bent his elbow, petrified him. He closed his eyes to block it out, but the vision of the needle working its way to the bone consumed every thought.

Off to his side a door creaked, and he heard the sound of someone barreling in.

"Ugh," a woman cursed in Chris's direction. "You need to stop moving around so much."

He watched her fiddle with one of the machines above him, adjusting the wires connecting the machine to his body. Chris turned his head toward her, forcing his eyes to pull her into focus. She couldn't have been much older than him, somewhere in her mid-thirties. Her hair was long and curled, her light brown skin accentuated against the blue scrubs.

"Where am I?" he asked, through a barely functional voice.

The nurse ignored his question and continued through her motions: checking his vitals, adjusting the machines, writing notes. She glanced at her watch and sighed in frustration, shaking her head.

"Hey!" His impatience rose to the surface, and his weak voice cracked.

"What?" she snapped.

"How did I—"

"Finger please." Before he could finish, she grabbed his left index finger and clipped a pulse oximeter to it.

"— get here? What... happened?"

The nurse sighed loudly, shook her head, and mumbled to herself. "They don't pay me enough for this."

Chris's question hung in the air until the sensor beeped. The nurse removed the oximeter without a word, placed it in her pocket, and disappeared out the door.

Ten seconds later his molasses mind caught up with the present, and he realized he'd been rudely ignored. His eyes burned and his jaw tightened. Chris attempted to lift himself from the bed, and immediately electric pain shot through his body, and he collapsed back into the bed with a loud groan.

"Probably oughta listen to that nurse." A subdued, Brooklyn accent cautioned him from behind the curtain on his right.

Chris wheezed through the pain and released a slow leaking breath. "What? Who's... there?"

"I'm ya conscience." A sarcastic, ghostly voice returned, cracking into a chuckle. "Just kidding. Names Troy. I've already told you that a couple of times, but I'm sure your head's a little fuzzy after everything you've been through."

"What I've been through? What *have* I been through? How did I get here?" Words slurred into sentences as his consciousness revved up.

"Well." Troy strained and grunted softly as he shifted in his own bed. "I can tell ya what I've pieced together from the broken conversations I've overheard between the doctors and nurses."

Chris closed his eyes tight and listened.

"Supposedly you were wandering around downtown, in a neighborhood over by the university when some schmuck, from what I can gather was texting or something, swerved off the road and you were the poor sap who just happened to be standing in - and then under - their path."

Chris forced his swollen eyes open and stared at the ceiling, taking in the annoying white noise of medical devices all around him. He felt like his mom had just broken the news about Santa Claus for the first time. That moment when fantasy gave way reality and his joy faded away with all things childlike and innocent. It all made sense: the plane crash, moving from one strange place to another, the bear that could swallow sounds, and other impossibilities. They were all injury-induced hallucinations. Memories of people, important people, who had altered his perception, manufactured by his own subconscious to deal with his pitiful life.

"So what happened to the guy who hit me?"

Troy cleared his throat. "Well, from what I heard, it sounded like the girl who tried to flatten you was more upset about the damage to her phone than the fact she nearly killed another human being. I think she ended up in the slammer."

"Good."

"I'd say. Sounds like she did a number on you. I mean you've been out cold for like three days. You didn't start blabbering until earlier this morning. I honestly thought you were brain dead or something. I swear you sounded like Frankenstein. Started wondering if maybe you were gonna hobble over here and suck out my brains or something."

"Wait a second. How long did you say I've been out?"

"Three days." He paused. "I think."

Chris tried to sit up again and collapsed in pain. "Has anyone been here to see me?" He cringed. "A woman with a couple of kids?"

"Nah. I heard 'em say you weren't carrying any ID when they brought you in."

"Argh." Chris cursed at himself. "I left my wallet on my desk when I stepped out." He felt a sudden surge of panic as he thought about Emily and the kids. He looked around, found the handset controller for the bed, and began pushing the large, red help button at its center over and over again. Several minutes of neurotic button pressing passed before the nurse burst back through the door, livid.

"What!?"

"Where's my phone!?" Chris demanded.

She made a beeline over to the shelf, pulled out a bag, and placed it onto his tray table.

"Here!"

Before he could say another word, she was gone. Wrapped up in his own emotions, he really didn't care. He struggled awkwardly to get the bag opened and then dumped the contents onto his tray table. Bloodstained clothes, the drawing Kira had made for him, shoes and his phone. He held it up and stared at the shattered screen. He held the power button down for several seconds. Nothing. He cursed, slammed the phone onto the tray table, and then moaned at the pain that flowed from his shoulder down his back and into his legs.

When it finally subsided, he lifted himself as much as he could and began scanning the room for a landline. Nothing. He picked up the remote to the bed and returned to his button-jabbing.

"Hello!?" He yelled into the speaker just below the red button. "I need some help in here! Hello!?"

After shouting at the plastic controller he sank back into his bed, aching and exhausted. For several minutes he lay there in silence, trying to catch his breath.

"Hey buddy," Troy called out from behind the curtain. "I know you're in a bad place right now. I know you're hurting, but I can tell you from experience that shouting at the nurses and being a jerk, it's not gonna help you're situation."

"You know what, it's their own stupid fault. You heard the way she treated me. Do they do that with all the patients around here?"

"Well," Troy paused, "I don't really know what happens outside this room, but from what I've observed over the last few days, yeah, customer service seems to be lacking."

For several minutes, Chris marinated in his bitterness. He

was ticked off at Troy for insinuating that *he* was a jerk. Ticked off at the nurses for the obvious. Ticked off at the world for putting him here. Troy seemed immune to it all, almost content to be stuck in the hospital, which also ticked him off.

"So why are *you* here?" Chris sighed, temporarily accepting his powerlessness.

"Oh, that's a very interesting question."

A fleeting déjà vu moment tickled the back of Chris's mind. Memory flashes of the people he had interacted with in his accident-induced, hallucinogenic dreams.

"I suppose you could say..." Troy cleared his throat and seemed to be composing himself. "... my choices sorta caught up with me."

His response lingered in the air for a solid minute. Chris wasn't sure if Troy was waiting for him to respond or what.

"About two weeks ago, I thought I was pretty hot stuff. My firm and I represented some of the biggest names in both the corporate world, the film industry, and we had our share of under-the-table deals in the political space. We made *a lot* of money. Went to a lot of parties, downed a lot of booze and other substances which shall heretofore not be mentioned. In fact, had my life not taken the turn it did a couple of weeks ago, I probably woulda been out getting smashed right now."

"So you were a lawyer?"

"That's right. Anyway, we had this big case we'd been working on for months that was a total shoo-in and the pay-off was *huge*. Sorta like God himself had handed us this gift." Troy paused again for an unnaturally long time. "Huh, now that I think about it, I wouldn't be surprised if that's exactly what it was."

After another long awkward silence Troy continued bending Chris's ear with how the shoo-in case turned south and how he and his firm had overextended themselves financially in anticipation of the big pay-off. He tried to dig himself out but had burned all his bridges on his ruthless climb to the top of his profession. Eventually, because he had so much riding on this case, he decided his only option to win was to manipulate some of the evidence, which backfired terribly for his firm, his status as a lawyer, and the outcome of the case.

"I knew after that trial that my days as a lawyer were over. Shortly thereafter, I received a notification from the Bar Association that I had been effectively disbarred. On top of that, my client was furious and issued a counter suit to recoup their expenses. With my income stream shut off I pretty much knew that I was about to lose everything I owned."

"Anyway, one night, my friend Jack Daniels and I stayed up late trying to drown out that all-consuming fear that had overshadowed my life. After downing an entire bottle I came to the realization that hell couldn't be a whole lot worse than what I had gotten myself into, so I wrote a final note to my family who I hadn't seen in years, cause like everyone else, they meant about as much to me as yesterday's weather report. The letter anyway was just a long-drawn-out justification for why I was right and why everyone else was wrong, and a bunch of lies, so I crumpled it up, flushed it down the toilet, walked over to my tenth story balcony and jumped."

"Geez," Chris gasped. His entire body tensed up at the images swirling through his head of Troy's body careening toward the asphalt below.

"The next thing I know, I'm waking up here in the hospital wondering why hell looks like an operating table and how I ended up with a shattered back, busted hip, a lot of internal bleeding, and a couple of broken legs. It took me a couple of days before I could recall the fact that I was the one who was responsible for my predicament. And that's the long version of the story about how I got here."

For a long time neither man spoke. Chris had no clue

what to say to a person who just survived a suicide attempt. Congratulations? Sorry? Good luck?

"So, you didn't tell me your name." Troy finally said. "It would appear we might be roomies for a while."

"Chris."

"Nice to meet you, Chris. Or should I say the voice of Chris since I really have no idea what you look like with this stupid curtain. Although you probably wouldn't want to see my hideous mug. That little fall definitely did a number on me."

"So where you going from here?" Chris asked. "Sounds like you don't have a whole lot to go back to."

"You know, Chris, that question has been running through my head ever since I regained consciousness. The second my foot lifted off that balcony, I knew I'd screwed up big time. You know how people say their life flashed before their eyes? I was only in the air for maybe three seconds, but those three seconds seemed like an eternity.

"My desire to live was like a drowning person's desire to breathe. And here I'd gone and thrown it all away in a moment just because I'd let myself get wrapped up into some really messed up thinking about myself and others. It was like there was this dark cloud blocking out my ability to see the reality of what was going on. Here I'd convinced myself that there was only one road out of the mess I'd gotten myself into. If I'd just been patient and waited for the fog to clear—and had been open to changing some things about my life— I'd of been able to see a dozen different ways to get out of my predicament. But I was a blind man, Chris. I was so blind."

Troy sighed, began coughing, and then attempted to mask the involuntary moaning that followed.

"Anyway," he continued after the moaning subsided, "you want to know the first thing I'm gonna to do once I get out of this joint?"

Chris listened.

"I'm going straight to Wendy's for a Big Bacon Classic. You know the one that's sorta like a BLT but with a hamburger added to the mix. I don't know where I'll get the money to buy one. Maybe I'll see if I can get a job there. But man, I am really tired of this nasty hospital food they've been feeding me."

"After that, I'm gonna do everything I can to repair those relationships I destroyed."

Chris chuckled softly through his nose. "Really? If it were me, I'd pick up the pieces and move on."

"Oh, I definitely plan on moving on. That choice has already been made for me. But I made a real mess of things Chris. If I just moved on, I'd have to carry the weight of my past with me every day for the rest of my life. Plus, if I don't at least make an attempt to clean up the messes I made and repair my past, then how am I any different from the guy I was before I jumped off that balcony?"

Chris heard a rattle from behind Troy's curtain as he shifted, followed by quiet, mumbled swearing.

"You know, Chris," Troy groaned, "I've done a lot of thinking over the past few weeks, and you know where I think I went wrong?"

"Where's that?"

"Blame."

"Blame?"

"That's right. It's almost more terrifying to admit to myself that I had anything to do with the way my life turned out than it was to step off that balcony. Life's easy when you can blame Melissa for losing the case, or Spencer for being late to the client meeting, or the weather for rear-ending someone at a stoplight. Blame gave me an out. You know what I'm saying? One less thing I had to deal with, you know.

"The problem with the blame game though is that eventually

everyone loses. You can't fix a problem if you keep covering it up with blame. Eventually all the holes you dug to bury your problems get filled and there's nowhere left to bury 'em."

Chris cringed at the dull pain swelling throughout his hips and legs.

"Let me put it this way, whenever I'd blame someone, I basically absolved myself of any wrong doing or any responsibility for whatever bad thing happened in my life. If I wasn't responsible or it wasn't my fault, then that makes me look and feel superior to the person who was—at least in my own mind. You wouldn't believe how masterfully I threw people under the bus. I elevated myself so high. I thought I was the greatest thing that ever happened to the legal system.

"Not only that, blaming others put me in a position where I didn't have to change anything about myself that mighta contributed to the problem. I mean, what would I possibly need to change if it's not my fault? It's the other guy who needs to change, you know. It's sorta like, if the weather caused the crash, then why should I feel any obligation to change my speeding and tailgating habits? Eventually though, justice catches up with us. Most bad drivers, who don't make course corrections, eventually end up paying the price in one way or another.

"So anyway, I got to thinking about all the relationships I'd incinerated, the bridges I'd burned, and it occurred to me that most legal cases that I was involved in were no different. I mean if you think about it, legal action is typically founded on one or two parties blaming someone for something. Both sides throwing blame at the same time they're dodging it. From a lawyers perspective, almost universally, both sides have something to do with the problem. My job was to unearth and exploit that so my side won.

"But here's the deal: I was doing the same thing in my personal life, and I didn't have a clue. Sort of like some of the doctors around here who preach good health practices with their patients and then turn around and screw with their own health by eating crap, not exercising, and smoking in the boys' room.

"I started thinking about how many of the cases I'd worked on that could have avoided the courts all together. If both sides had sat down and admitted to each other that they were both to blame for the problem, and then worked together to come up with a solution, they could have saved millions of dollars.

"That's when the scaffolding really started to fall. I started thinking back to all the relationship fiascos and other problems I ran into throughout my legal career, and I realized that in most cases, in one way or another, I had contributed to almost every single problem.

"Sometimes my part was only 5 percent, and other times it was 90 percent. It about killed me to think of all the damage I'd caused over the years. No pun intended."

Chris snickered quietly.

"To think that if I would have taken ownership of each of those problems, I coulda done something to resolve 'em, maybe not for both of us, but at least for me. If I would've done that, I probably wouldn't be laying here right now.

"My point is, you take ownership, you empower yourself to deal with it, and then you free your life of that particular problem. Blame others and you sentence yourself to a life of stagnation and an endless stream of problems. That's what I did Chris, I sentenced myself." Troy's voice waivered. "I just kept sliding downhill, deeper and deeper into a hole I couldn't dig myself out of. Ya know?"

The room got quiet. Troy's breathing came loud and deep through his nose. Chris wasn't sure if he was tearing up or trying to hold back. He felt tired, exhausted, like he was back in the dream, listening to another complete stranger wax philosophical and wished for a moment that Troy would shut up and let him rest.

"But now, Chris ..." Troy continued.

Chris rolled his eyes and felt instantly guilty.

"...Now I'm out of that hole. I'm out of the hole, but I left one hell of a mess climbing out, and to tell you the truth, I'm scared out of my mind to take that next step."

Chris sighed imperceptibly. "Yeah, and why's that?" His voice was tired.

"I have to admit to everyone I burned that it was my fault, even if it wasn't entirely, and then ask them to forgive me."

Chris wanted to close his eyes and fall asleep. But Troy's comment struck a nerve. He thought of all the people who had wronged him throughout his life. Actions he had little or nothing to do with.

"If it was the other person's fault, then why should you have to apologize? Shouldn't they be coming to you?"

"My thoughts exactly."

Chris furrowed his swollen brow in confusion and waited for Troy to continue.

"But here's the thing with that. If I'm feeling annoyed, frustrated, screwed over, or inconvenienced by the actions of someone else, then whose problem is that really? The other guy doesn't care how I feel. Probably doesn't even know I feel that way. So it's my problem, and if I want that problem fixed, then I have to do something about it. If I say, hey it's Melissa's fault, I basically hand over any power to make things better to Melissa, and I stay miserable for the rest of my life.

"But I can't do anything about it if I don't get off my high horse and serious ask myself what my role might have been in making the problem worse. Don't matter if my role was big or small, if I can't figure it out I'm stuck.

"So anyway, after having a few weeks to lay here with my own thoughts, I sorta came to the conclusion that since I'm the problem, that makes me the solution. The only thing that's left for me now is to admit that to everyone I've offended, apologize to them profusely, and try to right my wrongs where I can. The tricky part is gonna be getting them to believe that I mean it. You should try it with that nurse you were rude to."

The anger volcano fired up again in Chris's head and he clenched up at the accusation. "*I* was rude to? Did you see how she treated me?" A searing pain shot down his lower body and he groaned.

"You're right, it's all her fault," Troy replied sarcastically, while Chris's legs seized up. "You had nothing to do with it."

Chris closed his eyes and breathed through the pain. "That's right." He mumbled feebly, his confidence waning.

"So seriously, when you repeatedly pushed that call button, and then demanded that she help you, you don't think that in any way contributed to the problem?"

"Well, I wouldn't have been ticked off if she wasn't such a jerk about everything."

"Why was she a jerk, Chris? Huh?"

"I don't know! How am I supposed to know that? Someone peed in her Cheerios. I don't know."

"Maybe," Troy continued, ignoring Chris's defensiveness, "but you really don't know, do you? You're making an assumption."

"What does that have to do with anything? I don't understand why you're suddenly on my case about this." Chris was fuming now, but in too much pain to do anything more than gripe.

"Look, all I'm saying is that, for all you know, her mother died today, her kid is desperately ill, or her car broke down and the boss just threatened to fire her because she isn't keeping up with the load. Believe me Chris, I get your frustration and anger about this. You wouldn't believe how painful it was for me to try and convince myself that I was wrong, that it was my own stinkin' fault that I ended up disbarred and in the hospital."

For several minutes Chris lay there smoldering. His thoughts danced around erratically, trying to find a reasonable argument to convince himself how right he was and how wrong Troy had been.

"So what if she had a rough day? Look at *me*. My day hasn't exactly been all that peachy either."

"So you admit then that your reaction didn't help?"

"Well, no..."

"Come on man."

"Okay, my reaction didn't help. Are you satisfied? I still don't think I should be the one who has to fix *her* problem."

"Then you're screwing yourself over Chris, cause this ain't just her problem."

Chris didn't say anything.

"Here's the thing." Troy continued. "Bad relationships persist because neither side has the guts to apologize and start the process of making things right. They're both a bunch of namby-pambies.

"If you asked that nurse right now, she'd probably say that you're the one who's being the jackass. But then as far as you're concerned, she's the jackass. You're both stuck at a crossroads staring each other down, and neither of you can get anywhere until someone does something about it. If neither one of you does anything about it, you'll both stand there for the rest of your time in the hospital shootin' nasty glares at each other, becoming more and more unhappy, cynical, and bitter. It's like you're both trapped in the mud and sinking deeper with each passing moment because you're too stubborn to help one another grab the branch that will get you both out.

"On the other hand, if you're not a *sissy*, and can pull yourself out of your own stupid pride and accept the fact that you had something to do with the problem, then you might just empower yourself to stop the boneheaded staring contest and move on with your life. The sooner you take that first step, my friend, the sooner you break free of the staring contest and deal with your part of the problem, and the sooner you put yourself in a position to grow and move past the bitterness and cynicism."

"That's why I'm gonna apologize to every single person I threw under the bus and tried to screw over. It's the only way to free myself from the prison I've locked myself up in. They might not want to give me the time of day when I try and connect with 'em. They might not be willing to forgive me and move on themselves, but I don't have control over that. The only thing I have control over is my own actions, and I can either do nothing and live with the guilt, animosity, and resentment the rest of my life, or I can try and make amends and clear as much of that up as I can, while I have a chance. Then I can move on to better things knowing that I did everything I could to fix the problems I caused."

Troy stopped talking for a few minutes, while Chris aggressively grazed his upper lip with his teeth, unwillingly processing what Troy had said.

"So are you gonna do it or what?"

Troy's question startled Chris. "Geez!" he whispered to himself. "Do what?" His tone still defensive.

"Apologize to her and see what happens."

"Man, I don't know." He was not in the mood right now, even though he knew Troy was right.

"Chris, a lot of people are out there suffering, because they're unwilling to do what needs to be done to resolve their conflicts. If people were a little more open and honest with one another about what's going on, if people spent a little more time trying to understand one another, they'd get over their pain a lot faster. You want to get over some of your pain? Apologize to the woman.

Troy stopped talking again, and Chris silently hoped that he'd fallen asleep or slipped into a coma. He could feel his body relax the more he marinated in that thought.

145

"Now, when you apologize to her, you can't just say, 'I'm sorry'."

Chris rolled his eyes and sighed as the tension returned. "You're not going to let this go, are you?"

"Nope. That's the thing about us lawyers, we're persistent and relentless. So you gotta make it clear what you're sorry for.

"To do that you gotta let her know what's going on in your life that made ya act like a doofus. Not in a justifying way, not in a blaming way, but in a way that lets her see your pain. You gotta take ownership of the problem with your apology.

"If you don't do that, the chances of her coming to the table are pretty slim. And if you can't get her to come the table, your chances of having a productive conversation and getting what you both want are basically zilch."

Troy paused to take a breath, and Chris wondered if the man would ever stop talking.

"Hey, I have an idea." Troy suddenly perked up at whatever his idea was. "Let's practice."

"This is getting a little weird."

"Come on, man, it'll be more fun than counting these ceiling tiles."

"No thanks."

Troy cleared his throat and began imitating an old woman from Queens. "Hi, you wort'less piece of scum. How's it goin'? I hope yuh extremely uncomfa'table because I'm here to change ya diapa'."

Chris chuckled involuntarily and rolled his eyes. "This is so bizarre."

"Dude, come on, roll with it."

"I think I'll count the ceiling tiles," Chris chuckled softly. "That said, you do make a pretty good geriatric nurse."

As if on cue, the door to the room swung open. Nurse grumpy-pants stormed in, released a frustrated sigh, and shook her head in disgust. She made a beeline to the first monitor, pushed a button, and wrote a few notes on her clipboard.

A ghostly voice whispered from behind Troy's curtain. "This is ya conscience again. Get off your freakin' high horse."

Chris watched her out of the corner of his eye as she moved about the room, checking the medical equipment and taking notes. After a minute he took a deep breath and closed his eyes. "Ma'am?"

She made an intentional effort to avoid Chris and Troy. Chris cleared his throat.

"What?" Her voice was stern and annoyed.

Chris took a deep breath.

"I, uh, I just wanted to say I'm sorry that I sort of lost it with you the last time you were in here. That was out of line."

"It certainly was." She mumbled as she wrote.

Chris closed his eyes again and took another slow deep breath.

"It's just, Troy here says I've been out for three days, and I have no idea if my family even knows I'm alive. You'd think they would've been here by now, and my wife... " Chris could feel a lump forming in his throat. *This is ridiculous. Why am I getting emotional about this?* "... She's been struggling lately with our baby and the other kids, and I'm afraid..." Chris stopped. He felt stupid for not being able to finish his sentence with a woman he wanted to deck twenty minutes earlier.

It took him several seconds to regain his composure. "Anyway, I'm sorry."

The nurse stopped writing and stared at her note pad without moving. She nodded almost imperceptibly and then turned and walked out of the room.

"Yes! Yes! That was unbelievable! I'd clap, but my arms are locked in this stupid body cast, so maybe I'll just cluck." Troy began wildly clucking his tongue.

"Okay, that's enough," Chris said. The whole thing felt embarrassing, but he couldn't help quietly chuckle.

"I was sure you were gonna chicken out, but you did me a solid."

"Yeah, well it sure didn't invite much of a *healing conversation* if that's what you were hoping for."

"Doesn't matter."

"What do you mean it doesn't matter?"

"That's right. How do you feel?"

"You mean besides annoyed at you for manipulating me into apologizing and opening up to a woman who doesn't care about anyone but herself?"

"That's right."

Chris resented giving in to Troy's advice. He thought it was stupid. Embarrassed, he tried to stop thinking about it. He wanted to sleep, but he couldn't seem to shut off the feeling that something *had* changed. He still didn't care for the woman, but the frustration he had felt earlier seemed to have softened.

To his side, the door to their room opened slowly, drawing Chris's attention away from his thoughts. His heart raced as the nurse stepped back into the room.

She sighed as she had done before, only this time something was different. This time the sigh was more exhausted than frustrated. She fidgeted for a moment and then cleared her throat.

"I, uh. I just wanted to say..." She took a deep breath. "... It's been a rough day, and... I'm sorry I snapped at you." Her eyes kept moving from Chris to the window on the far side of the room.

"Hey," Chris replied, clearing his throat, "no hard feelings. I'm sure you nurses deal with a lot."

"We do." She seemed distant, worn out. "Right now all our beds are full and we're extremely short staffed." She stopped talking and stared at the window. "But, that's no excuse. I guess I just... I've got a lot going on right now, and I guess this morning when you were lashing out at everyone, I took it personally and I shouldn't have. Anyway, I'm sorry." She turned to Chris.

Chris felt a wave of embarrassment wash over him. "I feel like an idiot. Did I really lash out? I don't even remember that. I'm sorry."

"It's fine. Trauma can do that." She looked down at her watch. "I know you probably have a ton of questions right now, but if you don't mind holding off on calling me unless it is urgent, that would be helpful. I promise someone will sit down with you eventually."

"Sure thing." Chris felt completely flustered by the sudden turn of events but managed to summon his best professional, facade-manufacturing, auto-mode. *Stupid Troy.* "What's your name by the way?"

"I'm Cynthia."

"Nice to meet you, Cynthia. I'm Chris, but you probably already knew that from my chart."

"Actually no. I forgot about that." She reached out the door and grabbed his chart. "You didn't have any ID on you when they brought you in. Let me go grab the CNA and see if she can gather that information from you."

She tossed Chris a half-smile and turned to leave the room, as Chris remembered why he needed her earlier.

"Oh, hey. Just one thing. Sorry."

She paused as she was closing the door and exhaled.

"Do you have a landline I could use? I swear I won't bother you again for a while. I just really need to call home and make sure my family is okay."

She relaxed at the request and pointed to the side of Chris's bed.

"There's a phone right there, just press nine to dial out."

Chris looked over to his side at the phone within arm's reach. He turned back to Cynthia to thank her just as the door closed behind her.

The second she was gone he reached for the phone and a shot of pain knocked him back into the bed. He breathed slowly, allowing the pain to pass, and then lifted himself cautiously until he was able to grab hold of the phone.

Over the receiver the phone rang while Chris endured one of the most painful waits of his life. "Come on Emily, pick it up."

Chris fidgeted nervously in bed until he was at last redirected to a generic message informing him that her voicemail box was full. He hung up, dialed again, and waited. Nothing. "Come on. Come on. Come on. Where are you, Emily?"

After several attempts he collapsed back into the bed. The emotional pain lumped up in his throat and overshadowed the pain coursing throughout the rest of his body.

"Hey Chris. Thanks for humoring me. It's been nice to work through the thoughts that have been stewing around in my head the last few days. Sorry I pushed you so hard there."

Chris felt tired, absorbed in the labored weight of his own breathing. "I guess your theory was spot on."

Outside the door they could hear urgent voices shouting to one another and the sound of a bed being rolled quickly past their door.

The two men settled into silence and Chris became increasingly aware of the pain calling out to him from his lower body. He searched his memory to piece together fragments of the accident that could help him make sense of what had happened. A bridge between this reality and the reality he knew before passing through that strange dreamlike illusion he had awakened from.

He thought of the people he had met. People who never were. People his mind had manufactured to make sense of his painful reality, and help him find a way out. Ideas now caught in his awareness.

Maybe I should write those down, he thought. But it hurt to move.

He could feel his mind slipping toward dreams. Slipping back to the altered reality from which he had come. He let go and watched quietly as his pain faded into the recesses of unconsciousness.

CHAPTER 6

Waking Up

I n the ocean of sleep, he dreamt he was alone in a way that he had never been alone before, as though he had been dropped into the midst of a dark nebula, floating in deep space where even the light of the stars could not reach. He looked down and became aware of his body, illuminated from all sides, despite the absence of a light source.

How strange.

The instant the thought passed through his awareness, strange images formed around him like pulsations in the nebula's mist. He could feel the nebula flutter against his skin. Not quite water, not quite dust, not quite air: a strange material that seemed almost connected to him in some way. Images pulsed through the material and flowed through him and from him. He called out to see if anyone was there, but the sound traveled no more than a few inches from his mouth, as though he were floating inside a vacuum, surrounded by a thin atmosphere of air.

I'm dreaming. The nebula pulsed again. He attempted to force himself awake. He thought about Troy, about his family, the nurse, and the surges of pain he'd felt in the hospital. Pain that was no more.

With each thought, more random images flashed through the cloud, accompanied by bursts of sound like lightning moving along neural networks, crackling through the haze and into him. The sounds mixed together, creating a dreadful cacophony of noise: thousands of people trying to speak, machines grinding, music playing, nature singing. The more his thoughts raced, the more spiraling and unstoppable this dream felt.

In the space between thoughts, the clutter faded, and the noise died—ebbing and flowing like erratic ocean waves. He began to recognize the connection between the images, the sounds, and his own thoughts. He closed his eyes hard and attempted to calm his mind, but even with his eyes closed, he could still see. With his ears covered, he could still hear. The harder he tried, the worse it became.

"Is anyone there?" he screamed through the endless projections of blurred images and jumbled sound.

Smells worked their way into the chaos, overwhelming his olfactory senses: sweet and foul, stale and lurid, putrid and salty. Sandpaper passed over his skin, followed by bubbles, then jagged shapes, then silk.

"Oh God!" he groaned into the expanse.

His heart beat so fast that he could feel an electric hum radiating through his entire body, penetrating outward. Burning. He could feel himself hyperventilating and looked downward. His arms and legs began to tremble, then shuddered violently. Chris curled into himself, trying to regain some imagined level of control. Trying to stop the corporeal volcano from reaching its explosive end in three, then two, then one.

Chris's entire body exploded, his back arched, his arms, his legs locked wide. Light and energy burst from his center for an infinitesimal fraction of eternity, and the universe went silent.

Whether moments or decades had passed when his fingers finally twitched, he couldn't tell. Time did not exist wherever he was, nor did unconsciousness. Yet something he had once held close was now broken, dissolved into the vastness of space.

When his mind emerged from the stillness that once was, the images returned, clear and focused now, across a vast and glassy sea beneath him, formed of the nebula. Over its undulating waters, memories of his family appeared and then disappeared—his children vegetating in front of the television on the food-stained sofa. Anxiety rose up inside of Chris, and the waters became agitated. The swell rose and then fell, and he ached to hold them.

The images shifted with his thoughts and he saw his wife staring vacantly at him from the bedroom. He could hear Simon crying somewhere nearby. The swell rose again and then faded as he pondered on how the world must seem through those sleepy-hollow eyes.

His thoughts returned to the living room clutter, and the image on the glassy-black surface did the same. The sight of clutter drew him to the kitchen, and the image shifted again. He saw food embedded in the tile grout, caked on the drawer handles where the kids had placed their sticky fingers. Kitchen smells brought back memories of the lunches he packed most days for work, and across the obsidian-like sea he saw himself sitting at his desk, eating while he passed his days away at the computer. Another swell of stress rose and fell, and he looked on with regret at the life he was now living.

From his desk, he was carried off to his last meeting with the executive cabinet, before the plane or the crash or whatever had brought him to this space. "Chris, I admire your optimism," his boss condescended, "but the changes you and your team are recommending, while laudable, would be difficult to institute here from both a cost perspective and a cultural perspective." He turned to the Chris hovering above the water. "You're a failure and a disappointment."

The words bounced off the surface of the black sea and echoed off invisible walls. Chris closed his eyes and turned his head, cringing. "A failure and a disappointment. A failure and a disappointment. A failure and a disappointment." The surface of the water began to vibrate and dance. Rows of tiny waterspouts leapt in sync and cycled around. "A failure and a disappointment."

No!

The image faded, and the water stopped dancing.

For a time without beginning or end, the images came and went over the surface of the sea. Occasionally, strange and incongruous images flashed just beyond the limits of his conscious: subliminal thoughts that carried seeds of emotion. Seeds that sometimes took root, magnifying the swell of emotion, and other times they simply floated away on some imaginary wind into the darkness of the lake.

As an experiment, Chris began consciously placing thoughts onto the stage of his mind and watched the glossy black sea. Memories of playing at the park with his children, graduating from college, playing basketball with his friends, his first date with his wife, all appeared across the ocean as he brought them into being. These slippery thoughts floated along invisible currents and acquiesced to the draw of other thought streams, seamlessly blending from one image to another. The effort required to stay on any one thought eventually wore him down, and he relinquished to the magnet of his mind's will.

In endless space, he accepted his fate as an observer, contemplating the strange connections between one thought and another. The more he wondered, the more he noticed, and the more the images faded, along with the ocean screen, until once again he floated alone. Content—free of pain, free of worry, free of obligation, free.

"Nice, isn't it?"

Chris could feel David's voice brushing softly against his ears. He lifted his head and saw David a dozen arms away, sitting on a large, meteor-like rock.

"The human mind is a fascinating place." David looked off into the emptiness of space contemplating something Chris could not perceive. He eyed David curiously.

"You're not real, are you?"

David's gaze stopped wandering, and the corners of his mouth turned down. For a time he shook his head and said nothing.

"How is it that in a place of such clarity you allow yourself to return to obscurity, like a dog to its own vomit? How is it that in less than two hours you've gone from embracing this miraculous gift to dismissing it as though it were nothing more than an accident-induced dream. In this narrow space between chatting with Todd and exploring the recesses of your mind, you allowed your perception of reality to close your mind to an experience that is probably more important than anything you have encountered in your life so far.

"Chris." David paused and clenched his jaw, his deadly serious eyes pierced Chris like a venomous arrow. "If you spent the rest of your life trying to figure all this out, you would *never* fully understand the mechanics of this experience you've been gifted. *Let. It. Go.*" David shook his head vehemently and shuffled as though he were about to leave. "I am really tempted to end this whole thing right now and release you back to your miserable life. You *know* this isn't a dream. You *know* this is important, but you just can't let yourself accept it."

The sea rose like a giant bubble and then collapsed into itself, sending vast swells of shame along its surface and into Chris. David was right. Dreams were nothing like this. Dreams were clouded in fog. It was obvious that this was no dream, that none of this had been a dream.

"I'm ..." Chris closed his pain-filled eyes and floated lifelessly in space. "You're right. I'm sorry."

In the emptiness of space, neither David nor Chris spoke. David on his boulder, Chris in the absence of all things.

"The day I pulled you out of your reality, Chris, that moment when you sat there on that park bench, the world collapsing in on you—how would you describe what was going on inside your head?"

Chris thought back to the moment. He relived the rapid and overwhelming succession of negative looping thoughts. Thoughts that spiraled his mind beyond control, that drove him out of his office and into the street. He thought about the noise, the endless noise of impossible expectations floating around inside his head and the constant distractions stealing away his ability to focus on any one thing.

"It was..." Chris thought some more. "It was like I was trapped inside a fiery tornado on the verge of being torn apart."

"And when was the last time the weather of your mind was quiet?"

Chris shook his head as he searched his memory. He could recall nothing.

"That is because you, like many others, have fallen prey to the insidious snares of excessive busyness, distraction, and distortions in your perspective. Traps, laid both intentionally and unintentionally by others, that led you to that park bench. Traps that are so masterfully hidden that most people go through life completely unaware that they have lost their freedom at the hand of their own thoughts, choices, and behaviors.

"This mental clutter obscures your ability to see your situation clearly. And without an undistorted view of the world around you it's impossible to make those wise decisions that lead you toward a truly fulfilled life where you achieve your full potential.

"Have you ever felt like you have so much on your plate that there never seems to be enough time or space to get to the things that you are most excited to work on and accomplish? That you don't have time to think or even relax?"

Chris puffed a quiet, insincere laugh through his nose and shook his head. "Every day for the past several years."

"Well, you're not alone." David allowed the statement to linger in the air for a beat. "But the good news is that it's your beliefs and choices got you into this mess, and if you are the problem, then you are the solution.

Chris nodded slowly.

"That solution lies in overcoming the two major traps that invite clutter into your life and inhibit clarity.

"We humans, Chris, are social beings, which is a wonderful thing. We want to feel loved and accepted by others. We want to connect and share our lives with others. When we do that, it brings joy into our life. But sometimes, when those around us make requests, or ask favors, or invite us to do something, we subconsciously fear that a failure to say yes could potentially jeopardize that relationship, so we commit.

"We say yes to taking on a task. Yes to attending the meeting. Yes to helping with the party. Yes to installing the latest social media app on our phone. Yes to watching the show everyone is watching. All to preserve those relationships. Pretty soon our plates are so full of other people's ambitions and to-do lists that we no longer have space for our own.

"As noble and as important as it is to help and serve others, the more we say yes to things that don't align with who we are, the more we relinquish our ability to accomplish those things that we, with our own unique talents and abilities, have the greatest potential to influence. Be it spending more time connecting with those we love, working on projects where we can best leverage our unique talents and abilities, or connecting with our own thoughts. We end up checking off a lot of to-dos but accomplishing very little of substance and meaning. Before we know it, we're traveling a road we don't enjoy toward a place we never wanted to be so we can please those we don't even like - empty and overwhelmed. That's the first trap."

Chris floated silently and listened.

"The second trap comes from being human. Humans, like animals, avoid pain and seek pleasure. We hide from sources of pain, which ironically are necessary for our growth and fulfillment. But we constantly look for pleasure opportunities, many of which end in pain. In fact, it's become so easy to entertain and distract ourselves from discomfort nowadays that we have nearly forgotten how to deal with pain, boredom, and moments of silence. But it's in *those* moments where we find creativity, answers to our problems, and connection. Absorbed in our digital devices, we waste away our lives pursuing trivial stimulation, a step away from the door that leads to lasting fulfillment.

"Now there's nothing wrong with seeking pleasurable moments and experiences, but when we choose sources of pleasure that have been designed by individuals and organizations to attract and retain paying customers, if not careful, we allow them to draw us into their own money-making agendas by hijacking our desires. Entertainment media, news media, social media, video games, junk food, pornography, drugs, are all carefully designed to keep us ravenously consuming more, filling every spare millisecond of our time and our lives with activities that increase their bottom line and our dependence on their product.

"It's a subtle and cunning trap. Even though you know, in the dormant recesses of your latent potential, that something is horribly amiss, your ability to figure out what it is has been substantially reduce because you have no time to reflect on why your life feels messed up."

David paused for a moment and watched the smooth, plastic surface of the sea rise and fall.

"There's a parallel, Chris, between mental clutter and physical clutter and the path to clarity." He leaned forward and casually rested his forearm on his knee. "Your line of work is heavy with policies and procedures, right?"

"That would be an understatement."

"Then I'm sure you are keenly aware of the mess that organizations get into as new policies and procedures are added over the years."

"It's mind numbing."

"Yes, it is. Policies and procedures can become so complex over the years that half of them end up lost in an ocean of clutter and largely ignored. Every new potential risk, real or perceived, results in new patches to the policy, and the beast continues to grow, consuming everyone's time and energy. Eventually trying to adapt and improve takes so long that by the time the organization figures out how to navigate the policy and implement any necessary changes, either the change has become irrelevant or the competition has run circles around them. It's a whole lot easier to navigate and resolve problems when you eliminate the clutter from your life and then put checks and balances in place to keep it from coming back."

"But where do you even begin when the mess is so monumental?" Chris asked.

The question hovered over the undulating sea.

"Physically or mentally?" David responded.

Chris thought about it. The correlation hadn't occurred to him. "Both, I suppose."

"Well, let's say you just started a job, and your boss opens the door to your new office that was previously occupied by one of the most disgusting and disorganized individuals known to man. The desk is stacked with papers; the doors are crammed with unorganized files; there are crumbs, ketchup stains, and dried Pepsi syrup splatters all over the place. It smells like moldy socks, and it hasn't been dusted for decades. Where do you start?"

"I'd probably start by taking a walk outside to breathe off the nausea."

David smiled and waited.

"After that, I'd make it sanitary. You know. Get rid of the obvious stuff that would make me and everyone else want to hurl."

"Sure. The stuff you know doesn't need to be there."

"Right. After that, I'd probably set everything aside and look through the papers when I had time, try to figure out what they were. Maybe put them in related piles, so I could do some research and see if they're even necessary."

"Good. Now let's compare that to both organizational and mental decluttering. The first and most important thing when it comes to freeing up physical and mental clutter is that you have to know what it is you want. Remember how Freda talked about purpose?"

"Sure."

"How can you decide what to get rid of if you don't know what it is you want? If you don't know what you want as an organization, you end up pursuing every shiny new initiative, trend, or tool that comes along. Same for individuals.

"On the other hand, if an organization has a clearly articulated purpose, let's say for lack of something better, it's *providing high quality, industry-driven education so students can land meaningful employment*, then anytime a new tool, trend, or initiative shows up in their field of view, they'll ask, *do our industry partners agree that this help us provide a high quality education to our students and lead them to meaningful employment?* If the answer is it might, they'll research it with that question in mind. Then if they discover it *will* help them achieve their purpose, they'll put it into immediate use or file it away for future use. Otherwise, they'll ignore the hot new tool or trend and continue to focus on to those things that move their purpose forward.

"If, as a father, you want nothing more than to have close, connected relationships with your children, then anything that gets in the way of that, you eliminate. That could be time spent absorbed in social media, excess time spent on a hobby, working more than you really need to. You know what I'm talking about. Anything that hijacks your goal as a father. That doesn't mean you quit your job and stop doing all those things you enjoy. But maybe you dial them back a little to make time for the things that really help you become a better father.

Chris nodded and the movement of his head caused him to rotate slowly to the left.

"That sounds simple," David continued, "but at first it can be tough to remove clutter like that from your life. But after about a week or two of decluttering, most people realize how little they needed those things. And they notice they suddenly have a lot more time and energy to focus on the people, activities, and projects that energize them, fulfill them, and help them to achieve and become a better parent, employee, community member, or whatever else they choose to become."

Chris nodded again and his mind drifted with his body. He floated through memories of a life cluttered with meetings, email, social media, and news. Obligations he wanted to run from but felt powerless to escape. Activities that added little or no value to his life. He could see that now.

He thought about all the extracurriculars his daughter had been involved in before her mother's collapse. Monday: dance. Tuesday: piano. Wednesday: swim. Thursday: soccer. Saturday, games and performances. He saw Emily running their daughter to school, taking care of her siblings, groceries, cooking, cleaning. His mind passed through her's and returned to the sensory cacophony that had assaulted him at the nebula.

"Geez. Her storm is worse than mine." His voice was barely a whisper. "No wonder she collapsed."

"It's hard to see the mess others are in when you're buried in your own.

"But don't be too hard on yourself, Chris. Clutter and chaos are an inevitable and necessary part of life. This sea of glass, where you now hover, where the mental clutter quiets down, is a place you visit, not a place where you settle into for the long run.

"My mother used to complain that every time she cleaned the house, five minutes later someone would inevitably come stomping through with mud on their shoes, toss toys on the floor, or drop a dirty shirt in the empty laundry basket. But each time that happened, she would simply wipe up the mud, pick up the toys, or do the laundry—or make us do it—and generally the house stayed clean.

Chris chuckled, "Yeah."

"My point is that messes and clutter will always exist in our life to some degree. We can avoid that by isolating ourselves from humanity and becoming obsessive-compulsive, or we can keep a watchful eye and tidy up a little when we see clutter arise in our lives or organizations."

The two men settled into silence for a time. David on his rock, Chris unattached in the vacuum of space.

"Well, Chris," David stood up and dusted off his clothes, "it's been a pleasure."

"Whoa. Hold on. You're not pulling that one again, Houdini."

David worked his way carefully off the giant stone, which wobbled as his weight shifted against it. At the edge of the space rock, he leapt into nothing and landed on a solid, but invisible, surface. The rock, propelled by the force, drifted away behind him as he wandered off into the darkness.

"You've done well, Chris." David neither turned nor adjusted his pace. "I hope this has been good for you."

"Seriously." Chris fumbled over his words. "What, what about…?"

David didn't flinch. Behind him the sea of glass and the strange nebula followed in tow, like a giant black, plastic blanket dragged by a single corner. Chris watched David fade into oblivion until only he remained; a floating, inexplicably illuminated self, in the nothingness of space.

CHAPTER 7

Caves

C hris closed his eyes, breathed deeply and then slowly released his breath. By the time he'd fully exhaled, something had changed. The darkness was heavier now—damp and cool—and it smelled like wet dust.

From beneath him an invisible stone hand cupped his body and reintroduced gravity. The surface of the hand, or whatever it was, felt sticky and uneven, like clay-coated rock. Chris looked down and could no longer see his body. He extended his hands in front of him and strained to make them out. He could feel his hands, hear the skin of his fingers rubbing against one another, but all he could see was endless black.

Beneath his body now, the uneven ground pressed hard against his bones. He lowered his hands to the floor to adjust his position and felt clay ooze through his fingers. He attempted to shake it off and thought he heard the distant sound of movement. Instinctively, he held his breath, and pressed his ear into the dark, humid air. For several seconds nothing happened. He shuffled again and pressed deeper against the midnight air. Soon the sounds of nylon brushing against a rough surface trickled into his ear, followed by a faint and questionable flicker of light.

Chris locked his eyes in the direction of the light until it flashed again. Strange and fleeting shapes flickered around him in the darkness and then disappeared. His heart began pounding as the shapes returned, lingering a little longer. He watched curiously as they changed from one odd, twisting shape to another.

As the light intensified and the sounds increased, Chris pieced together the world around him. Brown-gray, cavern-like walls twisted in the moving light, meandering off in several directions. He dug his hands into the soft clay to stabilize his position and felt his palm yield to the frictionless mud. An involuntary gasp softened the dull ache from his elbow smashing into the ground, and he slid helplessly down a knee-high slope.

As if on cue, the growing light exploded from behind the corner, blinding an already stunned Chris.

"Holy Hopscotch!" A voice from behind the light gasped.

Chris cringed and raised his arm to shield his eyes from the burning light. Beyond the halo, the man stumbled backward and then wheezed as he braced himself against the wall and struggled to catch his breath.

"Holy Hanna, John! Get your butt over here! There's a person in here." He turned back to Chris. "You scared the bejeebers out of me. You okay?"

"A person?" A muffled voice shouted back from down the passage. "I think you're losing your marbles, Shane. I told you to make sure that formaldehyde was sealed. Geez."

"Just get over here, will ya?!"

Shane turned back toward Chris who cringed again as the light brushed his eyes.

"Sorry 'bout that." He cocked his head to the side to redirect the light of his headlamp. "So how on earth did you get back here? I didn't see a car or anything at the trailhead."

Chris squinted as his eyes adjusted to the change in brightness. "That's a good question. Where exactly is *here*?"

Shane's concern faded away in the shadow of suspicion. He lifted his chin and sniffed the air toward Chris, his rosy, red nose wiggling above his dust-covered, strawberry-blond beard. "You haven't been messin' around with any of that wacky weed have ya?"

"Not that I know of," Chris responded.

Shane glanced around at the passage and shook his head as though he were trying to ward off the growing skepticism. "You're in Greenway Cave."

"Interesting." Chris attempted to maneuver his way out of the position he had landed in and slid around awkwardly until he found solid footing.

"You sure you haven't been messing around with—" He paused and brought his thumb and finger to his lips, smoking an invisible reefer, "—you know?"

Chris grunted as he attempted to stand. "Well, it's definitely been a strange couple of days, but I'm pretty sure no drugs have been involved."

Shane stared Chris up and down, took a deep breath, and then shrugged off the last of his doubt as John came grunting around the corner behind Shane.

"Dang. You weren't jokin'." John wiped the sweat off his face and stared wide-eyed at Chris. "Is he alive?"

"What do you mean is he alive? Of course he's alive. Look at him!"

The two men looked like near twins in their dark green coveralls and matching white helmets. The only difference between the two was the color and length of their hair, the thickness of their beards, and the extra fifty pounds John carried around his waist.

"How did he get here?" John asked.

"What're you asking me for? He speaks English for Pete's sake."

John looked over at Chris and cleared his throat. "So, how on earth did you get down here?"

Shane rolled his eyes and interjected before Chris had a chance to respond. "You know, if you wouldn't've stopped for the thirtieth time to fill your darn pee bottle—I swear you got prostate issues—you would've been here when we went through all that. He says he doesn't know how he got here, and I asked him about smokin' doobies, and he swears he hasn't been doin' that stuff."

"Dude!?" John tossed his pack on the ground in front of him. "You just said to ask *him*."

"Whatever." Shane rolled his eyes again and sighed. "Look, let's stop arguing and help this gentleman get outta here." He turned to Chris. "I'm assuming you wanna get outta here."

"That would definitely be nice."

"Alrighty then." Shane nodded and studied the passage, wrapped up in his thoughts. The nodding continued for some time before he turned back to Chris, perplexed. "How did you get down the pit?"

"Pit?"

"Yeah. You don't look like you've got any gear with you, and there's no way you could've gotten all the way back here without dropping down Cathedral Pit." He stopped talking and stroked his beard. "Well, unless you came through the bypass, but then no one really knows about that, and it is *way* easier to take the pit than to do the bypass route."

Behind him, John sank into the wall and stared at the ceiling while Shane worked through additional scenarios in his mind.

"Honestly," Chris finally interjected, "if I told you how I got here, you'd think I'd escaped from the mental hospital." He racked his brain for a way to explain how he'd ended up in the recesses of a cave. "I can't believe I'm saying this." Chris took a deep breath and sighed. "Sometimes you just have to accept that there are certain things you may never understand and then move forward with what little you do."

Shane locked eyes with Chris while he processed the comment and then nodded slowly. He took a deep breath and glanced over at John who shrugged in return.

"He seems normal enough to me." John said. "Let's just make sure he's the last one up the rope though, you know, just in case."

"Alrighty then," Shane said. He turned back to Chris, scanned him from head to toe, and then dropped his pack to the floor and began shuffling through it. "You're gonna need this," he said, and he tossed Chris a headlamp. "Watch your head though; I don't have an extra helmet."

Chris wrapped the band around his head and tightened the strap while Shane tied up his pack and slipped it over his shoulder.

"Well, best get goin'. It's gonna to take us an hour or two to get outta here." He turned to one of the side passages and then paused and looked back at Chris.

"You gonna be okay?"

Chris swallowed nervously and drew in a jittery breath. "Yeah. I uh, yeah." He nodded rapidly and drew in another shallow breath.

Shane raised his eyebrows, tossed a final glance toward John, and then headed down the passage. "Onward and upward then."

Travel through the cave was not easy for Chris. Tight meandering canyons narrowed to impassible slots where the only way forward was to wedge his body against the narrow walls and inch his way upward toward the wider upper sections of the passageway. The physical exertion required to do this brought Chris's muscles near the point of complete exhaustion.

In this state of utter muscular fatigue, he failed to notice a large boulder wedged in the passageway and cracked his head against the rock with panic-driven force. A warm stream of blood trickled down his face, soaking the sleeve of his shirt. Chris cursed a pathetic string of profanities, causing Shane and John to pause and turn back toward Chris.

After a quick look they assured him it was mostly sweat mixed with a little blood, nothing to worry about. They'd seen much worse they assured him, and if he was lucky, he'd have a sick scar to tell stories about later on. Chris didn't like the idea of scars. Didn't like the idea of blood either. And what did they mean by worse?

As they traveled on through the underground labyrinth, the passage dipped and narrowed until the three men found themselves on their hands and knees moving toward a two-foot diameter, tube-like crawlway. John took the lead followed by Shane and then Chris.

When they arrived at the mouth of the rock tube, John wrapped the strap of his small pack around his ankle and slithered head-first, on his belly into the crawlway. Chris could taste his own heart knocking against the back of his throat; a sickly, burning, acidic taste mixed with the flavor of his own smoldering sweat. In front of him, he watched in disbelief as the hole swallowed John, and then Shane with their packs in tow behind them.

Chris cocked his head and peered down the stone throat. All he could make out now were Shane's pack and boots knocking against the walls of the tube as he receded into the passage a few inches at a time, grunting and wriggling like a giant worm. Chris sucked in a jittery breath, shallow and unsatisfying, closed his eyes and leaned into the hole.

Immediately, the world closed in and swells of panic pressed against his body, held at bay by a single thread of brute force determination. His face scraped against the rock, tearing at his cheeks and forehead. He pressed forward and realized he could neither lift his head nor angle his body to see what lay ahead of him. Each breath ricocheted off the rock and into his face like an oven heating his sweat-drenched body.

Chris had entered the passage with both arms above him and quickly realized what a mistake that was. He attempted to lower his left arm down to his side to better position himself, but the diameter of the passage prevented him from bending his elbow more than a few inches. Sweat poured freely from his forehead and flooded into his eyes, obscuring his view. In a moment of desperation, he tried forcing his arm downward and became wedged in the passageway. He tried to reposition his trapped arm, but it wouldn't budge. A sudden uncontrollable urge to scream and push against the walls with all his strength overcame him.

"You never told us what your name was."

The comment startled Chris and drew his attention away from his situation and the futile convulsions about to go with it.

"Chris." His voice cracked. He cleared his throat to regain his composure. "Chris."

"Cool. I'm Shane, and my *fat* coworker up ahead of us, is John."

John shouted back at Shane's sarcastic remark, but the response was too muffled for Chris to make out.

"Well, if you'd lay off those double fudge Pop-tarts and get off your lazy bee-hind and out in the field more often, maybe we could get through this miserable passage a little faster."

Another inaudible response wafted down the passage fueling the banter.

"Whatever." Shane chuckled quietly and turned back to Chris. "So Chris, you been cavin' before?"

Chris let out a high-pitched, desperate grunt and his arm snapped back to its original awkward position in front of him. He couldn't believe how unnervingly calm Shane was.

Chris made a concerted effort to compose his trembling voice. "Besides, rrrgh, a couple of tour caves back home, ugh, not really."

"Well, I'll tell ya a little secret, since it sounds like you're about ready to lose it."

Chris felt like a bed-wetting toddler being dragged along by exasperated parents.

"Forget about where you *want* to be and deal with where you are."

Chris squeezed his eyes shut and clenched his jaw to keep himself from losing it. The last thing he wanted to deal with was being entombed and barely mobile inside the bowels of a mountain.

"I know that sounds kinda weird and new-agey, but I've done a lot of cavin' with a lot of different people, and after seven or eight hours in the cave, people start thinking about how far they've come, how far they still have to go, how much they don't want to be where they are, and how exhausted they feel. That's when the panic starts setting in and makin' everything worse." Shane stopped talking for a second and let the sounds of Chris's grunt-breathing fill the space.

"I'm in the same spot you are and I'm just fine. The only difference between you and me is our thoughts. Just forget about how much you don't want to be stuck in this here passage and accept the fact that you are where you are. And even though it's not pleasant, if you keep inching forward, before you know it, you'll be standin' up in walking passage. Just keep focusing your thoughts on those inches."

"Okay," Chris shuddered. He hyperventilated through pursed lips and rolled his head against his shoulder to wipe away the sweat. Chris was about a yard from Shane's pack now. Up ahead he could hear John's muffled voice carrying down the passage.

"Oh shut your yapper and keep movin'," Shane shot back.

Chris could feel the panic stacking up again the longer they lay there waiting for John to move.

"So," Chris asked, trying to get Shane talking again to ward off the panic, "what, what is exactly. I mean what exactly is it the two of you do? Is this a job or something?"

Chris waited for a response, but the only thing he could hear was his own pulse pounding in his ears. He held his breath and listened. Up ahead he could hear Shane breathing, deep and rhythmic, as though he had fallen asleep.

How on earth do you fall asleep in a place like this?

Shane shuffled and grunted. "Well, yeah, sort of. John here's an ecologist, and I'm a bat biologist. We've both been with the Bureau of Land Management now for the last ten years. Don't spend as much time in the field as I'd like, but I usually make up for it on the weekends.

Shane projected his voice in John's direction. "John, on the other hand, only gets out caving a few times a year because he's too lazy sittin' around playing *Fortnite* and *Call of Duty* with his virtual girlfriend, who's probably not even a woman at all. I wouldn't be surprised if she was a forty-five-year-old bald dude with no life who sits around in his underwear all day."

John grumbled and the line started moving again.

"So what, ugh, are you guys, rrrrrr, doing down here?" Chris grunted as he shuffled forward behind Shane. One inch. Two inches.

"Well, for the last fifteen years we've been keepin' an eye on bat and insect populations."

"Interesting." Chris responded without thinking. Five inches.

"Sure is. My favorite part of the job though is geekin' out on the data we collect. I used to be a data analyst in Cincinnati before I ended up here in natural resources. Lived, ate, and breathed data all day, every day. Natural resources data's a whole lot more interesting though than performance metrics and market trends. Plus, animals and insects don't gripe at you when the data tells you something they don't want to hear."

Chris stopped to take a breath and rested his forehead against the gravel-dirt floor, sucking in dust. "What made you leave Cincinnati?" he coughed.

"Mid-life crisis. I about had a panic attack when I thought about spendin' the rest of my life locked up in a cubicle, starin' at a screen all day. Went back to school and ended up here."

Chris saw he was falling behind and dragged himself forward as fast as he could. "I'd think, ugh, more people, rrrugh, would have a ppppanic attack, ugh, being stuck in here than they would, dang it, being stuck in a cubicle."

Shane laughed. "Yeah, I suppose they would."

Shane pushed ahead a few feet and then paused at inch one hundred and thirteen while Chris struggled to catch up.

"What do *you* do Chris?"

It took a second for the question to register between warding off terrifying thoughts and hauling his body along the gravel-dirt crawlway.

"I'm, ugh, in, rrrr, HR." Chris struggled to get the words out.

"Cool. You enjoy that?"

Chris collapsed in a heap and sucked in another lungful of the dust particles hovering in the air. He couldn't believe how effortlessly Shane could talk while squirming his way through this mole tunnel.

"I used to," Chris mumbled with his face flat against the floor.

"Well, don't let yourself get stuck there too long if things don't change. I waited way to long before moving on to greener pastures. Felt like some monster devoured part of my soul along the way."

Shane made another push forward while Chris ruminated on monsters.

"But don't give in too early either. I've seen way too many people bail from jobs they could've loved if they'd just given it a little more time and energy fixing the parts that were broken."

Chris's thoughts drifted away from monsters and toward the fact that despite how hard he pushed himself he was still falling behind. He clawed at the ground with his arms and feet for a hundred more inches until his body collapsed from the burn. He let out an exasperated sigh and cursed the never-ending inches.

"How you holdin' up there, buddy?"

Chris was too tired to lift his flattened cheek from the ground. "Schtill here. Def... definitely looking forward to that... walking section."

"Well, we'll be there soon enough."

The sweat on Chris's forehead mixed with the dust in the air forming a salty muck that worked its way into his mouth, gagging him with its acrid taste. Chris closed his eyes and mustered another wave of strength to get himself moving again. Up ahead he could just make out the sound of John pushing his way through something nasty. Two hundred-sixty-five inches, two hundred-sixty-six. Onward and upward.

"So Chris, you ever..." Shane finished his sentence with a soft gasp.

For a dozen seconds Shane didn't say a word. Worse-case scenarios trickled into Chris's head. Shane wasn't dead. Chris could hear him breathing. More seconds passed and the trickle carried Chris's thoughts to places he didn't want them to go. The walls around him began closing in. He could feel the grit in his teeth grinding as his jaw clenched down. Hot air pummeled his face and his respiratory rate increased.

"You okay, Shane?" His stomach wrenched into a nauseating knot as his thoughts enslaved him.

"Sorry about that." Shane cleared his throat, "There's a beautiful little Opiliones on the wall right here in front of me. Not sure how he got all the way back here."

"Opi-what?"

"Harvestman. Most people call 'em daddy longlegs."

"You mean," Chris's throat felt suddenly very dry and raspy, "there are spiders in here?"

"Oh, it's rare in caves like these unless you're near the entrance. Mostly just little guys. When I was in Mexico though, doing field work down there, they had these arachnids called amblypygi, or tailless whip scorpions. Those suckers were huge."

Chris felt his entire body tensing up as Shane continued.

"The body was about the size of a golf ball, but their legs extended like a foot in each direction, and man were they ugly. In fact, if you poked 'em with a stick, they'd even hiss at you."

Chris's voice rose an octave and nearly cracked. "Why would you poke them with a stick?"

"Oh, just to nudge 'em a little so we could get a better picture."

"Can we change the subject please?" Chris shook his head neurotically trying to purge the memories of his brother pinning him down and dropping daddy longlegs on his face.

"Not sure what's more interesting then Opiliones." Shane replied innocently.

"How... how much farther?" Chris felt like a child again, back in the rear seat of his parents' van on a long car trip. But he didn't care as long as it changed the subject.

"Well speak of the devil," Shane declared. "Looks like we're here. It's a good thing you're not fat, otherwise you'd *really* dislike this next part."

Shane took a deep breath and inched forward amid a series of grunts.

Chris could feel the blood rushing away from his head and the passage spinning as he nervously worked his way past the location of the Opiliones sighting; inch three-hundred and forty-seven.

"Now," Shane grunted, "just remember, it may look nasty and impassible," He cursed quietly to himself, "but it doesn't get tight enough that you won't be able to get through." He strained hard through his teeth and then released. "John made it through and he's probably fifty pounds heavier than you are, 'cause fat squishes down. So when you get to the really tight part, remember to breathe out before you push forward. And keep one arm up and one arm down. That'll angle your shoulders just right so you slip through like a greased pig. After that it's a hop, skip, and a jump, and you'll be in walkin' passage again."

Shane's last words fizzled out through another series of grunts, aggressive exhales, and boots pounding against the passageway. For several minutes Chris lay there, eyes closed, drawing in ragged, deep breaths.

When he finally opened his eyes, he realized the passage had opened up enough that he could angle his head upward and see down the passage. A hundred inches in front of him he watched Shane's legs flail as he struggled to push through the restriction. With each bodily convulsion, Shane slugged forward a few millimeters, until at last his ankles and feet slid through an incomprehensibly small hole followed by his tethered pack.

"All through buddy," Shane shouted back down the passage toward Chris. "It's like sittin' in the Taj Mahal up here."

Chris took several deep breaths to prime himself for the push, snuck a final glance at the hole up ahead, and heaved his body forward. With the passage temporarily a little wider Chris repositioned his left arm to fall to his side while his right took the lead.

Seventy-five inches later the passage closed in. His right arm slid through the restriction and Chris realized that it was now impossible to turn his head left or right. Pain radiated from the sides of his head as both ears scraped ceiling and floor. Unable to propel his body forward with more than his toes, Chris panicked and made a desperate attempt to force himself through the restriction. The violent thrust wedged his chest between the ceiling and floor so that he could neither move forward nor back.

He tried to fill his lungs but could only manage a quarter breath under the crushing grip of the cave. Panic overcame him and his body convulsed helplessly in a desperate attempt to escape. Any part of him that *could* move slammed itself against the walls of the cave. The little air he was able to inhale left him in a series of pitiful screams, which caused his heart to pound with such force that all he could think about was how much longer he had until it seized up forever.

Not like this. He thought. *Not like this.*

Inches away from his trapped head a muffled voice settled into the space between the heartbeat pounding in his eardrums.

"Chris?... Chris?... Chris?" Shane's voice was calm and fixed. "You got this man. The hard part's almost over, if you can just think through this with me. You've got like twenty-four inches to go and you're a free man."

Chris could hardly speak. His entire body trembled as he listened to Shane, another panic attack circling somewhere nearby, ready to strike.

"You with me?" Shane asked.

Chris exhaled in short, breathy pulses through his nose. "Mmm hmm."

"Good. Did you put one hand up and the other down?"

"Mmm hmm."

"Good. Now, like I said, you've only got about two feet to go and you'll be able to sit back and sip some lemon-lime Gatorade. Just make sure you don't grab John's pee bottle by mistake. I did that once, and it wasn't pretty."

Chris started to chuckle and began to cry.

"Sorry, that was probably neither the time nor the place for that comment. Anyway, as soon as you feel like you're ready, I want you to breathe out as much as you can and then push yourself forward with your feet and fingers as hard as you can. You got it?"

"Mmm hmm."

"You're perfectly positioned to push through this last little bit of nastiness, so whenever you're ready, give it a good push and you'll be through in about thirty seconds."

Chris nodded and closed his eyes to prepare for the push. With each sip of air, he could feel his mind creeping toward the edge of an inevitable cliff. The decision to push forward occurred somewhere far below his subconscious, as though a force beyond his own expelled the air from his lungs and pushed his body forward while his mind lagged behind, debating his options.

The first desperate surge to inch forward crushed his chest between ceiling and floor. He attempted to inhale, but his lungs couldn't expand. His entire body erupted into another panic spree, involuntarily clawing at the floor and walls with both fingers and toes, desperately attempting to worm his way forward.

Eternal seconds passed by. His feet rose and fell, scraping at the wall. The fingers on both hands were raw, and he could feel his energy waning. One inch forward. Another surge of adrenaline. Two, three, four. He could feel his chest and back sliding against sandpaper walls, tearing at his shirt and grating his skin. Twelve inches now. The passage released its grip. He surged again and air rushed into his lungs and he screamed at the hole giving birth to him.

The ceiling above him rose and he pushed against the floor to lift himself onto all fours. Breathy and desperate moans spilled out of him with each hobbled crawl-step toward the middle of a room just wide enough to stretch out in, tall enough to almost sit up.

At the center of the room, Chris collapsed onto a flat rock half sobbing, half moan-breathing. John and Shane watched while they nibbled a snack.

"Guessing you probably need a minute," John said as he shoved a smashed, Ziplock-wrapped, peanut butter sandwich into his mouth and then extended it to Chris. "Hungry?"

Chris looked over at John through drunken eyes and shook his head. "Huh-uh."

"Suit yourself." He squeezed the sandwich mush out of the bag and into his mouth. Off to his side, Shane slouched up against the sloping wall and gnawed on beef jerky.

In his complete exhaustion, Chris couldn't believe how quiet it was, as though they were in a soundproof booth recording foley of John slurp-chomping his PB&J.

"So, guessing by how you handled Golum's Squeeze, I'm thinkin' you *probably* didn't take this route back to where we found ya."

Chris watched the wheels turn in Shane's head as he attempted to piece the Chris mystery together. The relief he felt, now that he was free of the death crawl, overshadowed any discomfort from Shane's attempts to figure out how he ended up in the cave.

"So you must've taken the longer route down Wizard's Way. Most people don't know about Golum's Squeeze and the fact it can shave off about four miles on your return trip. Hmm."

John nodded and mumbled something unintelligible, through his PB&J-stuffed mouth. Shane stared at him blankly and looked back over at Chris.

"Anyway, you're a lucky man, Chris. There's only about four people who know about this route. You're gonna see some spectacular passage up ahead. Just promise me you won't tell anyone about this area. It only takes one malintent person to wipe out hundreds of thousands of years of nature's underground handiwork. The only tool we have to protect that is keeping that information under the radar."

Once John had licked the last of the paste from the inside of the plastic bag, he stuffed the empty Ziplock into his pack, tossed it over his shoulder, and began crawling down the passage. Chris watched Shane follow suit until their light began to fade and then rolled off the rock he'd settled onto and dragged his beaten-up body down the passage behind them.

When the passage finally widened and the ceiling rose, Chris, who had been lost in exhaustion, barely noticed. Breathing felt labored and his unstable legs were on the verge of collapse. He craved sleep like a starving man craves food, but thoughts of falling behind in the darkness of the cave terrified him, and he kept moving.

With each step his mind and movements lagged a heartbeat behind in a dreamlike state of total exhaustion. It took several minutes before the present and past connected and allowed him to register the transformations in the cave around him. Massive dripstone formations hung from ceiling to the floor. Rock fountains rose from the ground, decorating nearly every square inch of the immense passageway; tiered cakes, bulbous, rolling monoliths, and cascading chocolate waterfalls frozen in stone along the walls, as though time had somehow locked in place their liquid motion.

Tucked away in obscure corners of this alien rock forest, white needle-like clusters adorned the walls like beachball-sized crystal bubbles, surrounded at times by organic-looking, orange and bulbous ridges of shelf-like rock. Within them, pools of sometimes clear, sometimes emerald water sat motionless, stirred only by an occasional drop of falling water. In the ether of silence, the collective droplets orchestrated a symphony of sound that reverberated off the rock walls.

"This is incredible," Chris slurred, admiring for the first time what exhaustion had blinded him to.

"It's pretty special." Shane glanced back at Chris to make sure he was all right and then continued.

At the far end of the formation gallery, the cave continued across a vast desert valley. By Chris's estimates, the passage could have easily accommodated a fleet of passenger jets. Gray, dust-covered mud cracks blanketed the floor. Their endless pattern continued unbroken except for a solitary set of rust-orange footprints that cut through the center of the passage and disappeared into the darkness beyond the reach of their light.

At the edge of the desert, John and Shane paused and turned to Chris.

"I'm not sure how familiar you are with cave conservation ethics Chris," John said, "but most cavers live by the motto *take nothing but pictures, leave nothing but carefully placed footprints, kill nothing but time*. The second part of that motto is extremely important here. You need to make sure you step exactly where Shane and I step. Okay?"

Chris nodded wearily, trying to keep his eyes open.

"Everything to the left and the right of you, even the ground you are stepping over, hasn't been disturbed for thousands of years, and we'd like to keep it that way. You understand?"

Chris nodded again. "Yeah." He took in the scene before him trying to comprehend how such a vast underground wilderness had come into being.

"Good." John stared at Chris for a moment longer and then turned to the desert.

At the edge of the hardpan John placed his right foot into the first footprint and then continued forward. Shane and Chris followed behind as the three men carefully maneuvered their way through the passage. The farther they traveled, the larger the passage became until the walls and ceiling extended beyond the reach of their light leaving the three travelers to wander a vast desert on a clear and starless night in a world of perfect silence.

The line between this new reality and the distant reality he had once known in the vastness of space blurred to oblivion. His exhausted mind drifted between conscious states. He wondered whether he had been transported once again to another strange surreality, alone with empty thoughts, together with fellow travelers, lost in the monotony of each meticulous step. A monotony that drew his focus away from the massive shape emerging from the darkness ahead.

When the shape finally registered, monotony gave way to curiosity. A dozen steps more and Chris could make out the gray and lifeless face of a massive rise, extending twenty or more stories to the ceiling. At the base of the cliff, a large boulder pile fanned out for hundreds of feet across the Martian floor. The three men approached the periphery of the mound, where multi-ton boulders rose up from the featureless hardpan complicating the way forward.

John and Shane climbed effortlessly for several minutes before summiting the pile and beginning the long scramble down the opposite side. Chris trailed a fair distance behind, held up by endless obstacles: car-sized boulders, teetering on a point of near-perfect balance, shifting under Chris's weight and sending him toppling helplessly off to the side. Treadless loafers and tight-fitting khakis limited his traction and flexibility. Uneven gaps between the rocks ensnared his shoes and nearly tore them off his feet. Chest-high boulders challenged his physical limits, forcing him to flop and wriggle his way over them like a fat toddler trying to climb into his highchair.

When Chris finally reached the base of the rubble mountain, Shane and John sat waiting for him. A single strand of rope dangled from the darkness above into a disheveled pile on the shattered rock floor in-between the two men.

John and Shane looked over at each other. "I can head up first," John commented to Shane as Chris collapsed on a seat-like boulder nearby. "That way you can follow Chris if he runs into any problems, and I can help out from above."

"Yeah, that'd probably be the best way to do it." Shane turned to Chris who had hunched over and was sucking in air. "You done any climbing or rappelling before?"

Chris looked up at the rope disappearing into the darkness and shook his head. "My church group took us rappelling once when I was like twelve."

"Ah, you'll be fine then."

A few feet away, John stood up and tightened the straps of a harness system he had put on while waiting for Chris to navigate the boulder pile. He did a final check of several points along the system and then stepped up to the rope. Chris watched as he unlocked a couple of metal clamps, attached them to the rope, and pulled down until the rope went tight and he could sit back in his harness. He then placed his foot in a loop hanging down from one of the clamps and stood up. The movement lifted John off the ground a couple of feet. He rotated slowly in the air for a moment, made a final adjustment to his pack that was hanging from a tether connected to his harness, and began his ascent.

Chris watched with trepidation as John climbed the rope; arms up, legs up, arms up, legs up. Lifting and standing rhythmically. With each movement John receded into the darkness above him until the only sign of his existence was the flicker of his light far above.

"Here ya go." Chris glanced over as Shane tossed him a

granola bar and then settled into a makeshift rock sofa. "You're gonna need fuel to get up that rope."

Chris caught the bar and tore open the wrapper. As he downed the chewy Quaker Oat chocolate he noticed that only a single button remained on the shredded rags of his once neatly pressed shirt.

"You know, the nice thing about climbs like these is that after fifty feet or so ya really can't see the ground. Makes it easy to imagine you're not that far off the ground."

Chris watched the tiny yellow dot above rotate slowly as he finished chewing. "Or that you're hovering over a bottomless pit," Chris added.

Shane chuckled. "I suppose you could see it that way too if ya wanted."

Time passed and the light above began moving erratically. Back at ground level Chris noticed the rope rising and falling a foot or two. Something felt off.

"Ooooooff roooooope!"

The long bellowing cry electrified Chris. It reverberated off the distant walls and he half expected John's body to come crashing into the ground in front of them. Instead, he noticed the mass of excess rope piled at the bottom of the climb began snaking upward until the tail end lifted off the ground and disappeared into the darkness above.

"What, what's he doing?"

Shane didn't budge.

"We only have two sets of vertical gear, so he's gonna send his back down for you to use."

Chris stood there for a moment staring up into the darkness and then collapsed back onto his rock seat.

A few minutes later, another bellowing call came down from above, and the rope began its descent.

When the package arrived, Shane unclipped it from the rope and helped suit up a trembling Chris. The jumbled mess of ropes, straps, and metal dangling from his body felt anything but safe.

"Alrighty. Onward and upward," Shane said as he tightened the last buckle and pulled the rope toward Chris.

Chris took the rope, and Shane walked him through how the system worked. Once he was connected to the rope, Chris wiped the sweat from his eyes with trembling hands and glanced up at the rope fading into the darkness above. The dizzying view threw him off balance and he toppled backward into the harness. A half-suppressed cry slipped out of his mouth before he realized the equipment had done its job.

"It's okay. You can let go now," Shane instructed Chris as he rocked back and forth clinging to the rope in terror.

Chris released his grip slowly and allowed his weight to settle into the harness as though he were sitting in a floating chair.

"Now it's just a matter of standing up and sitting back over and over again until you reach the top."

Chris placed his foot in the foot loop, straightened his legs and rose eighteen inches. He sat back and then attempted to stand again but the ascender wouldn't budge. He pressed harder. Nothing. Panic swelled up again and he pushed with everything he had, screaming through his teeth. This time it moved, but it felt as though it were tethered to a fifty-pound drum.

"Whoa there, buddy. Take a breath."

Chris hugged the rope and tried to breathe. "I can't. It won't go up."

"Follow the rope that's danglin' off your ascender, and you'll find out why."

Chris looked down and realized he'd been pushing down with his feet at the same time he was trying to lift the ascender his feet were attached to. He lifted again and bent his knees this time.

The ascender rose effortlessly.

"Calm minds solve problems, troubled minds create 'em. Remember that as you're climbing. If you need a break or feel panicked, just sit back, take a deep breath, shake out your arms, relax, and think."

Chris shook his head and then lifted and stood a few more times. He rose above Shane's head and watched Shane settle back into his earthy couch. Each step up felt awkward and exhausting. At twenty feet he realized he had rotated slightly. He waved his free arm and leg to turn himself back toward Shane and immediately his foot popped out of the loop at the same time his hand slipped from the upper ascender. Any sense of false security that existed before toppled into the darkness, followed by an involuntary shout for survival. He flailed helplessly trying to regain the rope while Shane watched calmly from below.

"Calm minds," Shane called out from below.

Chris lunged for the ascender, hugged the rope, and counted down, waiting for his breathing to slow to a functional pace. Ten. He sucked in a jagged breath. Nine. Another. Eight. A little smoother this time. When he arrived at one, he opened his eyes, took a final deep breath, assessed what had gone wrong and carefully repositioned his foot back inside the loop.

Steps now, not inches. My mind is here and nowhere else. He lifted the ascender and stood up. One. He sat back and lifted again. Two. Lifting, standing, lifting, standing.

Time inched along with him up the rope. Chris had to pause every meter or so to rest, but his thoughts remained with him. At seventy-six steps up he glanced down and could barely make out a closed-eyed Shane, nestled among the rocks.

With each rise and fall, the world below him faded into the darkness until only he and the rope remained. All around him dust and moisture particles danced in and out of his beam, moving and drifting with the currents of the air. Along the outer limits of his light, a gray haze blurred the dark world beyond, creating the illusion of something lurking beyond the darkness. Deep sea creatures, pulsating in their transparent skins, passing in and out of his light before he could completely register their form.

With no point of reference, it was impossible to know how high he had climbed or how much rope he had left to travel. He was where he was: on a rope, suspended in space, drenched in sweat, arms and legs burning, locked in an eternal climb.

"Hey there spelunker. How was the climb?"

John's light hit him, and Chris's pupils contracted painfully, knocking him out of his zone and into the reality that he had arrived at the top. He cringed, and John turned his light away.

"Sorry about that." He looked down at Chris from the top of a twelve-foot rock slope. "Man, you look like death warmed over."

At the base of the slope, a metal bolt fastened to the wall kept the rope from rubbing against the jagged rock. Beneath it, Chris sank back into his harness and let his arms fall limp. In his utter exhaustion, he wanted to cry, but even that was too much effort. He released a pathetic, whimpering groan and took the last two steps to the bolt.

"Okay, now to get over that bolt, you're gonna attach that biner hanging off the black rope on your harness—that's called a cow's tail— to the line that goes from the bolt to me."

Chris looked down, fumbled with the cow's tail, and clipped it to the rope above the bolt.

"Now go ahead and take your foot out of the foot loop and then remove the hand ascender and attach it to the same line."

Weak, tired, and aching, he could barely grip the clamp with enough strength to remove the ascender. The thought of disconnecting himself from the rope while dangling above a multi-hundred-foot pit terrified him beyond belief. Every time his mind wandered down the pit, he forced it with everything he had back to the task at hand.

"Perfect. You've got two points of attachment now. The next thing you're gonna do is put your foot back in the loop there and unclip your chest ascender at the same time you step up. Once you're unclipped, you can climb the last ten feet to where I am."

Chris struggled his way through John's instructions and then hobbled up the last stretch of the climb, collapsing against the wall to John's side.

"Off rope!" John shouted down the pit while Chris whimpered.

A moment later, a deep and muffled reply, padded by the abyss, arrived topside.

"Dude," John turned back to Chris, "not bad for your first time ascending. The bigger, nastier pit up ahead should be a breeze for you."

Chris jerked toward John, his eyes bulging. "There's another one?"

John sat down across from Chris and started laughing. "I'm just pulling your leg. It's straight forward from here on out."

"Man, you guys are relentless." Chris hunched back into the wall.

The laugh petered out, and John reached in his pack and pulled out another bag of PB&J mush. A few minutes later, Chris heard a shuffle from down slope and watched Shane clear the edge.

"You gotta be kidding me!" Twelve feet below him Shane crossed the bolt, unclipped the carabiner hanging off it, and wandered up the slope with ease. "That took you like ten minutes."

Shane smiled, dropped his pack beside Chris, then turned back and began pulling up the rope.

"Man, I feel like a wuss. You guys aren't even fazed by all that, and here I am flopping around like a drunken penguin."

Shane ignored the comment and continued hauling at the rope, piling it into a nest at his feet. When the tail end finally cleared the ledge fifteen feet below, he took the knotted end, stuffed it into his pack, and began feeding the rest of the rope in after it.

"You know, you shouldn't beat yourself up like that. There's nothing wrong with taking your time and looking a little awkward your first go at something."

He continued stuffing the rope in the pack. Chris opened his eyes and looked over at Shane.

"Too many people are afraid of doing anything that might reveal that they're less than perfect. Which is ridiculous because who on earth was ever perfect the first time they tried something?"

Shane, lost in his thoughts, punched the last of the rope into the pack and tightened the drawstring. He kicked the stuffed pack onto its side, took a seat, sighed, and turned to Chris. "The only way to make yourself feel like you're perfect is to avoid doing anything that might prove you're not. My grandma told me that the only perfect parents are those who don't have any kids. It's easy to believe you're perfect when you never have to prove it; because once you try to prove it, you only discover you're not. Perfection is a never-ending false snipe hunt that does nothing but exhaust those who think they might one day achieve it."

John stopped chewing and stared blankly at Shane, a dollop of mutilated PB&J hanging out of his mouth.

"You and all your philosophical mumbo jumbo."

Shane rolled his head from John to Chris and then gestured toward John. "For example."

John rolled his eyes and continued chewing.

"Sounds like my seven-year-old." Chris added.

John hurled a pouty glare at Chris.

"No, not you. My daughter." John relaxed and returned to chewing. "She hesitates to do anything until she's certain she can do it well, and then if she screws up, she comes down hard... on... herself." The second the words escaped his mouth, he realized the hypocrisy in his comment. "Guess the apple doesn't fall too far from the tree, does it?" Chris sighed.

Shane and John shrugged and glanced at each other.

"Anyway," Chris closed his eyes and took a breath, "my five-year-old is the complete opposite. He'll dive in even when he probably shouldn't. The initial results usually aren't pretty, but he gets super fixated and usually masters whatever he is doing in about one tenth of the time it takes his sister."

Shane turned pensive and nodded. "That's an interesting thought." He paused for a beat. "We should all take time to think about things and prepare before we take that first step, but eventually you gotta act. A lot of people get so stuck in over thinking their insecurities that by the time they take that first step, those who plunged in early on are already miles ahead of 'em. No amount of thinking about it is ever gonna make that first step any less painful and clumsy. So you might as well jump in sooner than later and get it over with. It's like cheetahs."

Chris turned to Shane with a puzzled look.

"Cheetahs don't avoid chasing a gazelle because they think there's a chance they might not catch it. They don't tell themselves, *if, I don't catch one I'll be a failure for the rest of my life and everyone'll think I'm a loser.* They don't sit there and say, *well today the wind's a little too strong and coming from the wrong direction and the light's a little off, so I think I'll go hungry today and try tomorrow.* Trying and making mistakes is a daily part of what cheetahs do.

"If a cheetah misses a catch, she'll take a breather and try again from a different angle until she catches the impala. And the cool thing is that each new angle she tries sharpens and diversifies her hunting skills, which makes it easier for her to adapt when the environment changes and her previous skills become obsolete.

John stuffed another empty Ziplock into his bag and sighed with intentional force. "At least let's keep moving. I finished the last of my food waiting for you to finish your sermon, and now I want Cheetos, thanks to your stupid story."

Shane chuckled as John threw his pack over his shoulder and headed off down the passage. He stood up, grabbed his own pack, and turned to Chris. "We better go. The last thing we want is to be stuck in this hole when John starts to get hangry."

"I heard that!" John yelled back from up ahead.

Chris rose up and staggered down the passage behind Shane.

"Anyway, I feel sorry for people who can't see the role they're thoughts are playing in holding them back."

"Definitely," Chris mumbled, and he watched the lights of his two companions fade off down the passage as he lagged farther and farther behind.

The separation from the others, and the monotony of his movement, dipped his conscious mind into the dreamlike sea of semiconsciousness. Disparate phrases drawn from his memory began repeating over and over, tormenting him as he wandered.

Let's spend a little more time doing additional research. President Reed repeated over and over. *Let's not jump into anything too disruptive too soon. To soon. Tu soon. Two soon. Two. Three. Four. Chickens just back from the shore.*

Dragging himself out of a cave became a metaphor for dragging himself out of the exhausting life he had lived up to now; out of the hole he had dug to protect himself; out of the desire to control; out of the fear of failure.

Up ahead a muffled shout, drowned out by a sickening thud, pulled Chris's mind back to the cave and his labored steps, and he mustered the strength to press forward a little faster. A hundred steps later the muffled sounds came into focus and tortured screams intermingled with forceful fits of coughing.

He rounded the last corner, and in the middle of the passage lay John, helplessly sprawled out on the floor, his lower leg jutting off at a very unnatural ninety degree angle to his right. Shane had dropped his pack and knelt beside John, trembling and pale.

"What happened?" Chris could feel his own legs flushing with ice, ready to buckle.

"I don't know." Shane seemed hyper-alert. "The rock just shifted and came down hard on his leg and then rolled off." He paused and then looked at John. "You with me John?"

John nodded. He peered reluctantly down at his leg, started to hyperventilate, and then looked up at the ceiling and screamed again.

"We gotta get him out of here." Shane wiped his mouth nervously and looked up at Chris.

"How much farther until we're out?" Chris asked.

"Not far. Probably a couple hundred more feet, maybe five minutes tops if we were movin' at a normal pace." He stared nervously at John. "Hang in there buddy; we're almost out."

Shane helped John drag himself a few inches to a large rock and got him into a reclined position.

"What do you want me to do?" Chris asked.

Shane looked around, assessing their options. "There's a radio in the truck. We can get ahold of the field office from there, but it'll probably take Search and Rescue a couple of hours after dispatch to get here. Plus, it's about a forty-five-minute hike down to the truck once we're out." Shane brought his hands to his mouth and scanned his mind for options.

"Let's see if we can at least lift him up this next section. It's a lot flatter and more comfortable up there. Good place for the two of you to wait while I head down to the truck and call for help. It's not ideal, but I'm not sure what else we can do."

With no medical training, Chris felt more than uncomfortable with the plan, but the thought of wandering off into the wilderness to look for a truck was equally terrifying.

"Okay." Chris leaned up against the wall to keep himself from toppling over and looked ahead down the passage.

Thirty paces away, the passage took a steep turn upward and then leveled out several stories above. Climbing the steep slope looked challenging for someone with two good legs.

"How on earth are we going to get him up that?" Chris shook his head and felt like he was going to pass out.

Shane looked at the ground and sighed. "I don't know. Maybe if one of us helps him from above and the other braces him from below, we can help him inch his way up. I don't know. What do you think John?"

John nodded between hacking coughs. "Let's give it a try before the endorphins wear off."

Shane closed his eyes, took a deep breath, and nodded slowly. "Alrighty then."

Decision made, Shane squatted down next to John and helped him wrap his arm around Shane's shoulder. On three, the two men rose up on John's good leg, while his bad leg flopped into a more natural looking position. John paused at the top, closed his eyes, took several deep breaths, bit his upper lip, and nodded.

Shane moved carefully down the passage as John hopped alongside him on his good leg. After traveling a dozen paces toward the slope, John began to sway.

"Man, guys, I don't feel so good." The color left his face, and he started to tremble.

"Shoot. Shoot. Shoot." Shane braced himself and attempted to lower John to the floor as John lost control and began heaving uncontrollably. PB&J remains splatted across Shane's side and onto the floor. Shane cursed and attempted to dodge the fallout without dropping John.

Once the heaving stopped, Shane lowered John back to the floor. Chris watched John's eyes roll and his head flop to the side

"Can you lift his feet up, Chris? I think he's going into shock."

Chris repositioned a large stone next to John's feet and

carefully maneuvered John's legs to rest on top of it. Once his feet were positioned, Shane lowered John's upper body to the floor.

"Let's give him a minute. Let the shock pass before we attempt the ascent."

Chris was dumbfounded that they were still even considering climbing the slope.

"Here." Shane dropped his pack and extended it to Chris. "Why don't you take the rope to the top of the slope there. I didn't bring a pully, but there's a feature at the top of the slope that we could swing the rope around and build a makeshift counterweight system. That should keep John secure while we help him up the slope."

Chris stared at Shane wide-eyed and confused.

"A counter-what system?" The amount of stress flooding his body had Chris questioning his own ability to hold down his granola bar lunch. The thought of climbing a multi-story slope alone and setting up a rope so they could rescue an injured man was more than he could mentally deal with.

"Right. First time caving." Shane bit his lower lip and sucked in a hard, deep breath. "So, at the top of the slope there's a large boulder. You'll toss the rope around the base of the bolder, pad it with the rope pad, and send both ends of the rope back down to me. When you're done come back down here and I'll walk you through the rest. Does that make sense?"

"I think so." Chris could feel his mind racing, trying to piece together how this was going to work.

"Good. Why don't you grab my pack then and head up to the top while I hang out here with John and wipe down my coveralls before I puke too." He glanced down at John who seemed to be breathing normally now.

Chris slipped Shane's pack over his shoulder and nervously maneuvered through the passage to the base of the slope.

The closer he got the more intimidating and insane the whole thing seemed. At the base of the climb, however, Chris realized it wasn't nearly as bad as he'd made it out to be. Fist-sized pockets swallowed his hands, and small ledges made the ascent feel more like climbing a ladder than scaling the sheer cliff he'd imagined.

Halfway up the slope, he turned around to check on John and Shane, and the walls immediately began to spin. He closed his eyes. *Don't look down. Don't look down. Don't look down,* he repeated until the world stopped spinning and he could open his eyes and continue the climb.

For the final stretch, he kept his attention fixed on the wall in front of him, moving at a sloth's pace; slow, intentional, refusing to release one limb until the others had reiterated their unwavering commitment to his life.

When he finally arrived at the top, Chris collapsed on flat ground and tossed his pack onto the twenty-foot wide, soft, dirt floor. The thought of having to climb back down made him physically ill.

For several minutes he lay there trying to catch his breath, trying to convince himself to get up again, to not lay there and let himself die.

"Everything all right up there, Chris?" Shane shouted from below.

"Just taking a little breather." He called back.

He took a deep breath, lifted himself to seating, and staggered over to the massive boulder leaning against the wall. The thing was enormous. It reminded him of a collapsed tower that had unhinged itself from the ceiling; the pointed front-end pierced the ground and the base lodged precariously against the wall near the ceiling.

A few steps from the boulder, Chris hesitated. He couldn't fathom how a twenty-ton boulder could have come to a rest on point no wider than the palm of his hand. The idea of wrapping a rope around its base and then putting weight on it seemed insane. He stepped closer and leaned against the rock to get a closer look. Immediately, he swore he felt the boulder shift.

He jerked his hand back and gasped several quick breaths.

"Are you sure this thing is stable?" He shouted down to Shane.

"That rock hasn't moved an inch since we found this cave. In fact, we used to rappel off it before we realized it was easier to down-climb the darn slope. We even got a bunch of guys once and tried pushing the thing over, just in case. I think we spent an hour hammering on it before we decided to give up. There is no way on earth that rock is moving."

Chris turned back to the boulder, shook his head, and sighed loudly. *This doesn't seem right.* He opened Shane's pack, grabbed the tail end of the rope, wrapped it around the back side of the boulder, and pulled the rope through until he thought he had pulled enough to reach the bottom.

"You ready?" Chris shouted down.

He heard shuffling below as Shane worked his way over to the base of the climb.

"Yep. Go ahead and toss 'er down."

Chris grabbed the pile of rope he'd woven around the boulder and tossed it over the slope.

"Got it! You can go ahead and toss the pack down the other side."

Chris followed instructions and waited for Shane. He heard more shuffling but no confirmation. After a few minutes Chris glanced down the slope to see what was taking so long and felt the space around him begin to spin. Without thinking, he braced himself against the boulder to keep from toppling over. The second he pressed his weight on the giant stone it began to slide.

Instinctively, Chris dove for cover, screaming to the others below. Behind him the giant stone toppled forward with a deafening boom that seemed to rattle the entire mountain. Chris turned and watched in horror as the immense, wedge-shaped boulder lumbered toward the top of the slope and then split in two behemoths with a high-pitched thundering crack. He screamed until he could scream no more, until his lungs had filled with dust. Hoping to defy the inevitable. Hoping to will John and Shane to safety.

This isn't real, he lied. *Just a dream.* A dream where a powerless Chris lay frozen in fear, helplessly watching two unstoppable bus-sized slabs pass the point of no return and accelerate like a roaring freight train on an inevitable collision course toward the exposed men below.

CHAPTER 8

A Call to Act

W hen the dust finally settled and the endless stone fragments had come to rest, an eerie silence rested over the cave. Locked in the fetal position at the top of the slope, somewhere inside a mountain, Chris trembled and sobbed. He called out for Shane and John, but no answer.

When enough time had passed and his tormented sobs had dissipated with the dust, Chris picked himself up and peered over the edge of the drop. Down below a pile of shattered boulders and rocks covered the area where John and Shane once waited. A sickening, inconsolable feeling of guilt and hopelessness settled over Chris. He knew they were both gone and he knew there was absolutely nothing he could do about it. He stood there staring for a while, wanting to cling to some microscopic thread of hope that he might have overlooked. But it was all in vain.

When he finally found it within himself to accept that they were gone, he reluctantly turned toward what he hoped was the entrance. As he dragged his tired body and soul toward the mouth of the cave, a strange and undeserving peace settled over him—as though both Shane and John were walking with him, guiding him toward the light he knew he had always been searching for.

In the silence of the cave, in the solitude of his travels, he could both feel and hear his heart beating within his chest. Pounding with resolve to live a better life than the one he had settled into over the past year, so that when his time came, he would be prepared to close that final chapter.

✻

The farther he traveled, the warmer the air became. Whether it was a physical change in the environment or his own exertion, he couldn't say. Up ahead a hundred twisting shapes materialized on the wall beyond the reach of his light, and Chris realized his own journey had come to another beginning.

He rounded the final corner, and an explosion of sunlight forced his eyes closed. Swallows and wrens filled the desert air with their calls, and a beaten Chris collapsed onto a large rock at the center of the gaping entrance. The whole world seemed more luminescent than he had ever experienced. The air cleaner, the sun warmer, the colors more vivid.

From the auditorium-sized, mountain window, a vast arid landscape extended out toward the horizon. Rows of mountains faded to blue in the atmospheric haze. Foothills covered in juniper and pinion pine descended toward a valley covered in rabbitbrush and sage. Two solitary dirt roads intersected the expanse; the only signs of humanity.

At his feet, vibrant red Indian paintbrush flowers dotted the rocky terrain leading down the mountain. A collared lizard scurried across the cave floor and came to rest on a slab of limestone, just outside the cave, warming itself in the sun.

"Beautiful, isn't it?"

Chris turned to the far corner of the entrance as David stepped out from behind a rock and made his way toward him. When he saw the pain etched across Chris's face, he paused and approached slowly.

"Please, David, tell me none of this is real."

David sat down on a large stone next to Chris and exhaled. A gentle breeze stirred the dust at their feet.

"The accident, Chris, would have happened whether you had been there to witness it or not. Their time had come just as yours will someday. *Your gift* was to learn from them before that moment came."

"But I'm the one who made the boulder fall. It was my fault."

David nodded slowly and turned to Chris. "*Your fault* that you ended up in the cave? *Your fault* that the rock fell on John and injured him, forcing you and Shane to figure out a rescue plan? *Your fault* that a massive rock, the size of a bus, that had been stable for years finally gave?"

Chris leaned forward, staring at the ground.

"What you *feel* and reality are often two very different things. That rock, Chris, had been shifting for months and would have fallen regardless of what you did. Spending your life blaming yourself for something you had little to no control over will only sentence you to a life of pain and misery. What's done is done, and there is nothing you can do to change that. The wheels that turn this life are infinitesimally bigger than you or me. Forgive yourself. Follow Shane's advice and learn from your mistakes and failures, and then pick yourself up and press forward."

David turned to his side, toward something or someone Chris could not see.

"I'm pretty sure both Shane and John would want you to do that. Don't let their only legacy for you be one of regret and self-loathing."

Chris bit his lip hard and shook his head. Another lizard settled in on a small rock in front of them and waited for an unsuspecting ant to enter its strike zone.

"I want to ask you something, Chris."

The lizard bobbed up and down on its front legs.

"When you were up at the top of that slope, contemplating the placement of the rope, the thought came to you that anchoring the rope on that big boulder was not a good idea, right?"

"How, how did you know that?"

"Just answer the question, Chris."

"Well, yeah, but..."

"Why then did you decide to ignore what you felt you needed to do and follow Shane's instructions instead?"

"I don't know." Chris paused and stared at the ground. "I guess I figured that Shane knew what he was talking about better than I did."

David nodded. "He did. But he didn't have the perspective you had, Chris. Let me share a story with you.

"Once there was an intern at an aerospace facility, touring an airplane during the manufacturing process. During this educational tour he noticed what he thought was a loose bolt in the elevator control mechanism on the tail of the aircraft. He felt the same way you did. What did he know? He wasn't an engineer yet. Why would anyone listen to an intern about a loose bolt? Even if he said something, they'd probably just make him feel stupid, point out it was nothing. So he kept his mouth shut and tried to suppress the need to say something.

"Several weeks later that same airplane took it's first commercial flight. The day it took off that little loose bolt rattled itself free, the plane pitched uncontrollably, and all seventy-eight people died. Why did they die?"

Chris chewed his lip and stared at the lizard.

"Most of the time, Chris, the consequences aren't as dire as those that you and this intern experienced, but they can be significant."

Chris nodded quietly.

"For example, what do you think will happen if you ignore the conflict that now exists between you, Kyle, and Tara? What do you think will happen if you don't apologize to your boss and the other cabinet members for losing your cool? Or if you give up and distance yourself from your relationship with your wife and your children?"

"The boulder will fall," Chris mumbled and bit at his nails.

"The boulder *will* fall. So the sooner you speak up and address those things that seem off in your life, the less likely you are to end up in a position where the boulder has passed the point of no return and it's too late to do anything except watch helplessly as the world falls to pieces.

"I'm such a screw up." Chris kicked a small rock and the lizard scurried away.

"We all are in some way. But it's nothing we can't fix, if we try."

David rose from the rock and stepped from the cave's shadow into the sunlight. The light embraced him, and for a moment he lost himself in the view.

"The problem, Chris, is that most people, when they feel they need to say or do something, seldom do. They mull over it for a time, searching for good reasons not to act, and then allow those initial impressions to fade into the shadows of regret."

David turned to Chris and his eyes penetrated Chris's soul.

"You *know* what you need to do, Chris, but you just can't do it. And that inability to act, that inability to follow through on what you feel you need to do, is keeping you from becoming the husband, father, and HR director that you have the potential to become, *and* from living a happy and fulfilled life."

Chris fidgeted with his wedding ring and looked at David through tormented eyes. "How do I overcome that, David?"

David smiled, and the correctional facade melted away.

"That, my friend, is a very good question.

"Do you remember when you approached the base of the climb and saw the rope dangling there?"

Chris nodded.

"How did you feel when you looked up that rope and contemplated the idea of ascending it?"

Chris cast a wide-eyed, incredulous glance at David.

"Are you serious? I was terrified out of my mind."

"That's right. And that is what most people experience when they're mulling over how they're going to get from where they are in their life to where they want to be. Whether that's mending a broken relationship, becoming a great leader, or improving your health. Imagine if the fear had been so great that you absolutely refused to get on that rope. Where would you be right now?"

Chris thought about it for a moment. "I'd still be at the bottom."

"It's a scary thought, isn't it? But you didn't refuse; you chose to climb because you wanted something."

"Yeah, I wanted out."

"Exactly. Now imagine if you'd been so desperate to get out that you ignored Shane's advice and tried to brute force your way up the rope in a panic. Like a lot of people do when they desperately want something. What do you think would have come of that?"

Chris shuddered at the thought, recalling how horrific the first thirty feet had been. Images of freak-out Chris, suspended in the air, appeared across the screen of his mind.

"I mean that's virtually what I did until Shane got me to calm down and talked some sense into me. If I hadn't listened to him, I probably would've passed out forty feet off the ground or given up or had a heart attack and died there on the rope."

"That's right. Trying to defy the natural order of things almost always results in failure or burnout. So what finally got you to the top then?"

Chris closed his eyes tightly and shook off another flashback of the boulder pile covering Shane and John's body. "I took Shane's advice and climbed one step at a time. Stopped worrying about how far I had to go or how miserable I was and focused on steps. I had to rest about a thousand times, but," the analogy David had been making clicked and Chris's voice trailed off, "it wasn't nearly as bad as I imagined it would be once I got going." He paused. "Right."

"It almost never is."

Chris sighed and looked at David. "But how do I even make time to take those steps when I'm constantly drowning in other people's demands and overwhelmingly busy?"

David thought it over for a moment as he walked the shadow line. "You can be busy doing just about anything. How many people do you know that are so busy playing video games they don't have time to socialize or exercise or even shower for that matter? The problem isn't being busy, Chris. The problem is what you choose to be busy with; what you choose as an excuse *not* to do the things you know you should be doing.

"There are things you can do with your time and energy, Chris, that will fulfill you, and there are things you can do with your time that will leave you feeling empty and defeated at the end of the day *and* at the end of your life. The sooner you start choosing the best things and then identify the small steps you need to take to make those things happen, the better off you'll be."

"It just seems like every time I try to choose those best things someone puts a penny on my track and the train derails."

David nodded.

"It can definitely seem that way. The reality though, is that most of the time, we put those pennies there ourselves. *You* are the one who decides what you will fill your time and your life with. The problem is that, up to this point, you've unintentionally allowed others to decide for you by saying *yes* to their requests or expectations. Sometimes you have to do that, but often you don't."

David watched Chris struggle with his thoughts and returned to the stone bench beside him.

After a time, David leaned forward and turned to Chris. "Change is hard. Saying *no* is hard. But whose fault is it that you are busy with things that don't matter, that you barely have time for the things that do?"

"It's mine." Chris nodded.

"That's right. And if you are the problem, then..."

"I am the solution."

Chris turned to the unsolved puzzle-of-a-man beside him as the sun touched the horizon and the shadow line faded.

"Welp." David patted his lap and rose from his rock. "I've got something I want to show you, Chris, and then we'll wrap up this little adventure and have you back to your sweet wife."

Chris attempted to rise from his own rock and felt his entire body lock up in pain. He paused, took a deep breath, and moaning, forced his defiant legs to stand.

"Yeah, those muscles will stiffen up quick after a beating like the one you took. Gotta keep 'em moving." David shimmied to illustrate and then gestured toward the cave. "Back to your old friend, darkness. Don't worry, though. No belly crawls, pits, or boulders this time."

The thought of going back into the cave electrified Chris's nerves. He sucked in a ragged breath but couldn't seem to fill his lungs. He tried again, and David shuffled into the darkness.

"Whoa, whoa, wait up."

Chris limped along behind him as quickly as he could, his legs and upper body burning with each step. Underneath his clothes, cuts and scrapes burned like fire each time they brushed up against the fabric. Flaps of his dirt-encrusted shirt, held together by a single button, swung open as he moved, exposing swollen, red and bloody lines running the entire length of his stomach and chest. Tears in his slacks revealed similar wounds in the early stages of healing.

The farther he hobbled into the cave, the darker it became. He pressed the power button on his headlamp but nothing happened. The darkness was absolute now.

"David?"

CHAPTER 9

Parallel Paths

Beneath his feet the floor of the cave seemed to change with each step. Soft dirt at first, then flat. Tile maybe? He held out his arms to keep himself from smashing his head into the low cave ceiling, but the ceiling never materialized, and the clip clop of his shoes against the polished floor now echoed across the darkness.

Far ahead of him, a tiny rectangular pinpoint of light pierced the darkness. Instinctively, he turned toward it, arms in front, sweeping the floor with his feet every few steps. The farther he shuffled, the more he forgot about his pain, about the dust, the shredded clothing, and the scars across his body. Forgot about them until they were nothing more than a distant dream.

Within a few minutes the shuffling became pointless as the rectangular light grew and illuminated not only the floor but a now healed and well-kept Chris. It was a door of some sort. Not a stand-alone door propped up in the middle of an empty room but a door that was somehow connected to the darkness, welded to an endless, rubbery, black wall.

A step before he passed the door's threshold, Chris paused and examined its solid, pale, wood surface and metallic, lever-style handle. The door felt unsettlingly familiar. He reached out to turn the handle and hesitated. He didn't know why, but something inside him was not ready. Not ready for change. Not ready for an end and a beginning. For all *this* to become memory.

His arm sank back to his side, and for a several minutes he stared at the handle, knowing that time would eventually leave him no choice but to open it. No choice but to see, to move forward, to accept whatever the door gave him. Wondering. Imagining. Unsettled.

When that time finally arrived, he pushed the handle and stepped forward.

The opening of the door brought with it a stream of fluorescent light that flooded his eyes. Behind him, the door closed slowly. He half turned and realized he had stepped out of a custodial closet and into a hallway. Buckets, mops, and chemicals cluttered the tiny room behind him that had once been void of all things.

The door latched closed, and the hallway settled into focus: administration building, one floor down from his office, north end. He felt like a stranger in a foreign land, afraid to move, uncertain of what might come next.

At the hall's end a suited figure stepped into view. Chris cursed to himself and tried to look for an escape. It was Angela. The same woman who had sent him spiraling on the day he disappeared. The tension filled his chest with each step she took toward him. He tried to compose himself and hide his discomfort.

"Chris! How are you?" she called out warmly. "Wasn't sure you were going to make it in today or not. How's your family doing?"

Chris blinked hard and couldn't believe what he was seeing. The last thing Angela Price, the Vice President of Student Affairs, had ever been with him was warm and friendly.

"Chris?" He stared her up and down, bug-eyed. "You okay?

You seem a little lost or something."

He cleared his throat. "Okay?" His mind retreated, and he sputtered out a robotic response. "I mean, yes. I am okay." His eyes danced back and forth between Angela and the floor.

Angela eyed him suspiciously. "Well, I just wanted to say thanks for all the work you and your team have put into the new people and culture programs. I think the way you've proposed rolling out those new initiatives will really help ease people into some much-needed change."

Chris's eyes widened again. "Yeah." He nodded rapidly, looked for something to lock his attention onto. "I...thought... that...would be best."

Angela squinted and stepped back a little, examining Chris. "You sure you're okay?"

Chris nodded rapidly. "Yeah." His voice cracked. "Doin' good."

Angela continued to monitor him and then glanced down at her watch. "Well. I've got a meeting I need to get to." She adjusted the shoulder strap on the bag she was carrying and eyed him up and down. "Do me a favor, Chris." The rapid nodding returned. "Take a day off or something; you look like you need a break. This institution would be in a world of hurt if you burned yourself out."

Angela continued down the hallway and disappeared around the corner. Once she was out of sight, Chris collapsed against the wall.

"That was bizarre," he mumbled.

The second the words escaped his mouth, the pale-yellow walls pulsed, and the world twisted like a rag. Ripples rose up along the ceiling and floor, pulsing and undulating, as though the world around him had become liquid, altering not only what he saw but time as well. Everything around him lagged. The sounds of shattering crystal and cartoon-like rubber balls bouncing across the hallway reverberated across his ears. Three seconds later everything stopped, and the hallway returned to normal.

At the end of the hall where Angela had appeared before the blip, another suited woman rounded the corner and made a beeline down the hall.

"Dr. Price?" He whispered.

Chris turned back to where she had disappeared a few seconds earlier and then glanced back to Angela two. The second they made eye contact, she flashed a fake half-smile that longed to be a sneer, turned to her phone and barreled past him.

Chris felt as though a brick had knocked him across the back of his head. He stood there glancing up and down the hallway, trying to make sense of what had just happened. After standing there for several minutes, he decided to make his way to his office before something else happened.

At the end of the hallway, he passed through an open office space lined with cubicles, surrounded by permanent offices. All around him employees chattered on their phones, pounded email responses on their computers, and wandered the office disseminating gossip. He shuffled through the commotion in a surreal daze, like a man without form meandering an irrelevant world.

At the end of the space, Chris passed through a door that opened into a large common area. Clusters of students hunched over their laptops bleeding out buckets of stress. Others scrolled on their phones while others flirted awkwardly. In a corner at a round table, amateur philosophers solved the world's problems while scarfing down corn dogs. In the background, soft, popular music wafted through the air, largely ignored.

Midway through the common area, he made eye contact with Kyle and Tara who had sequestered themselves at a table off to the side. When they saw Chris, Kyle quickly broke eye contact, whispered something to Tara, and then sat back in his seat.

"Hey, Chris." He made brief eye contact and then raised his

eyebrows at Tara.

"Hey. How's it going?" The whole interaction felt forced and unwanted.

"Oh, you know. Same old, same old." Kyle glanced briefly at Chris again and then turned back to Tara who raised her eyebrows and looked up at Chris with a brief, fake smile.

Chris stared at the two, waiting for someone to break the silence, while the discomfort mounted with each passing breath. "Well, I don't want to interrupt anything, so I guess I'll see you around then?"

Kyle and Tara smiled insincerely and watched Chris turn and walk away. The second he turned they huddled back into their near-whisper conversation.

A step beyond earshot, the world froze. Tables vibrated rapidly, and the floor swelled beneath a low-pitched hum. A second later, a loud thunk returned the commons to their original state.

"Chris?"

Chris turned at the sound of his name. Kyle and Tara were no longer huddled together in secrecy but seemed genuinely excited to see him.

"Oh good. It is you. Hard to tell from behind sometimes. Do you have a second?"

Chris looked around the commons confused, wondering if he was part of some bizarre joke. "Okay." He walked slowly back to the table shaking his head in disbelief.

"Hey, Chris. Have a seat." Tara gestured at the seat across the table from them. No more hesitancy. No more fakery.

Chris sat down, and Kyle leaned in closer, ignoring the confusion draped across Chris's face. "So this morning I was talking to Jamie over in the Development Office, and she had this brilliant idea that one of her business donors mentioned in passing that could really increase accountability and employee development. It's a bit unconventional, but she said this donor was willing to back it if we ever decide to pilot it."

Tara nodded enthusiastically toward Kyle. "It really is brilliant."

"Anyway, I set up a meeting with the four of us to discuss it next week." Kyle paused and stared at Chris. "Hey man, you okay? You look a little spacey. Kids keep you up again last night?"

Chris snapped into focus and cleared his throat. "No." His eyes drifted. "It's just been a really weird day."

"Well, I know all about weird days." Kyle joked. "Anyway, I just wanted to let you know."

"Thanks." Chris felt completely lost. "I appreciate that. Sounds like a real opportunity."

The three stared at each other in awkward silence, with Chris drifting off into no man's land.

"Oh. I almost forgot. Your wife was trying to get a hold of you. She texted me to see if I knew where you were. I told her you probably left your phone on your desk and stepped out for a breather or something like that."

"Emily?"

Kyle chuckled. "Uh, yeah, unless you have another wife that we don't know about." His smile faded, and he looked up at Chris with concern. "You sure you're okay?"

Chris brought his hand to his mouth as his mind drifted home. "Yeah. I'm fine. Just a really, strange day. I should get going." He rose from the bench. "Thanks for flagging me down."

Chris walked to his office like a ghost in a world where he no longer belonged; everything disconnected. There was the world, and then there was Chris. He didn't even know why he was going to his office when going home was a car ride away. Maybe he just needed time to process, time to re-connect to the world of the living. Maybe he didn't want to go home yet. Regardless of what it was, his office was where he needed to go.

✳

When he opened the door, everything was exactly as he had left it. The only thing that had changed was him.

Chris walked over to the window and looked down at the swarming walkways below. It was nearly four-thirty, and university employees trickled out of the surrounding buildings toward whatever final destinations relieved their pent-up stress or created more.

When the mesmerizing monotony of watching river-like crowds lost its draw, Chris reached into his pocket and pulled out his phone. The device looked as though it had been run over by a herd of wild horses. Spiderweb cracks branched out from a dozen impact points and deep scratches covered the entire back surface, caked with dirt.

Chris brushed off what he could with his hand and then blew hard to clear the dust. A cloud of clay dissipated into the air and settled over his desk. The movement activated his phone, and he noticed a missed call from Emily. Seeing her name made his heart race until he could feel it in his throat. He stared at the phone for a moment and realized his hands were shaking. He squeezed the phone tight and pressed call.

"Hey handsome man." A friendly voice answered on the other end.

"Emily?" He couldn't remember the last time she sounded warm or enthusiastic about anything, let alone hearing his voice.

"Of course, it's me. What did you expect, one of your other

women?" She chuckled softly.

"It is so good to hear your voice." Chris breathed.

"You sound like you haven't seen me in a month. Is everything okay?"

"No, everything's fine. I just." Emotions rose up, and he sent them back down. "It feels like I haven't talked to you in weeks." Chris collapsed into his office chair.

"You're making me blush, Chris." Emily giggled, sighed, then returned to business. "Anyway, I was just wondering when you might be home tonight? I know you've been really busy lately, and I wasn't sure if you were going to make it home in time for dinner or if you needed me to stick something in the fridge for you?"

Chris shook his head and stared at the ceiling. He couldn't believe what he was hearing.

"Hello? You there?"

Chris cleared his throat. "Yeah. Yeah. I'm here. I."

"Sorry, thought I lost you. So?"

"I should be heading out in the next fifteen minutes."

"Great." She perked up. "I'll see you soon then."

The call disconnected. Chris sank deeper into his chair and the room spun and the windows drooped like a Salvador Dali painting. Walls on every side of him pulsed giant ripples through once solid sheetrock. As soon as it began, it was over, and the phone rang.

Chris picked up the shattered phone and saw a picture of his wife on the spider web screen.

"Hey."

"Are you home yet?"

"Is everything okay?" His anxiety demons beat down the door he had locked them behind.

"When are you coming home?" Her voice quivered on edge.

The demon door flung open, and he could see where the call was headed. "I'll be on my way in just a few minutes."

"You always say that!" Emily choked. "I don't know what we're having for dinner tonight. I need you to pick something up for the kids."

A child shouted in the background, and a fight broke out. Emily screamed at the children, and the sound passed through the receiver and tore Chris's eardrum. He cringed and held the phone at an arm's length to keep the piercing sound out. His hands were shaking again beyond his control.

In the background the kids quieted down and began to sob.

"I've gotta go." Emily bawled and the line went silent.

Chris leaned forward and curled up into his desk.

"David," he whispered, "what are you doing to me?"

After several deep breaths, he stood up and paced in front of the window trying to dissipate the swells of anxiety. Beyond his office door, he could hear his coworkers wrapping things up for the day, wishing each other habitual good nights. He stopped again, peered out his office window, caught his reflection and remembered. Remembered running down the street. Remembered the plane, smashing into the ground, the moment his old life gave way to something new. The moment he began to see, to regret, to hope.

Down below, the swarms thinned, and the sun dipped lower in the sky. Chris noticed a gray-haired man, heavyset, mid-fifties, sixties perhaps. He walked slowly, head to the ground, shoulders in. Where was he headed? What would life be like for the gray-haired man thirty minutes from now? Would he be in bed? Watching TV? Writing a novel? Arguing with his family? What insights about life might he impart if given the chance?

The old man passed by a young woman, mid-twenties. Fit, dark skin, frosted black hair in shoulder-length coils. She seemed pre-occupied, distant, lost in her phone. She walked quickly down the sidewalk, oblivious to everyone. Oblivious to everything she passed. What was she doing? Was that really who she was or was she lost in a facade? Her unique insights buried deep within her like a gold coin at the bottom of a deep well.

As the sun continued its progression toward the horizon, Chris lost himself in the people below. His will to run home was swallowed up by some inescapable force that compelled him to wonder. He drifted rhythmically from one person to the next. Seeing them for who they were, who they had the potential to become. Wondering. Loving. Reflecting on what it all meant.

CHAPTER 10

Choices

B y the time the lights in the surrounding buildings began flickering out so too had the anxiety stirred up by his conversation with Emily. Along the shallow edges of his conscience, it felt wrong experiencing the absence of fear and pain while his wife continued her own suffering. But deep down he knew that everything would be okay in time. As though he were no longer locked up in his own distorted views of the world, but a distant and curious observer of his own life, standing at the top of the world, seeing for the first time the truth behind his emotions and hers, the truth behind the illusions and distorted perceptions.

He turned to leave and felt another glitch in the fabric of reality. Different this time. But a glitch all the same.

✸

Outside the building the air was comfortable and quiet, and the walkways now illuminated by vintage-style streetlamps. Chris hesitated at the front of the building, feeling an almost physical, magnetic draw pulling him to the right. He thought about his parked car, thought about home and Emily and the kids. They were a block and a half down the walkway to his left, and a twenty-minute drive to his house. The longer he hesitated the stronger that unseen force pulled against his will to go left until a voice that was not his own rose up from the recesses of his mind.

"Those feelings are not coming from within Chris. You would be wise to learn to follow them. Your family will be fine."

He closed his eyes, inhaled deeply, and turned right.

✳

Two blocks to the south, he stepped into the terraced-house neighborhoods bordering the campus and began weaving his way through a maze of rectangular blocks, following the pull. Above him the dusk-sky faded to black, and all around him the traffic thinned to nothing. The sound of distant engines reverberated off man-made, city canyons, snuffing out any would-be silence, while townhome windows glowing soft and yellow, or flickering pale blue, illuminated the shadows between streetlights.

As the evening waned on, Chris felt more and more lost. Mirrored streets and a sickly orange sky that absorbed the city lights and drowned out the stars made it impossible for him to orient himself. The more he wandered, the more unsettled he became. Street signs disappeared and rows of houses replicated; the same ten brightly colored homes stretched on for a quarter mile. Up ahead the street between blocks looked as though it were folding in and stretching away. Chris picked up his pace to escape the brick-and-mortar jaws in a dream world that had become all too common now.

The more he ran, the slower the jaws of the city closed, and the more the buildings sank into their familiar position. At the end of the street, the city park—vibrant with quarantined greenery inside raised stone beds and lined with short, decorative, cast-iron fences—welcomed Chris home. He followed a stone walkway through the beds, past old-growth live oaks draped with ferns and Spanish moss, and arrived at the bench where it all began. A bench once kissed by a falling plane.

He stared at it curiously for a moment and then sat. Immediately, a soft and familiar presence stepped into his periphery.

"Much better here without all the..." David stepped out from behind the twisting shadow of the old oak and searched for the word, "... detritus, debris, wreckage? It's quiet. Peaceful. I can see why you were drawn here."

Chris half-turned toward David as he came to rest on the bench. For several minutes the two men sat in silence in the evening streetlight illuminating the urban jungle, lost in its depths.

"I want you to close your eyes for a moment, Chris."

Chris glanced slowly toward David whose attention was fixed on the meandering shadows. David ignored Chris's silent inquisition and then turned to him and raised his eyebrows. "Go on."

Chris shook his head, reclined a little, and allowed his eyelids to fall shut. Immediately, the red glow of skin covering his eyes intensified. Heat from the streetlights pressed against his face, passing through his clothing and warming his skin.

"What do you see?" David asked.

"It's bright."

Chris cringed as the glow burned brighter. Red became pink, and then the back of his eyelids gave way to a vast and intimate field of blinding white. Blurred shapes fused around him in various shades of gray, brown, and yellow. He watched the shapes change slowly into a focused dream and an arid landscape unfolded before him across unwalkable distances.

"Okay?" David nudged.

"This is so wild." He could feel his eyelids blanketing his eyes, and yet they had never been more open. He could feel the bench pressing against his back and legs, and yet here he was standing on an infinite expanse. "I'm at a crossroads on a gravel road branching off in four directions."

"Yes, you are. And where do you suppose those roads lead?"

Chris scanned the horizon and traveled each road with his eyes. The road to his right continued for a hundred paces, became paved, and then split off in three directions. Some of those paved roads looped back to the original fork while others divided exponentially into a vast network of dendritic connections branching across the mud-cracked valley. The roads to his left and in front and behind him did the same.

He looked to the horizon, and the mesh of roads blended into a hazy gray, where a large urban city rose up. Skyscrapers of varying sizes vied for dominance along the skyline.

He turned to his left and followed a meandering dirt road toward a cactus-strewn desert, where red and orange cliffs dropped into jagged, terraced canyons, carved out by slithering, green rivers. Along the top of the canyons, roads connected ranches with poplar tree perimeters. Some ranches looked completely derelict and abandoned, while others appeared operational and modern, outfitted with large barns and massive Quonset huts.

Farther along the canyon, a pine forest rose from the red rock toward high mountains where glacier topped peaks pierced low lying clouds. The farther the range extended toward the horizon, the darker the clouds became and the more coal-like and barren the mountains.

Behind him, on the precipice of visual reach, beyond the valley of endless roads, multi-million-dollar cabins lined the shore of a placid lake surrounded by a darkened forest of evergreens and deciduous trees. On one side of the lake, time passed, and the motionless waters held their breath. On the other side, a hurricane force wildfire consumed everything within its path.

Disaster zones, desert oases, ghost towns, churches, carnivals, beaches, swamps. Roads of every variety and quality divided and merged like a vast neural network connecting an endless variety of places.

"Nowhere and everywhere." Chris finally answered.

"It's interesting, isn't it, the number of choices available to us at any given point in our lives? Sometimes we don't even realize those choices exist. We just make them. Traveling down familiar roads without even considering where those roads might take us."

David closed his eyes and breathed in the cool night air. He released his breath slowly and turned to Chris.

"Where you're standing right now is the convergence of all the roads you've chosen to travel up to this point in your life. The choices you've made consciously or unconsciously. You, Chris, are the sum total of your choices. The problem is that you've made a lot of choices without thinking."

Chris bit his lip and nodded quietly.

"You've probably noticed, though, that there is nowhere on that vast landscape of your mind where the roads cease to divide. No one place where you can arrive and choice no longer exists."

Chris scanned the landscape and realized David was right.

"The moment you stepped out of that custodial closet, you were given a gift to peer into a version of your life governed by a different set of choices. Roads you could have wandered over the last nine months but chose not to. Roads that lead you to consequences not only for your own life but for the lives of those you interact with. Roads that will always exist here in this vast network of choices and that you could still potentially travel *if* you choose to do so."

"But how do I know which roads are the better roads to travel?" Chris stared at the maze of complexity before him.

"*That* is a very good question." Chris felt the bench wobble as David shifted. "The reality, Chris, is that the only wrong roads you can walk are the ones that get you nowhere. Endless loops. Like bad habits that become so comfortable that idea of traveling better roads or developing better habits becomes less appealing the longer you travel them. But you obviously can't make choices about which roads to travel if you aren't even aware that they're there. Take a look behind you."

Chris turned and beheld a dark, industrial wasteland. He noticed a single set of footprints exiting the urban, zombie-scape toward where he now stood. Gray smog settled over rust-encrusted factories while smokestacks pierced the acrid air, pumping their poison back into the noxious cloud. Crowds of people wandered through the maze along fractured sidewalks and through post-apocalyptic alleys. Some flaunted the latest fashion trends, others sported suits and skirts, and others cowered before them in modest, casual attire or oversized tattered rags. There were men, women, old and young, every race and nationality. Lost souls whose faces hung down in varying forms of frustration and confusion.

"We can only ever see that which we are willing to see. Most of the time the answers are right in front of us, but in our stubborn fixations we force our mind closed, shut our eyes, and refuse to see them." David continued.

Through gaps in the flowing crowds, Chris caught glimpses of individuals who had collapsed along the human riverbank, hugging their knees, eyes locked in hollow, distant stares. Inside the flow, the masses varied in their paces along central walkways. Walkways which split off into loops small and large where the current of people circled in eddies over and over again, oblivious to forks that branched off from the loops and out of the polluted mess.

The biggest loops carried the few who had been caught in their flow to the perimeter of the wasteland, where beautiful English gardens, a stone's throw from the loop, flourished in the afternoon sunlight. Small decorative, gravel paths branched off these loops and wove their way deep into the gardens where enthusiastic children scurried throughout the gardens, exploring the nooks and crannies. Occasionally a child would plunge back into the smog-shrouded wasteland, disappear for a time, and then come bursting back into the garden, covered in soot and beaming with joy.

Chris watched as crowds of adults moved curiously to the perimeter of the wasteland and studied the gardens but refused to enter them.

"I don't get it." Chris watched them puzzle over the view for a time, before one by one, they continued along the loop, back into the wasteland. "Why don't they leave?"

David reached over and gently tapped Chris on the back of his head. "See for yourself."

The second he felt the tap, his vantage point shifted. At his back, he could feel the industrial soot and its corrosive influence. In front of him the crowds of people he had been observing pointed and commented at the scene in front of him. Chris pushed his way through the crowd and hesitated. The gardens, the children, the stone paths were gone now. Beyond the perimeter path, red-orange, desert sandstone plummeted into a vertigo-inducing gorge that extended nearly half a mile before it rose again and plateaued onto the vast network of roads and trails weaving across the great valley.

Where are the trails? The second the thought crossed his mind the gorge closed up and the valley closed in and the trails appeared.

He turned to the woman next to him, who stared forward and refused to breathe. "Did you see that?" he asked.

"See what?" She glanced suspiciously at Chris, hands over her mouth, and glanced rapidly between him and the desolate valley.

"The gorge. It closed up."

She stared at him uncomfortably, shook her head, and began backing slowly away.

"Dude. The only thing out there is a death wish." A tall, muscle-shirted man commented, turning away from the gorge and toward Chris.

"What are you talking about? There's a path right here." Chris pointed at the path a step away.

"It's a freaking gorge dude!" The man's temper began to rise.

"Look. I'll show you." Chris stepped off the loop and onto the path. The crowd gasped, and the man and a couple nearby lunged for Chris.

"Dude, what's wrong with you?" The man cursed. "What are you, stupid?"

The man, and the couple, and the crowd shook their heads and began to dissipate. One by one, they flowed back into the charcoal cloud, some glaring at Chris with contempt, others snickering condescendingly, a few voicing their concerns—begging him not to try anything like that again. Most, however, made obvious efforts to ignore the fact he had even existed.

When the mist had finished consuming the last of the crowd, Chris turned back to the valley and stepped out onto the trail.

Where is the garden? He stepped again. The gravel along the trail crunched against his shoes.

Another step and he glanced reluctantly over his shoulder. Perhaps the strong man was right, and it was he who was consumed by deadly illusions. He who was about to plummet to his own death down a gorge he could not see. He extended his foot in front of him brushing it over the surface of the trail.

When he was certain it was solid, he shifted his weight to his foot, and the landscape blossomed before him. Rolling hills, swaying willow trees, and various beds of perfectly manicured flowers sprang out across the foreground like a pop-up book. The children he had seen running, playing, and exploring the garden earlier reappeared, as though a veil had been lifted from his eyes.

Chris scanned the scene and noticed a solitary adult walking along the path. He hadn't noticed adults in the garden before, but now he counted perhaps ten, maybe twelve adults walking among the hordes of children.

Like the adults in the wasteland, they came from all walks of life. One woman's fingers danced across her phone as she wandered a blue-stone path. A young man in a business suit moved hurriedly to the top of a hill. Others meandered through the garden in pairs, engaging in rigorous, friendly debate, serious conversation, and reflective silence. In nearly every way they seemed to be engaged in activities no different from those in the wasteland, but here, in the garden, everyone seemed unencumbered, liberated from some suffocating, unseen force.

Chris continued along his own path into the garden where he could see more clearly. The air healed those who breathed it. The sounds quieted turmoil, and the colors filled the mind with possibilities.

At the center of the known garden, Chris paused and turned his attention back to the fringes of the wasteland loop. A new group of solemn sojourners emerged from the smog and congregated at the scenic viewpoint on the edge of their uncrossable chasm.

"I still don't understand. Why do they refuse to see? Why are they so stubborn?"

"Stubborn?" David rested his hand on Chris's shoulder. "Or afraid?" David closed his eyes again and inhaled the night air.

"Think back for a moment to the last few years of your own life, Chris. How many of those days or months or years have you wasted your life away tolerating your circumstances? Wandering endless loops and allowing your mind to bombard you with toxic thoughts and the emotions that come with them. Forever moving forward but never progressing. All because you too were afraid of what *might* happen but never *did* happen."

In the world within his eyelids, Chris turned to the enslaved pilgrims. He watched with hopeless empathy as replicas of himself studied the uncrossable ravine and then one by one returned to the wasteland.

"You've been given a marvelous gift, Chris. The gift to temporarily step beyond the smog-shrouded world and examine the possibilities from a new vantage point. A gift to see with greater clarity, a re-creation of sorts.

"The problem is, like all recreational adventures, the thrill of the adventure fades the moment you return home. The moment you step back into that old environment, where your deeply engrained habits sustain the status quo, the vision of what could be quickly gives way to the intimidating reality of what is.

"So even though your mind has been opened and you've recognized the need to change, you're still the same Chris who collapsed on this bench a few days ago on the verge of mental breakdown. Those habits that shaped your yesterdays are poised to continue shaping your tomorrows. Your wife still struggles. Your coworkers think you're a lousy boss. Senior leadership is still frustrated to no end with your arrogance.

"You might feel inspired and ready to change now, but as the days grind on and your efforts become entangled in snares, what will happen to you then? *That* is the million dollar question."

Chris closed his eyes tightly and watched the fringe people stare despondently into the distance. "I don't want to go back to that, David. I can't go back to living like that again. What do I do?"

The people on the loop faded, the gardens receded, and factories folded up. Chris could feel the heat from the garden's sun dissipate and the red glow of his closed eyelids returned. He opened his eyes and turned toward David.

227

"Well, for starters, you need to stop putting off doing what you feel you need to do."

Chris's gaze drifted away from David and toward the ground.

"Time, Chris, is fear's favorite meal. The longer you hold off acting on those things you feel you should do, the bigger your fears become, until eventually you're serving your ability to act to fear's ravenous appetite.

"The sooner you act on what you feel you should do, the sooner you'll discover that the fear of change is significantly more painful than the actual process of making that change and facing your fears. Not acting invites your rational mind to manufacture justification for not taking the steps you know you need to take." David paused and squeezed Chris's shoulder. "Don't grant your mind the time or the opportunity to do that."

Chris nodded slowly and then turned to David shaking his head. "I feel like everything's been such a mess though. Where do I even start?"

David nodded and slapped Chris hard on the back. "You're a smart man, Chris. I'm sure you'll figure that out." He leaned forward on his knees, nodded for a moment, and then half-turned back to Chris. "But if it were me, I'd start by writing down insights I'd gathered over the last few days and make note of the things I felt I needed to change. There's one more thing that might help." David rose from the bench and extended his hand toward Chris. Chris rose, and David began shuffling through the brown, leather, shoulder bag he'd been carrying. "It's hard to change habits and behaviors that are making your life miserable if you aren't even aware you have them."

"Yeah. Tell me about it."

"But it's a problem that's easily solved," David added, removing a thin, beautifully bound, leather book. "Now, you don't *need* a book like this to identify hidden bad habits in your life any more than you need a map to get to where you want to go. But maps like this one can definitely come in handy at times, especially when you're trying to figure out where to start."

David turned the book over in his hands, examined it, and then extended it to Chris.

"So, here's your map. Drafted by cartographers who have walked similar paths to those you now travel. Cartographers who found their way out of the loops."

Chris turned the book carefully in his hands, examining the fine leather craftsmanship. It was as though the book had been printed a hundred years ago and then carefully preserved. Weathered by time and yet in mint condition. The font was equally exquisite in its craftsmanship and design.

"There's something important you need to know about this book, Chris."

Chris stopped examining the book and looked up at David.

"Very important." David was serious now. "You can't force a tree to grow any faster than it has the ability to grow. The laws governing your own growth and development are no different.

"The first steps down any new road are rarely what we expect. It can be easy to convince yourself, when you don't immediately experience the results you expect, that the thing you are trying for the first time is not working or that you've made a mistake.

"But no one ever became a concert violinist after practicing the violin for a week. Most likely, after that first week, all they experienced were sore fingers, sore ears, and a lot of frustration. The road to concert violinist *demands* that those traveling it face the struggle with patience. It *demands* years of practice before the muscle memory and coordination create fluid, effortless, and beautiful music. Becoming an influential boss or a patient and forgiving husband or a connected father or a high value employee is no different."

David stopped talking and bore down on the gate to Chris's

soul. His eyes burned through Chris who struggled to maintain eye contact under the weight of David's gaze.

"Chris." David tightened his lips, shook his head, and aimed an arrow-like finger toward Chris's heart. "You promise me that you will not let this book sit idle. That you won't just set it on your shelf and watch it collect dust. That you will use it until you've arrived at the fringes of your own map and have begun forging new roads with the help of those around you."

Chris looked up timidly at David and nodded. "I promise." He felt the book in his hand, gripped it tighter, and cleared his throat. "I promise."

"Great." The fire in David's eyes faded away, and he shifted the shoulder strap of the bag. "Then this is where I say goodbye and send you off on the next leg of your journey." David looked distracted now and turned his attention toward a small side street branching away from the park.

Chris raised his eyebrows and widened his eyes. "There's more?"

"Oh yeah, and this next part is way more challenging than what you just went through."

Chris felt the color wash out of his face. David rolled his eyes as the sarcasm sailed over Chris's head.

"I'm talking about going back to your normal life, Chris."

Chris exhaled loudly. "Geez David." He glanced around at the park and took a deep labored breath. "I'm not sure I'm ready for that either."

David slapped him on the arm and smiled. "Come on, Chris. You'll be fine." He turned to the street he had been eyeing and drifted toward it. "Just remember that everything you need is right there in the book you're holding as well as in the people around you and in the lessons you've learned over the last few days. If you get stuck, ask others for help. I'm sure they'll be *more* than happy to give you their opinion."

David receded a step at a time toward the magnetic street while Chris struggled to wrap his tired mind around the inevitability of unanticipated endings. When it finally clicked, he panicked.

"David, wait!"

David paused and glanced back at Chris, and Chris knew the lessons were over. Chris closed his eyes and tightened his face, then shook his head and looked up at David.

"Thank you."

David tipped his head, turned to the street, and faded into the shadows of the city.

✳

Chris couldn't say how long he stood there staring into the night when his phone tinged. He reached into his pocket and pulled out the device.

WHERE ARE YOU!!!!? UGH! The lock-screen message faded as soon as he saw it. It was 9:04 PM.

Chris took a deep breath and closed his eyes.

He held the phone in his hands for a breath and then began typing.

I'm so sorry for how I've acted lately and for all that I've put you and the kids through, for not being there for you. I know this sounds like another shallow apology, but I am sorry and I'm on my way now. I'm going to do better now. See you soon.

Chris pressed send, returned his phone to his pocket, and hurried down the dimly lit street toward his family.

Epilogue

To my friend on this shared journey we call life.

I congratulate you for opening this spine-bound map. Countless ordinary women and men have shaped these pages with their wisdom. Insights gathered in those moments of perfection speckled across the vast desert of their imperfect lives. Lives valiantly traveled toward something better.

The world through which you now travel is, like theirs, full of endless opportunities, distractions, and demands, and it can be easy at times to fall victim to misguided voices, both within and without, that lead you down endless loops. Voices that obscure the simple and beautiful paths all must wander to experience peace and happiness while you sojourn along this infinitesimally small and yet astronomically great adventure.

This book, this map, is a guide for those moments when you find yourself staring at dead ends or coming back to the same fork over and over again. Wandering unsettling paths where the world feels clouded in smog, or floating adrift on an ocean of pain where you see nothing but endless horizon. No point of reference. No indication that you are moving toward anything. No sense that life will be different today, or tomorrow, or the next day, or ever. And yet just beneath the undulating blue carrying you along its rippled surface, there is always a steady and unwavering current that carries you onward toward a horizon that will one day lift you onto dry ground. Perhaps it is that very current that brought you here today.

Regardless, you are here today because of the paths you have chosen to wander over years or decades of your life. Some of those have been wise and productive choices that have carved out profoundly beautiful attributes that you've likely dismissed and can no longer see, while others have eaten away at your soul, leaving behind deep scars and imperfections that have carried you here today in search of a new path.

Choosing the wrong path is never the end of the road. Wrong paths can help you see the right paths if you allow them to. They are an essential part of carrying you to your ultimate destination. After all, what kind of life would it be if there were only one easy road across endless hard pan. Through the bitter we know the sweet. By darkness we see the light.

To begin a journey along the right path requires nothing more than a single, small step. Many travelers however, put off taking that first step because the perception of that step and those that follow seems so monumental and overwhelming that they cannot bring themselves to take it. The problem is not that the step is monumental, the problem is that the traveler is not focusing on the step, which is small, but on the immense distance between where they are and where they want to go.

At other times the initial step seems so small and insignificant that the traveler fails to see how taking it can get them from where they are to where they want to go in the timeframe they wish to arrive at their destination. But it is against the physical laws that govern this world to expect shortcuts along the road of life. The only thing that matters is that you press forward consistently along the right path. A year, or two, or ten may seem like an eternity, but if you cast your eyes over the years that have passed by you will discover that they have flown by like a fleeting dream, and that you are who you are today because of the small steps you have taken across those years.

Now, one last thing before you continue. No one can take the first step down a new path with the same mindset that got them stranded in the wilderness or lost at sea. To discover new ways forward you must set aside your biases, and stop searching for excuses to not change the things that deep down inside you know are making your situation worse. You must silence that brutally unkind voice inside your head and question everything it tries to persuade you not to do. You are better than that voice. Its disapproving and pessimistic statements are filled with lies.

Do not limit yourself by dismissing principles that fail to align with your deeply engrained personal beliefs. Don't let that voice tell you that true principles are relative to the individual. While we are all unique, we are also all the same. In fact we are more similar than we are different. We all bleed. We all feel pain. We all struggle. You can no more say that you can obtain peace through continuous conflict with others than you can say that fueling and hydrating your body are irrelevant to your survival. Principles of well-being are as universal as the principles of survival, and you would be wise to accept that lest by holding your ground you sentence yourself to a life of stagnation and regret.

The man or woman who spends his or her life arguing their point so they don't have to move forward, despite that deep and nagging suppressed feeling that something is amiss, will never travel beyond the base of the foothills. Their perspective will forever remain limited and their ability to understand those things which matter most in this life will be lost to their view. Those, however, who press forward against the vehement attempts of their own ego to defend their way of seeing, who listen closely to the whispers of true principles, will find themselves, as the years roll on, at the top of the mountain where the view is clear and their understanding of the world has guided them to things which matter most.

This book is but a small sample of universal truths passed on through all humanity, independent of any one person. A mid-point to help ground you in your journey and propel you toward those who can help you discover more throughout endless reaches of time. This map does not lead you to wealth or fame or anything else that you may think will make you happy. It invites you to take those single small steps that overtime will lead you to a life fulfilled, to peace amidst chaos, and to joy in the journey despite the inevitable setbacks you will encounter.

Thank You

Dear Reader,

I would like to end this book by thanking you for taking the time to read through its pages. I hope that *Cursing at Mountains* has been as beautiful a journey for you to read as it was for me to write.

If you would like to discover ways the principles in *Cursing at Mountains* can be applied to your own life, I have created a free *Cursing at Mountains Workbook,* which you can request on my website below.

If you have enjoyed this book, I would invite you to share it with someone who you think might benefit from the many lessons embedded within its pages. Lessons that countless people, whom I have been blessed to associate with throughout my life, have shared with me.

Also know that I would love your feedback: what you have enjoyed, what you think I could improve, and how this book has made a difference in your life. You can post those comments where you purchased this book or send me a message via my website: www.brandonkowallis.com.

May you have a wonderful journey wherever the waves of life may carry you!

Brandon

* 9 7 8 0 9 9 6 4 5 9 7 1 6 *